MUNGO'S DREAM

Mungo's Dream

J. I. M. STEWART

New York

W · W · NORTON & COMPANY · INC ·

Copyright © 1973 by J. I. M. Stewart

Library of Congress Cataloging in Publication Data
Stewart, John Innes Mackintosh, 1906–
    Mungo's dream; a novel.
    I. Title.
PZ3.S85166Mu3 [PR6037.T466]   823'.9'12
ISBN 0–393–08669–0   73–2933

PRINTED IN THE UNITED STATES OF AMERICA

1 2 3 4 5 6 7 8 9 0

CONTENTS

Part One
ENGLAND

'HOWARD FOUR, FOUR,' the porter in the bowler said, consulting a typewritten list. The porter was committing the solecism known in Mungo Lockhart's youth as Wearing your Hat in the House. Indeed, he was indoors twice over, since he inhabited a glass box built into the gate—'gate' being the word for the lofty yet claustrophobic tunnel which pierced the entire thickness of this part of the college. But although the bowler must therefore be a token of dignity its wearer's attitude was friendly. If you were nervous (as Mungo was) you might suspect it of being commiserating, but probably it was simply designed to hearten. It was true that the man gave no hint of how to find Howard 4, 4 (which must mean a quadrangle and staircase and 'set' of rooms). But that was perhaps by way of putting it to Mungo that he now belonged to the place, and was not to be supplied with information like a tourist. Mungo picked up his two heavy suitcases with a comforting lack of effort and walked on.

He had, after all, been here before—for the interview that had turned him into an Oxford undergraduate. So his nervousness wasn't terror or anything approaching it. 'Mungo,' his headmaster had said, 'we despatch you with confidence among the Sassenachs. There's been plenty of porridge gone to the making of you. And we'll hope it was of the same boiling that nourished John Keats.' This had been a humorous allusion to Mungo's poems in the school magazine. 'Not too much of that impulsiveness,'

he had added seriously. 'Still, don't sit on it.' And he had
shaken hands. It was almost the first time Mungo had
attained the dignity of being shaken hands with, except
by the minister after Sunday school.

Howard turned out reassuring; it was a small, almost
domestic, quadrangle opening unexpectedly off a corner
of a very large one. It had, indeed, a disproportionately
large gate of its own, which gave on the outer world (if
any part of Oxford was to be called that) and was
crowned with an incomprehensible Latin inscription. But
it was nice to have this note of almost private grandeur,
and Mungo decided that he was going to like his corner
of the college. Perhaps they put the quieter undergraduates here: those he had seen termed in old-fashioned
novels 'the reading men'. He was a reading man himself,
although not always of the books enjoined upon him,
and for a time at least he was prepared to be moderately
quiet. So they had guessed right about him.

He found his staircase. It must shelter a reading man
who was musically inclined, since on the ground floor
somebody had just begun to play what might be a cornet.
Only it was an odd sort of cornet—or rather not a
cornet at all. Could it be, of all things, a hunting-horn?
Mungo had just admitted this odd conjecture when it was
substantiated by a sudden outburst of yelling, view-
hallooing, tally-hoing, and gone-awaying in surprising
proximity to his left ear. Some of the reading men must
be hunting men as well. Their hullabaloo, although it
ceased at once and was apparently no more than a brief
ebullition of animal spirits, had conveyed, in its sudden
eruptiveness, rather a spine-chilling effect. Not that
Mungo's spine would have registered much change on a
thermometer. If faced by a band of savages (and these
people sounded virtually that) he would still have had
the advantage of being six-foot two and in the modest

habit of regarding himself as a fairly reasonable specimen all round.

The rooms down here were numbered 1 and 2, and had people's names in white paint over the door. Number 4 must be on the next storey. Mungo flexed his arms to cope with the suitcases, and climbed. He stopped on a small landing and looked at a door on his right. Here was 4, sure enough. And over the lintel it said:

THE HON. I. A. V. O. CARDOWER
MR M. G. LOCKHART

Mr M. G. Lockhart eyed the announcement with misgiving. But, he thought, you probably went through this door and found two other doors. Perhaps Cardower—it was a faintly familiar name—was a don and so extremely eminent as a lawyer or something that he had been made a Privy Councillor. But no—that wasn't right. Privy Councillors were the *Right* Hon. And plain members of parliament weren't Hon., although they referred to each other formally as honourable. Straight Hon. like that was what was called a courtesy title. Cardower was probably an undergraduate, after all. Perhaps the two of them were going to be on either side of a little corridor.

Mungo put down one suitcase, turned the door-handle, picked up the suitcase again, and barged through. He found himself in a large and lofty room. Its walls were panelled, and had been painted white rather a long time ago. The furniture looked as if it had started quite high up on the social scale but been through a good many junk shops since. This was as much as Mungo noticed before he became aware that there was a young man of his own age in the room. The young man had been lounging in a window-seat, but now he stood up—almost as if Mungo were a lady, Mungo thought.

For a moment they looked at one another in a faint

surprise which was to become memorable.

'Oh, hullo,' the young man said. 'Are you Lockhart? My name's Ian Cardower. We're going to be doubled up.'

'With laughter?' Mungo asked, and felt foolish. He hadn't intended a feeble joke. It had just been that the phrase held no other association in his head.

'Not exactly.' The Hon. Ian Cardower hadn't stared. 'Sharing this set.'

'Oh, I see. I didn't know. Does everybody do that?'

'Not the Scholars. They have their own sets from the first. Just the Commoners—the ignorant gnomes like you and me—in their first year.'

'I wasn't told.' Mungo disapproved of being called an ignorant gnome, even if some element of irony had been intended. At his Scottish school his gaining a place in an Oxford college had been regarded (except, perhaps, by his headmaster) as an intellectual triumph of the first order. Mungo himself had been viewing it rather that way. 'I suppose we can manage,' he said—and was aware of an ungracious note. 'Loneliness is said to be the awful thing at Oxford. We'll have one another at whom to glower, Cardower.'

'So we shall.' Cardower was decently quick to extract a whimsical rather than a surly intention from this. 'One way or another, we've both mucked in with unknown characters already, I suppose.'

'Not me. I've never been away from my aunt, you see. It's traumatic.' Mungo was furious with himself for producing this twaddle, and also aware of being under a level and judicial gaze. 'What does the set consist of?'

'This, and a small bedroom each. Even in my grandfather's time, the sets used to be used the other way: this as a dorm, and two little rooms to go away and work in. Not that I imagine *he*—' Cardower checked himself.

'And mod. cons. in the basement,' he added. 'As for the bedrooms, they seem identical, so I've just moved into one straight away. I'll help you shove yourself into the other. If you think there *is* a difference, we can toss.'

As he spoke, Cardower stooped and picked up one of Mungo's suitcases. He did it as effortlessly as Mungo himself would have done, and he had to stoop as far. Mungo had only noticed that his room-mate was slim and fair; now he saw that he was tall as well. In fact he was very tall. They were alike in that, if in nothing else.

The bedroom had running water and a new-looking bed. Otherwise it was shabby and seemed to let in the damp. A previous owner had abandoned on the wall an enormous unframed photograph, now torn and flapping, of a lugubriously erotic chunk of Indian temple-sculpture. The same man, or another, had left a stuffed badger, upon which some depilatory art appeared to have been practised, under a cracked marble-topped table.

'It's not just the Hilton, is it?' Mungo asked. The sight of the bedroom had somehow cheered him up.

'Well, no—but the Hilton wouldn't run to *that*.' Cardower was pointing to the monstrous photograph. 'Complicated, isn't it? You can lie in bed and try to work out just what's going on. Decent of me to let you have the benefit of it.'

'I'll keep it for long lazy Sunday mornings.' Mungo wasn't going to shy away from a bit of bawdy. 'Doesn't your room run to anything of the sort?'

'No—but otherwise it's just the same. You can come and look. They'll do very well, it seems to me.'

'I suppose it's quite something to you—a bedroom of your own.' Mungo's good-humour grew. 'After some awful dormitory.'

'Dormitory? At my—' Cardower again stopped abruptly. 'Your aunt did you better, I dare say,' he said.

'Well, yes—but I agree with you they'll do very well. Each of us retires into his hutch, and continues to scowl at the other through the wall.'

'I do hope not.' Ian Cardower said this with an assumption of mature politeness which Mungo felt to be distancing, although it was perhaps only a hint that more in this vein would be tiresome. 'By the way, we have to trundle over our own trunks from the lodge. But that can keep. Let's return to our common ground and relax for a bit.'

This they did, with a literalness which involved a sprawled posture on the room's two sofas.

'I wonder how they work it out,' Mungo said. 'Pairing boys—men—off, I mean. You'd think they'd do it by schools.'

'Not unless people ask, I imagine. Are there many people from your school here?' In the instant that Cardower asked this a curious twitch—perhaps what they called a tic or habit spasm—passed over his face. Mungo, who wasn't slow, realized that Cardower felt he'd put a foot wrong—and that this was one of the major crimes in his remote and alien code.

'None at all,' Mungo said easily. 'And not in the whole university.'

'There are plenty of mine. Even some on this staircase.'

'I've heard them,' Mungo said composedly. 'The young barbarians at play.'

'The young—? Oh, I see. It occurs to me that it's perhaps according to what we're going to read—the doubling us up, I mean. Are you reading History?'

'English.'

'Then that isn't it. Do you think it might be by inches? The tallest chaps in the loftiest rooms.' Cardower was using this fancy as a friendly lead in, Mungo supposed. 'What are you?'

'Six two and a quarter.' Mungo almost didn't carry on
—but that would have been uncivilized. 'What about
you?'

'Six two exactly.'

'Ho-ho!' Mungo said mockingly—and wondered why
this juvenile signal of amiability felt a little forced. He
was all keyed up, after all, to plunge into things utterly
new, and a mob of Etonians or Harrovians or suchlike
seemed certainly that. But feelings he hadn't much suspected in himself were stirring in him, and in part they
appeared prompted by humiliatingly superficial things.
For this business of 'coming up' to Oxford he'd put on
his best suit. And Cardower was wearing what Mungo
(whether rightly or wrongly) conjectured to be his best
suit too. Only they weren't the same sort of suit.

This species of awareness was so squalid that Mungo
grabbed at something more reputable. All the exploring
he was going to do would be under the eye of a chap
who wouldn't himself be exploring at all. Cardower had
brought all the answers up with him. His venerable grandfather, summoning the young scion to the ancient ducal
seat or whatever it was, had given him the entire gen.
Life at the varsity is essentially unchanging, my dear
boy. Get your wine from Sucksmith's in the High. A
thoroughly sound claret, and they take away the empty
bottles. Bless you, my dear lad, and be a rowdy credit to
your ancient name. That kind of thing.

With these thoughts Mungo Lockhart was on his own
ground. He wasn't too good (although he wasn't all that
bad) at the general run of school subjects. But he had
always come top in English, and from as far back as he
could remember had enjoyed verbalizing whatever day-
dreams visited him. More recently this innate endowment, as it seemed to be, had been exercising itself—often

restlessly and urgently—on actual people and situations.
His acquaintances had taken to talking *in absentia,* as it
were; they formed surprising combinations, landed themselves in queer predicaments, quarrelled and made love,
all inside his head. So much had his brain become a kind
of story-telling machine that he had lately formed the
conclusion that something sober and permanent would
have to come of it.

So the paradoxical consequence of Mungo's sudden
burlesque glimpse of the old duke who must be Cardower's
grandfather was to turn him serious.

'Do you know?' he said. 'I think the real reason they
put you and me together is that they have some theory
of social motility.'

'Of—? Yes, I see.'

'The melting-pot idea.' Mungo thought a less abstract
vocabulary might be better accommodated to a young
barbarian. 'It can't much be managed in schools—not as
they still are. And I expect it doesn't much happen afterwards, when we're in jobs—not as *they* still are. But there
are a few years for it here. Dons may have well-meaning
notions of that kind.'

'Well-meaning? You think it's bosh? You wouldn't
play?'

'No, not that a bit.' Mungo saw that Cardower was
being serious too—although rather with the air (he told
himself perversely) of a liberal-minded laird anxious to
get on with a difficult gillie. 'Only I don't know that I
want it shoved at me. To be honest, I'd rather have, at
least, my own base—although I don't think I'd just sit
and sulk in it. You see, it's less of a bore, this doubling-up
business, for you than for me. You've got things laid
down—settled lines and expectations, established friends
who'll be in and out of this room. But I've got to push
around and see what's what.' Thus launched, Mungo was

really a little enjoying himself. 'The simple Scottish boy,' he said.

'You're a damned articulate Scottish boy.' Cardower had been listening with grave attention. 'For that matter, I'm a Scottish boy myself.'

'Then you're a shockingly anglicized one.' Rather against his will, Mungo grinned disarmingly. 'I'm sorry rather to talk rot,' he said.

'If you like, we can go to the Senior Tutor or the Bursar or whoever arranges these things, and make him change.'

'*Make* him?'

'Yes, of course.' It seemed to surprise Ian Cardower that there could be any doubt on this point. 'As a matter of fact, my father rather wanted me to have his old rooms in Surrey. But I said I'd prefer just to drift into the place and see what happened. My own modest impulse to push around.'

'Oh.' This information deflated Mungo. 'Perhaps we'd better give it a go.'

'I suppose so.' Cardower stretched himself lazily, as if some small matter had been casually determined. 'What's the M. for?'

'The M?'

'In M. G. Lockhart.'

'It's for Mungo. And the G's for Guthrie, which was my mother's maiden name. You've told me I's for Ian. But what about A. V. O?'

'We'll come to that when there's an idle half-hour.' Ian Cardower smiled for the first time—urbanely (Mungo told himself viciously), like a young *chargé d'affaires* who has successfully rounded a difficult diplomatic corner. 'I'm not sure there aren't Guthries in my family somewhere.'

'It's a pretty common Scottish name,' Mungo said. His

new room-mate had spoken as if there could be only one
lot of Guthries in the world—or one lot of Smiths or
Browns—just as there was doubtless only one lot of Cardowers.

'Did they call you Pongo at school?'

'No, they didn't, and they're not going to here.'

'Sorry. I suppose Mungo's a family name?'

'No, it's not. It's just that there's a Mungo Lockhart
in a Scottish poem my father's said to have been rather
fond of.' It was with some surprise that Mungo heard
himself offer this unnecessary confidence.

'Sir Mungo Lockhart of the Lea?'

'Yes.'

There was a silence in which the lodgers in Howard
4, 4 regarded one another with a fresh access of caution.
The line from William Dunbar's *Lament* had acted (the
imagistically resourceful Mungo told himself) like an exchange of visiting cards, and the information conveyed
hinted that they might have some things in common. But
clearly nothing of the kind ought to be explored at the
moment, and Ian Cardower signalled his grasp of this at
once.

'Have you got a trunk over there?' he asked.

'Yes—and a crate with books and things.'

'So have I. Let's get them and settle in. They keep little
trolleys in the lodge, the kind they have in railway stations.
You just borrow one.'

Mungo wondered how Cardower could have come by
this particular piece of local knowledge. Undergraduates
could scarcely have trundled around their own luggage,
he supposed, in the dear old duke's time.

They unpacked their trunks and suitcases each in the
privacy of his own bedroom. But of course it was otherwise with the books and miscellaneous minor chattels.

These, although really much more private than shoes and
ties (or even vests and pants), go prescriptively on display
—and indeed it was only in the large panelled apartment
that there was provision for them.

'What's this called?' Mungo demanded, as he gave the
Collected Poems of W. B. Yeats honourable prominence
on a shelf. It seemed inevitable that Cardower was going
to be in many small things his oracle. 'Living-room,
sitting-room, drawing-room, study—or what?'

'It hasn't got a name. Six centuries haven't found it
one. Those are our bedrooms. But this is just our room.'

'Do we keep in it?'

'I think that's Cambridge. We just live in it—or perch.
It's rather like lodgings at the seaside in some novel.'

This analogy wouldn't have occurred to Mungo. He
rather supposed that Cardower's home life took place in
Long Galleries and Double Cubes (such as he had once
viewed at Wilton), surrounded by Van Dycks and Cana-
lettos. In which case nothing even in this splendid college
was likely to feel particularly homey to him, with the
possible exception of its great hall. But at least he was
shelving a wholly unassuming collection of books. They
seemed to be history-books mainly, and so not particularly informative—except perhaps to the extent of hint-
ing that Ian Cardower had some tincture of reading man
in him too. Mungo kept a look out for anything suggesting what at school had been called extra-curricular interests. One would expect, he told himself expertly (for he
was a dogged prowler in public libraries), Surtees, and
Peter Beckford's *Thoughts on Hunting*, and Siegfried Sas-
soon, and volumes in something called the Badminton
Library telling you how to haul innocent creatures out of
the water or shoot them down from the sky. But nothing
of the kind appeared. All that did appear was a battered
copy of Richard Jefferies's *Bevis*. This made Mungo (who

was volatile in such matters) suddenly feel that he was
going to like Ian Cardower very much. And Cardower,
whose own books were the less numerous, was now giving
Mungo a friendly, but appraising, hand with his.

'You do cart around a lot of novels,' he said. 'French
ones, too. Do you reckon you'll read them all this term?'

'I've read a good many of them, as a matter of fact.'
Mungo felt it right to get a shade of apology into his
tone. 'But I thought I might want to rummage in them.'

'Rummage in them? Yes, I see.' Cardower didn't appear
to be puzzled. 'Solid rather than trendy,' he added, running his eye along the shelf. 'Hullo! Leonard Sedley's
An Autumn in Umbria. Well, well. Quite a milestone,
they say.'

'It's a marvellous book.' Mungo had become animated.
'But not exactly in a cosy way. Do you know it?'

'Know him?' Cardower seemed to have misheard, but
corrected himself. 'Yes, I know it—vaguely. I must have
read it a long time ago. Well, that's about the lot.' He
looked at his watch. 'My parents,' he said abruptly,
'brought me up.'

'Very nicely. Your manners are tiptop.'

'Silly ass! They've brought me up to Oxford in the most
old-fashioned way, and are staying for the night at the
Randolph.' Cardower's tone modulated from the casual
to the formal. 'I wonder whether you'd care to come
and dine with them? They'd be awfully glad to meet
you.'

2

THEY WALKED UP St Aldate's, which Cardower called
St Old's. Mungo didn't bother to be surprised about the
invitation he had received. Everything was so unfamiliar
that his head wasn't totally clear; he forgot his momentary persuasion that he was going to like this unexpected
room-mate (just because of *Bevis*); but he did remember
—or spontaneously feel—that he was ready for anything
that was going. He wanted at least to know about this
chap—and about his parents, if they were on offer. What
had happened, he told himself, was simply drill. Cardower
had gone into a routine. Suddenly confronted by the
simple Scottish boy, he had turned on the *noblesse oblige*
stuff. And Mungo would give it a go. Mungo judged it
very important to maintain in all things an enquiring
mind.

It occurred to him that there was one quite prosaic
enquiry that he ought to make at once. Who was the Hon.
Cardower's father, and how did one address him? And
who was his mother, and how did one address *her*? But
this social curiosity could not have been as lively as it
doubtless ought to have been, since in the act of imple-
menting it he was distracted by a shop-window. The shop
called itself an Academic Outfitter. The display was in
part of blazers, jerseys, scarves, ties, and anything else
upon which college crests or colours could plausibly be
displayed; and in part of gowns, caps, hoods, surplices
and similar adjuncts of the life of learning. Mungo halted
to view this useless gear with disfavour.

'Do they still,' he demanded, 'make us go swanking around in that stuff?'

'Oh, yes—every now and then. But it's not swanking. Academic dress is designed as a vesture of humility. Except, of course, if you're a nobleman.' Cardower produced this solemnly. 'Then your square—that's your cap—has a big gold tassel.'

'Christ! Are *you* going to have a square with—?'

'I'm talking rot. That was ages ago. And I shouldn't have one anyway. I'm not a nobleman.'

'I suppose not.' Mungo decided to let this nomenclature business be for the moment. 'I don't see anybody walking about in gowns.'

'That's vanished too—but much more recently. You only wear a gown at rather formal times, like dining in hall and going to see your tutor. And squares and white ties and so on are just for examinations.'

'Don't you still think it's a lot of rubbish?' They had walked on, and were waiting to cross Carfax.

'Oh, I don't know. There's something to be said for special clothes for special occasions. Going to a dance given by some awful woman for some awful girl, for instance: dressing up helps you to bear it.' Cardower suddenly grabbed Mungo by the arm. 'Come on!' he shouted, and they dashed successfully across the nose of a bus. 'Of course, I suppose I was a bit broken to *outré* clothes at school.'

'Didn't anybody rebel?'

'Rebel? Oh, I expect so. All sorts of people had all sorts of ideas, you know. And digging in their heels about this or that was among them.'

'With any result?' Mungo asked. He was a little baffled by this vague conjuration of strange territory.

'Result? None whatever—except, rather rarely, short sharp agony.'

'Oh, *that*!' Thus afforded some sense of a familiar world, after all, Mungo again felt an impulse of companionableness towards Cardower. 'Are you glad to have left?'

'I'm not sure that I know. Are you?'

'Yes—definitely. There are things at home I almost can't bear to have come away from. But not school. It hadn't all that scope. I'd had the place.'

'I see. Do you know? At school I felt like the chap in the Happy Valley—Rasselas. A land of contentment well hidden away—hidden away behind a popular picture of rigours and horrors, for one thing. But, in the main, just easy to be happy in. It becomes a bit of a bore, that.'

'I expect there were a few chaps lucky enough to escape boredom. Bloody miserable, in fact.' If Mungo said this roughly, it was in reaction to a sharpening sense that he had never talked to a contemporary like Ian Cardower before. He didn't yet know whether Cardower was in any way remarkable or particularly clever. But he was civilized (a History Sixth character who had read *Rasselas*!), and from a kid he had been able to listen to people talking as, for Mungo, they had talked only in books. He also seemed not to object to being serious, Mungo acknowledged to himself beginning to feel impressed.

'I say,' Cardower exclaimed, 'what awful women this town goes in for! No wonder sodomy is rampant among its young males.'

'Is it?' Mungo was startled by this sudden frivolity and impropriety in one whom he had just been crediting with higher qualities. 'I quite see'—he added, recovering himself—'what you mean about the females in this street.'

'But we'll range the countryside, you and I, in quest of unsullied virginal beauty. We'll leave Howard 4, 4 every afternoon at two o'clock precisely. There must be many a rose-lipped maiden between here and Bablockhythe.' Without pausing in what had become a quick march down the farther end of the Cornmarket, Cardower gave Mungo a swift appraising look. 'Correct?'

'Excellent plan.' Mungo had a notion that he was being required to vouch for the simplicity of his own sexual constitution. 'We'll start tomorrow.'

'And here we are. Lick your hand and smooth your hair, my lad. For in we go for our square meal.'

'Just a moment.' Mungo wasn't sure that the rustic admonition had amused him. 'What do I call your father?'

'Call him? Oh, I see.' Cardower had probably never been asked this question before. 'He's Lord Robert Cardower, but it would be a bit heavy—don't you think?—to Lord Robert him. Just give him the credit of his years, and call him Sir.'

'What does he—I mean, does he do anything in particular?'

'He's a diplomat—but not a strikingly successful one. Too honest or something.'

'But I don't call your mother Madam?'

'She wouldn't mind in the least—but perhaps not. You'll probably get away with calling her You. But if it turns out to be positively necessary to distinguish her from the barmaid or somebody, then it has to be Lady Robert. And that's that.' But on the threshold of the door Randolph Cardower hesitated. 'Sticking to names,' he said, '—do you mind if we start calling each other Mungo and Ian? Unless we decided to hate one another like poison, we'd be doing it in a few days, anyway.'

'For an Oxford man of six hours' standing, Ian, you do have a ruddy good grip of the customs of the place. Go ahead.'

Robert Cardower was as tall as Ian, and even slimmer. The clothes of father and son obviously came from the same tailor. Viewed side by side from behind (Mungo

thought—although this experience naturally wasn't being
offered him), they would probably strike you as being
twins. Even face to face, Lord Robert was to be distinguished from his son less by physical appearance than by
talking twice as fast. He couldn't have had a clue that
Ian, whose invitation had so clearly been a matter of sudden impulse, would be turning up with another chap. But
he had grasped the situation straight away, and in no
seconds at all slipped through every gear in the box.

'How do you do? It is so nice of you to come. My wife
and I have been looking forward with a great deal of
curiosity to meeting Ian's room-mate. I am very glad he
is to *have* a room-mate. In my last year at school I shared
quarters with an extremely clever boy who quite talked
my head off—and to my great advantage, since I was most
shockingly ignorant of virtually everything in the world.
Almost my only genuine expertise was in keeping tame
owls. And then I was sent up to Oxford—my father
thought it would do me good—and put by myself in some
rather large rooms in Surrey—the quad next to yours,
that is. I felt the lack of stimulus at once. I had acquaintances here and there in the college, but it wasn't at all the
same thing. It seems to me that a single companion, whom
one gets to know really well, is so much better than a
crowd. But tell me—what do you think?' Lord Robert
accompanied this sudden question with a glance of
anxious expectation, rather as if gathering Mungo's
thoughts on the matter in hand was a pleasure he had
been anticipating for days. Unfortunately Mungo's only
genuine thought was that any school-friend who had managed to talk Lord Robert Cardower's head off must have
been a prodigy worth knowing. So all Mungo managed
now—or thought he managed—was a mumble. 'I couldn't
agree with you more,' Lord Robert said, instantly and
convincedly. 'I think you are perfectly right. Elizabeth,

don't you agree?' He had turned to his wife as if she must no longer be excluded from a mature vein of speculation which Mungo had been developing. 'Ian, come over to the bar, and we'll fetch some sherry. I've booked a table—"reserved" it, as the man says—so there's no hurry in the world, no hurry at all.'

Elizabeth Cardower—Lady Robert—although neither so voluble nor so challenging as her husband, alarmed Mungo at first a good deal more. She was perfectly friendly, and she didn't hint the slightest sense that the youth was to be put at his ease. But her glance was cool and appraising, and you could see she was turning over the questions it might presently be possible to ask. Perhaps—Mungo thought—she did more in the anxious mother way than her husband did father-wise. She was wondering whether Mungo would be a good moral influence on her son. (For many years a similar concern about one boy or another had been a regular preoccupation of Mungo's aunt.)

'I think it very clever of the college not to team up men reading the same subject,' Lady Robert said. 'If you and Ian were both historians it would probably be quite fun for a time, but you would end up by boring each other fearfully. Among professional people there seem to be a lot of marriages of that kind nowadays. Particularly among the dons. If there's one at Balliol who knows all about Beaumont, he hastens to propose to a lady at Somerville, to whom Fletcher is an open book.'

'Were you at Oxford—and did you read English?' It was Mungo's habit to ask any question that came into his head.

'Yes, I was—and I did. I count myself almost a pioneer. Are you a pioneer—so far as your school is concerned?'

'Not exactly.' Mungo wondered whether this transition deserved to be called deft. 'Boys come from time to time, although most go to the university at Aberdeen or Edinburgh. There aren't any others at Oxford now.'

'The college has been very sensible about you and Ian, I do think. Or did you have any say in it? Did you take an initiative?'

'Oh, no. It was just a shock.' Mungo felt this was a fair reply. He wondered whether Lady Robert could suppose that he had written in to some Dean or Senior Tutor asking to be doubled up, please, with a good-class Lord or Hon.

'You mustn't let Ian's acquaintances be a nuisance to you. In your rooms in Howard, I mean. Just turn them out.' Lady Robert paused, and suddenly smiled charmingly. 'You have the inches for it. I do dislike stunted men.'

'So long as we don't try to turn each other out.' Mungo wasn't sure whether he'd liked Ian's mother making a kind of pass at him, however innocent. But second thoughts inclined him to think he did. 'It might be bad for the furniture.'

'Yes—it would be the tug of war. But it's convenient, isn't it? You needn't bother whose shirts and jeans are whose. Or shoes, probably. Ian raids his father's clothes ruthlessly. Incidentally, I wonder why two husky males can be so long in securing four glasses of sherry.'

Mungo wondered whether this was a signal to him to spring smartly to his feet and say 'I'll see'. He decided to stay put. Lord Robert might be seizing the opportunity to utter a few Polonius-like final admonitions to his son.

'But I'm grateful to them for not shoving at the bar,' Lady Robert was saying. 'I remember Oxford as a place where it was wonderful occasionally to encounter males just one at a time. They seemed always to hunt in threes and fours. Why are you reading English?'

'Why?' This abrupt transition took Mungo by surprise.

'Well, it was what I did best at school. Nothing much more than that.' Mungo was conscious that this was a guarded reply.

'Ian was quite good at it too—although there was very little emphasis on it at his school. We suspect he does some writing from time to time, although he keeps dark about it. Of course, it's in the family, in a distant way. But here they are.'

Mungo briefly wondered just how 'it'—which appeared to be writing—was distantly 'in' Ian's family. At once, however, he had to pay attention to Lord Robert, who was certainly paying attention to him.

'I do hope we have not diverted you from a pleasant first dinner in hall. But my memory is that not many people go in until Saturday. Some freshmen may be dining with parents, as Ian has so agreeably decided to do. Your own parents, I suppose, would have rather a long way to come, if they were to visit Oxford?'

'My parents are dead, sir. I live with an aunt, my mother's sister.'

'As a townsman or a countryman?' It was with his air of cordial, swiftly pouncing interest that Lord Robert contrived this skip-and-jump—but it was not before Mungo had glimpsed on his face the same tic or momentary grimace he had remarked in Ian earlier. Such things must be hereditary—and the father was no less displeased than the son that he had put a foot wrong. One oughtn't to take it for granted that the parents of even the most stalwart lad are in the land of the living. Mungo, however, who didn't even remember either his father or his mother, wasn't offended.

'Oh, as a countryman. My aunt, Miss Guthrie, lives at a little place called Easter Fintry, about half way between Forres and Nairn. I went to school in Forres.'

'How extremely interesting!' Lord Robert offered this gratifying but surely implausible comment with a curious abruptness; indeed, almost as if he had been told something startling. He turned to his son. 'Ian,' he began, 'do you realize that Lockhart—' But Ian was discussing the menu with his mother, and Lord Robert, as if thinking better of what he had been about to say, turned back to Mungo. 'I am delighted you are a countryman. Particularly as you are going in for literature. I have always thought that English poetry must be hopelessly mysterious to young people brought up in a town. Do tell me what you think.' This time, Lord Robert's anxiety to have Mungo's opinion appeared to have reduced him to a state of breathlessness, so that he actually paused upon his question.

'I don't suppose,' Mungo said, 'that it would make much difference with Shakespeare.'

'I quite agree! I couldn't agree with you more. But then Shakespeare is so absolutely universal. Consider Wordsworth, though. I've often thought how little I should make of him if I hadn't had the good fortune to be brought up in a quiet country home. Ian, have you gathered that Mungo—I may call you Mungo? Do say! —is entirely the countryman?'

'I've guessed it, more or less. He began to tolerate me when he saw I'd brought up a *Bevis*.'

'*Bevis* might be the favourite book of a boy in a Glasgow tenement,' Mungo said. He was impressed by Ian's sharpness of observation, but he hated anything like rot being talked about reading.

'Yes, indeed!' Lord Robert was all eagerness. 'But then *Bevis* is so *very* good a book. Wouldn't you say? When Ian and his sisters were young, I inflicted a great deal of reading aloud on them. It's a family habit, like tippling. And I started off with straight children's books. Do you

know the ones, Mungo, about Amazons and Swallows
and Coots and so forth by Arthur Ransome? He was a
dear man, and I liked him very much. But I'm afraid I
came to regard him as a most dangerous writer. You do
agree?'

'I'm afraid I hadn't thought,' Mungo said. Then, feeling this to be a lame response, he added: 'His kids are
rather an upper-class lot.'

'How very true! But what I chiefly felt was the un-
nerving absence of any darkness in their hearts. Traffick-
ing with exemplary characters is always bad for us. As I
recounted the adventures of these blameless young people
I felt I was piling up a dreadful sense of guilt in my children. Ian, whom I believe to be not wickeder than other
people, must have felt a moral outcast as he listened.
But the marvellous thing about Richard Jefferies's book is
that, even in their idyll, Bevis and Mark can quarrel.
Shall we go in to dinner? Just as you and Ian, if you become intimates, will certainly quarrel.'

'I don't see that we need. We're probably quite a tolerant pair.' Ian, who must be used to his father's philosophic vein, turned to his mother as they moved towards
the restaurant. 'What do you think, mama?'

'I'd rather you quarrelled than just disliked each other.'

'I do so agree!' Robert Cardower offered his wife the
same urgent and gratified acquiescence that he had been
offering Mungo. 'Quarrels are extremely horrid, but salutary in a fashion. Elizabeth, is this table perfectly agreeable to you? They remind us of the fallen creatures that
we are.'

'I don't see that I'm a fallen creature just because I
have a row with somebody.' Mungo's disinclination to
buy a theological view of the matter was so brusque that
he hastily added a softening 'Sir' to this declaration.

'Ah, not in itself. Shall we take evasive action before

the *table-d'hôte*? But a row can be a sudden perch from which one views a farther darkness which is darkness indeed. Dear me—upon what a morbid vein we have stumbled! Do tell me, what made you decide to come to Oxford?'

Mungo considered saying something like, 'I thought I'd take the measure of the spoliators of my country.' But finding himself to shrink from the expression of cordial interest such words would probably evoke, he found himself answering simply, and perhaps not less veraciously, 'I got the chance, so I thought I'd come and have a look.'

'Wandering scholar stuff,' Ian said, and turned to engage his mother's interest in the wine-list. It seemed to be his line to let his father make most of the going with casual guests.

'How much I would like to do that again myself!' Lord Robert contrived to indicate a friendly envy of Mungo's lot. 'There have been, I know, so many changes since my time. The colleges are said to insist on some decent appearance of a desire to study, and even the entrance requirements of the university itself are no longer derisory. The scene must be largely altered, indeed. I do so approve of that. The *dolce far niente* ethos was really a very great bore. Few of my undergraduate friends were absolute fools. Many of them are now in the City and the Cabinet and so on, where at least total imbecility must be gravely disadvantageous. But when up at Oxford we all considered idleness *de rigueur*. To cut things so fine that one ended up with a Fourth Class was very much the fashion.'

'But one reads in the newspapers about a lot of Cabinet Ministers having taken Double Firsts and things.'

'Perfectly true! And they are, of course, the invaluable men nowadays—and often extremely pleasant people to boot. Only'—and for a moment Robert Cardower looked perplexed—'one doesn't seem to remember them from that time.'

'Perhaps they were shut up in their rooms with their books, sir.'

'That must have been it. And I do feel very strongly how admirable that kind of concentration is. But one ought to find a mean. Don't you agree? Do tell me.'

'I don't think one should mug away just to impress a lot of examiners. But if something eems really relevant'— Mungo fleetingly wondered whether this vogue-word, recently arrived in North Britain, was already outmoded in the sophisticated South—'it's natural to shut yourself up and go after it while you have the chance.'

'That is so true! But, of course, a great deal of reading can be done in vacations. They are the proper time for the bulk of it, indeed. I try to impress that on Ian, who says he intends to peel potatoes at the Savoy for half the time, and spend the proceeds on the continent during the other. He tells us it is the usual thing.'

Mungo had heard about the impoverishment of the aristocracy, but understood it to be a myth cunningly fostered to secure them in their condition of unjust economic privilege. Yet there might be genuine cases, no doubt; and if that of the Cardowers was to this picturesque extent among such, he wondered whether he should be taking this fairly expensive meal off them now. But it might just be that Ian had a spirited notion of beginning early to pay his own way in life. Or perhaps his father was merely being funny.

'If we get on tolerably during term,' Mungo said, 'we could peel potatoes together, and have a garret where we'd encourage each other in studious habits at night.' This mild humour, although it wasn't quite Mungo's style, seemed acceptable to Lord Robert, who laughed agreeably. 'But the vacations do seem a problem,' Mungo added seriously. 'The long one goes on for months and months.'

'So it does. And when you are tired of the Savoy or Claridge's, you and Ian must simply come and scrape carrots at Stradlings. We are all fond of carrots. You will allow me to join you sometimes, and Elizabeth as well. We can think of it as a reading party in the Victorian manner.'

Mungo realized that, from Lord Robert, this was an invitation, and not simply chat. Although conscious of holding a fairly good opinion of himself, he didn't reckon to be a charmer of the fast-working sort, and there was something a little surprising, surely, in the speed with which these Cardowers were taking him on. Of course wealthy people had embraced D. H. Lawrence like that —and not always got a very good bargain out of it in the end. Perhaps Stradlings, although he had never heard of it, was a kind of Garsington Manor, where you had gone to tea and met characters like Aldous Huxley and Bertrand Russell. Mungo was modest enough to think that he wasn't yet, perhaps, quite ready to be an ornament of that sort of *salon*. However, it needn't be this that was expected of him. Probably it was Lord Robert rather than his wife who made the running in the way of moral concern about their young, and he had simply decided to spot in this wholesome and upstanding Scottish lad somebody who would be a good influence on his son. Ian might be a precocious *roué*, for all Mungo knew, or have taken to drugs or to haunting casinos.

'You must certainly pay us a visit,' Lady Robert said.

'I'd like to enormously.' Mungo offered this reply with as much of the politely conventional as his limited experience of such exchanges could manage. Lady Robert was almost certainly just obeying some rule in thus instantly backing her husband up. Her appraising glance was at work again. Mungo remembered Lord Robert's mentioning that Ian had sisters. Perhaps (like their mother) they disliked stunted men, and were not recklessly to be exposed to others differently proportioned. Mungo had a notion that people like the Cardowers would expect a grown-up son to make more or less what friends he liked, but to bring home only those whom they would describe as of an eligible sort. Mungo was some way from seeing himself as that.

But this business of putting himself wise about the Cardowers didn't—fleetingly, at least—altogether please him. He told himself that only three or four hours ago he hadn't known of their existence, and that—really and truly—he would be quite glad to stop knowing about it any moment now. If he must be doubled up with a public-school boy, he'd have preferred somebody from Fettes, or Loretto, or any other establishment not absolutely in the van of that racket. He saw himself arriving at this Stradlings place, and everybody being perfectly charming to him, and himself developing in consequence into a kind of Julien Sorel (for nearly a month Mungo had been regarding Stendhal as the world's greatest novelist): scheming, sensitive to imaginary affronts, hideously proud, very much out on a limb. That he wasn't, as Julien was, a peasant's son would make this all the more humiliating and absurd. The thing was to keep clear of the whole Cardower family-complex, and just see what was to be made of Ian Cardower by himself. He was pretty sure he liked Ian, and would continue to like him through any rows of the sort his father so cheerfully predicted.

Having arrived at this, as he felt, clear-headed view of the matter, Mungo found that he didn't particularly want to be shut of even the senior Cardowers, after all. As the dinner went on, he progressively came to believe that Lord Robert was genuinely anxious to learn what, on this or that, his son's new friend had to say. Mungo was aware

of having shamefully little to say—or rather of having
no technique for saying it at the tempo dictated by his
host. But this was precisely the situation in which Lord
Robert was astonishingly good. If you wrote him down
—Mungo thought—he would sound quite comical; almost
like Jane Austen's Miss Bates. But in fact his monologue
expertly created an illusion of your own scintillating par-
ticipation—so deftly did he take up, respond to, agree
with, question, qualify things you simply hadn't said, although you might have done, if your wits had been about
you. Perhaps this was what was called the aristocratic
embrace. Mungo still had the modesty not quite to see
why he should be hugged, but there would surely be
something almost bloody-minded in resenting it. He ended the evening feeling that Ian's parents could be reckoned among Ian's assets. He'd known a good many boys
—and girls, for that matter—about whom this couldn't
be said.

3

As soon as Ian and he left the Randolph, Mungo noticed that something odd had happened to the atmosphere of Oxford. To its atmosphere in the literal sense, that was; not as breathing the last enchantments of the Middle Age, and so forth. He didn't feel rook-racked, river-rounded or summoned by bells (although one bell was banging away somewhere or other with unnecessary reiteration). He just wasn't in contact with the ground as firmly as usual. It was precisely as if the air had thickened and was a little buoying him up. Or the terrestrial globe might somehow have lost a lot of its mass, so that the pull of its gravity was lessened, and one felt rather like the people who had taken to bouncing about the surface of the moon.

In whatever way Lord and Lady Robert Cardower were to be appraised in general, they were certainly not the sort to pour too much wine into a young man on his first night in the university, so Mungo was fairly sure he wasn't drunk. Or was he, all the same? His acquaintance with alcohol was so tenuous that he would have blushed to reveal it—even to Ian Cardower, of whom he was suddenly very fond. It did seem possible that a certain floating and insubstantial quality about the people in the street was a subjective rather than an objective phenomenon. There was undoubtedly something out of the way about them.

'Who are all those chaps?' Mungo demanded, coming suddenly to a halt by the steps of the Martyrs' Memorial.

'We're in a university city, aren't we? They don't look like students to me.'

'Why shouldn't they be students? They just happen to have disguised themselves as young heroes of labour from the motor-works at Cowley. Or they may be young heroes of labour disguised as students. Nobody can tell. And there's always a third possibility. They may be young villains. You'll know that if they put the boot in.'

'Nobody's going to put the boot in on me,' Mungo said truculently.

'Good Lord! You must have a head like a feather.' Ian, although amused, had put a firm hand on Mungo's arm. 'Back to college with you, my bonnie Hielan' laddie.'

'I'm not your—' But Mungo broke off. 'Do you mean I'm tight?' he demanded, shocked by this corroboration of his own suspicion.

'Of course not. It just sometimes happens like that after drinking only quite a little.' Ian was reassuring and know- ledgeable. 'For a minute or two after you go into the open air. We'll wander around for a bit, if you like.'

They wandered around: along the Broad, round the Sheldonian Theatre and Clarendon Building, down Catte Street, across the High. A great many of the build- ings—colleges, Mungo supposed—had recently had their walls cleaned or refaced; and on the inviting surfaces thus obligingly provided were scrawled all sorts of *graffiti*: plainly the work of rising young scholars in the university, but for the most part unintelligible even to Ian, whose line was so very much that of knowing all about Oxford already. Mungo, who found himself disapprov- ing of these doubtless sophisticated escapes of wit, ex- plained at some length that in Scotland they were perpetrated only by agitators and street-arabs.

'Keelies,' Ian said.

'Yes.' Mungo was surprised by this command of a

vulgar tongue. 'I didn't know—' But his attention was distracted by the moon. It was the harvest moon, now waning, and it had occurred to it to take up a position behind Magdalen Tower. The young men looked at the resulting spectacle with proper respect, and walked on silently for a time. They came into a cobbled lane. It was dimly lit and deserted; only in the Cornmarket, indeed, had there been the effect of a nocturnal urban crowd. 'In the deserted, moon-blanched street,' Mungo said, 'how lonely rings the echo of my feet.... But, look. There's an enormous meadow.' They had stopped before high wrought-iron gates set between equally high stone walls. Through these glimmered an extensive prospect of grassland and trees. 'It must be *our* meadow. Let's go in.'

'I expect—' Ian tried the gates. 'I thought so. Locked.'

'They've no bloody business to lock us out of our meadow.' Mungo's truculence returned to him. 'Let's climb.'

'Pretty high walls.'

'Not pygmies.'

'Right! You get on my shoulders and you're over, Sir Mungo. But you'll have to haul up my dead weight.'

'Can do.'

This feat was creditably performed, with the consequence that Mungo was able to judge himself sober again. In a shadowy indeterminate space beyond a railing sheep were wandering—or so it seemed until they realized that the sheep were wisps of vapour drifting up from the river. So they decided that the river was their goal, and found it at the end of a broad avenue of untidy elms. On these Ian pronounced in disparaging terms—rather as if he were a territorial magnate given to arboricultural pursuits in a big way. Mungo, who would have preferred to think of the trees dreaming in the moonlight as green-robed senators of mighty woods, found such airs irritating, and wondered whether he cared for Ian Cardower after all. But then they found themselves surveying a cluster of ungainly river-steamers at their moorings below Folly Bridge, and wondered whether they could signalize their arrival in Oxford by setting one of these craft in motion, steering it down the Isis, and leaving it tied up at Iffley lock. Nothing—naturally enough—coming of this, they contented themselves with climbing on board what Ian said was one of the few surviving college barges, and discussing what the water would be like if they stripped and swam.

This presently they had to do—for no better reason than that they had talked themselves awkwardly into it. In fact it was fun while it lasted, although they weren't without anxiety that the proctors (or even perhaps a party of women undergraduates, nocturnally perambulating) might turn up on their splashing and puffing. When they scrambled back to the deck of the barge, however, they began to feel foolish. They couldn't get inside the blasted thing to scrounge for a towel or something, since it was firmly locked up. So there they were on its deck—actually on view from Folly Bridge, if anybody was idle enough to be interested in them—and finding that the night air of an Oxford October was neither balmy nor possessed of any notable properties in the drying way. The screen of trees between them and the centre of the city had already shed enough leaves to provide them with the enjoyment of a vista of Oxford's dreaming spires. From Magdalen Tower, once more, on their right, to the answering terminus of Christ Church's Tom Tower on their left, there the whole bag of tricks lay expansed. It was everything that Matthew Arnold could have declared it to be—or Wordsworth, had he chosen to contemplate it instead of London from Westminster Bridge. Earth had not anything to show more fair. It was a spectacle which ought simultaneously to have elevated and calmed the mind. But Ian—perhaps from a sense of what was silly in their situation—reacted differently. He glanced at Mungo, and his eyes suddenly glinted maliciously in the moonlight.

'It's no like the wee laddie's Lossiemouth,' he said mockingly. 'And yon river's a muckle puir thing compared wi' the Findhorn.'

'Shut up, you!' Mungo was outraged by this brutal burlesque of his northern tongue.

'Or, for the matter o' that, wi' the bonnie Drochet burn.'

'What the hell do you know about the Drochet burn?' For a moment Mungo was bewildered. 'Put on that idiotic turn again, and I'll scrag you, Ian Cardower.'

'And now the young dominie's fashed. For it's that that the loon's going to be? A braw doup-skelper.'

Mungo hurled himself at Ian, and in a moment they were wrestling desperately. The barge, although it was a kind of house-boat and as massive as the Queen Elizabeth, swayed beneath them. Their naked bodies were cold, slippery, hard to get a hold on. It wasn't an expert affair.

'I can't take the pants off you,' Mungo gasped savagely. 'But I can take—'

'No, you don't!' Ian gave a violent heave that sent Mungo tumbling across the deck. In a moment they were at it again—warmed up, ready for quite a lot. Mungo did something clever with an instep against Ian's ankle, and this accession of skill was still delighting him when he was catastrophically confronted with its consequence. Ian, as he fell, had cracked his head against an iron stanchion. He lay quite motionless—no longer like a young man but like a big dead fish. Mungo saw that he had celebrated the first day of his university career by committing manslaughter. Ian sat up.

'Rupert!' Ian exclaimed rapturously.

'Gerald!'

They sprawled side by side on the deck, alternately
panting and laughing. The notion that they had been
comporting themselves like the nude gentlemen in
Women in Love amused them vastly.

'At least they had the sense to do their scrapping in a
well-appointed library,' Ian said.

'And before a large fire in a bogus baronial fireplace.
How's your thick skull?'

'Fine thank you. My private parts too.'

'Then let's get dressed, and off this bloody tub. You
frightened me, Ian Cardower.'

'And whose fault was that? But I agree. Let's briefly
put on manly readiness—as another Forres loon once
said.'

'Shut up, you!'

'Christ, are we beginning again? He was very respectable—a thane of Cawdor, and all that. I suppose we've
got to get back over that wall.'

'What about after that? Will the college be locked up?'

'Lord, no. We just walk in.'

'Offering a courteous good-night to the chap in the
bowler.'

'Just that.'

Chattering amiably, they scrambled into their clothes,
and retraced their steps along the New Walk. The moon,
having bestirred itself and moved off in a south-westerly
direction, was shedding impartial light on the most es-
teemed monuments of Oxford at large and Christ
Church's despised and outcast Meadow Building. Mungo,
whose aunt had brought him up on Ruskin as well as
Carlyle and Scott, rather liked this Venetian Gothic performance. He wondered when he would get to Venice.
There, he thought, people would be singing on the water

on a night like this. Monteverdi, perhaps. Monteverdi had been *maestro di capella* at St Mark's, but had by no means confined himself to sacred music. Here, there was only another bell or two at the moment; the sound came muffled because it had to leap-frog over the architectural mass before them. People had probably been tugging away at those same bell-ropes when Monteverdi was composing *Orfeo*—and Shakespeare rehearsing all that thuggery at Forres and Dunsinane and Inverness. Mungo began humming from the opera, and then broke off.

'Have you ever been to Venice?' he asked.

'Never been to Italy at all. My parents have a fixation on France, and were always taking us there, or bundling us off there. But I'll bet Italy's better. Particularly the girls. France for guzzlers, but Italy for passionate spirits like you and me. We'll go there in the Easter vac.' As Ian made this startling proposal in the most casual way, they found themselves before the high stone wall again. 'Brace your puny frame, my motile Mungo,' he said briskly. 'You're the ladder this time.'

It was nearly midnight, but there was quite a lot of noise in Howard. People were clattering up and down stairs, banging doors, shouting, and singing in ragged and raucous chorus. When the racket happened indoors it had one sort of resonance, and when it was continued in the quadrangles—for there seemed to be a lot of wandering from one part of the college to another—it had quite another.

'It sounds more like an end of term than a beginning,' Mungo said, his lately terminated schooldays in his mind.

'Happy reunion stuff, I expect. The terrified freshmen —that's you and me—cower in their attics.'

'We haven't got an attic.'

'True.' Ian had paused on the ground floor of staircase 4. 'And we're right on top of old Pons. Well, well.'

'Who's Pons?'

'You can see who he is, there above his door. P. de Beynac. I was at school with him.'

'Another freshman?'

'No, he came up last year. Seems to be quite holding his own, wouldn't you say?'

There was certainly a considerable volume of sound coming from the rooms of Mr P. de Beynac. They were the same rooms, Mungo realized, in which the hunting-horn had been in requisition that afternoon. He wasn't sure that he found all this exuberance exhilarating, and he was quite clear that he wouldn't care for it every night of the week. He'd rather supposed it to be an aspect of English polite life already on the wane in the time of Evelyn Waugh's Paul Pennyfeather. But apparently not. (A loud crash of splintering glass confirmed this negative conclusion.) Ian seemed quite uninterested. They climbed the stairs to their own rooms.

'Shall I shut this big outer door?' Mungo asked.

'The oak? No—I don't think that would quite do. In-hospitable. Somebody might want to call on us.'

Mungo thought poorly of this, but refrained from say-ing so. They tumbled on their respective sofas—certain rules for territorial behaviour were already forming them-selves in Howard 4, 4—and stared at each other with an attention much relaxed from that which had obtained earlier in the day. Ian yawned and Mungo yawned. But they didn't seem quite to want to go to bed. It wouldn't have been much use anyway—not till joy had a little abated around and below them.

'Ought we to be exchanging any more credentials,' Ian asked lazily, 'or be enquiring into each other's nasty habits?'

'They'll just emerge. But I don't mind a shot at credentials. Your room-mate comes of poor but honest
parents, long-since deceased. His father was a school-
master. It's why he didn't much like the term doup-
skelper.'

'I apologize,' Ian said quickly.

'You don't need to. We fought it out.' Mungo produced this robust etiquette seriously. 'I say, are we going
to find ourselves a bit different from all those chaps?'

'Not in the least.' Ian was surprised. 'Only rather more
articulate. That's because we both resisted much of the
education provided, and picked up our own instead. Curious that we've made the grade in this joint, really.'

'Certainly curious that I have.' Mungo was impressed
by the diagnosis just offered him; he thought it extremely
perspicacious. 'Why do you seem to know about Moray,
and even about the Drochet? Have you a seat there?'

'A seat? I haven't any seat, except the one I'm on
now. And it feels as if its springs are broken.'

'Your father, then?'

'Nothing of the kind.' Ian was impatient. 'We live in
a farm-house in Wiltshire. *Howard's End* kind of place.
You'll come and see.'

'But somebody?' In Mungo's voice was the suggestion
that Ian was being dishonestly evasive. 'Come back to
Moray.'

'All right, all right. My grandfather.'

'The dear old duke?'

'The dear old duke?' Ian, who had looked puzzled,
now frowned, and Mungo realized that he thought this
facetiousness poor form. 'There isn't any duke. Dukes are
a damned queer lot. My grandfather is a marquis, if you
want to revel in that sort of thing. Lord Auldearn. You
may have heard of him up there, since he does have a
house in Moray. Not that he ever goes near the place.'

'But you do.'

'Occasionally I do. Since they gave me a gun. The grouse and all that.'

'All that? You mean the blackcock and the golden plovers!' Mungo was vehement in a moment. 'And even the herons, because they eat your bloody trout. And a truck-load of hares and rabbits, just happily potted on the side. Not to speak of a gillie or two now and then.'

'Rubbish! That's out of a song by Tom Lehrer.'

'Gent fires, gillie falls. "Sir," gillie gasps, "you're ma laird: the guid God bless ye." Death of gillie. Gent has to catch a first-class sleeper south before the funeral. But he sends a nice wreath of English roses, scientifically packaged in dry ice.' Mungo paused, almost as breathless as if he had been the Marquis of Auldearn's younger son, Lord Robert Cardower. 'Well, that's it. I've feelings about all that in Scotland.'

'And enjoy flinging them around.' Ian looked at his companion dispassionately. 'I don't know that I've thought about it very much.'

'At least you're quite right about dukes. Do you know about the behaviour of a dead-and-gone Duke of Sutherland?'

'Haven't a clue, I'm afraid. I don't know the family at all well.'

'Christ! Well, ask the crofters he shoved into the sea.'

'Oh, come!' Ian had sat up. 'Quite a lot of prosperous crofters now. There are Commissions and things to see about it. Fisheries, too, in the islands. Really getting going again.'

'Man, do you know the load of debt put on a family there, if they're to have a boat and equipment that can fight it out against the big people round from Aberdeen?'

'Glad to know there are big people in Aberdeen.'

'Why, you blasted—'

But at this point in their discussion of the economics of depopulated regions Mungo was obliged to break off. The door had been flung open and there were four more young men in the room.

Three of the visitors were drunk and belligerent. The fourth (as is often to be remarked on such occasions) was a little less drunk than the others, and ineffectively disposed to play a dissuasive or moderating role.

'It's that bloody man Cardower!' The leading young man had come to a halt with a clumsy affectation of surprise.

'Hullo, Pons.' Ian, who had been confronting Mungo stiffly, resumed his relaxed sprawl. 'Try to remember your manners, my boy. And take them off to bed with you.'

'And who's that?' Having sheered away a little from Ian's reception, Pons de Beynac pivoted uncertainly on a heel, and stared insolently at Mungo. 'Why, if it isn't a young gentlewoman! Robin, it's a young gentlewoman.'

'So it is.' The youth appealed to nodded solemnly. 'And in college after hours. Let's put her out.'

'Wasteful,' the third youth said, and advanced uncertainly on Mungo—who, so far, had judged it incumbent upon him to imitate Ian's air of unconcern. 'Let's—'

'Oh, come on, you chaps. Let's go. This is a bore.' The fourth youth was waving vaguely towards the door.

'A winsome gentlewoman.' Pons, who perhaps believed that he was being enormously funny, advanced a little farther. 'A tight poppet.'

'Belt up!' Mungo had jerked himself erect on his sofa.

'Chuck her under the chin for a start.' Pons made a gesture as if to put this gallant proposal into effect.

'Get out!' Mungo said, and got to his feet.

The effect of this was to make Pons drop the gentle-

woman business. He took Mungo's measure, and spoke
with a great air of cold sobriety.

'Perhaps, sir,' Pons said, '*you* don't quite care for my
manners either?'

'I don't give a damn for your manners. But I don't like
your face. So bugger off.' There was a moment's uncertain
pause, in which it was Mungo's turn to assess Pons's phy-
sique. Pons wasn't a tall man. He barely came to within
six inches of either of his involuntary hosts. He reminded
Mungo, all the same, of a pocket battleship—the German
kind which, long before Mungo was born, had displayed
an awkward ability to take on craft twice their size. Mungo
saw no appeal in a sustained gladiatorial encounter. He'd
had one with Ian, after a fashion, not much more than
an hour before. So he repeated his injunction to Pons,
only turning it up a bit. 'Fuck off,' he said. 'I'm going to
count three. If you're not making for the door by then,
I'll lay you out.'

Pons de Beynac's very proper reply to this was to take
a swipe at Mungo. And at this Mungo, decisively rather
than expertly, hit Pons on the chin and put him flat on
the floor. Since Pons was so drunk, it was an inglorious
victory—and the more disagreeable in that Pons promptly
vomited. And at this Pons's friends took him by the
heels and hauled him out of the room. Then one of them
turned and politely shut the door. There was the sound
of a bumping progress down stairs. It seemed time to go
to bed.

'Well, well!' Ian said, and stretched himself. 'The scout
comes in at eight o'clock with some cheery nonsense
about a beautiful morning. But you needn't pay any attention to him.'

'Informative to the last.' Mungo, deciding against clearing up the mess, made for his bedroom. 'Good-night, Ian.'

'Good-night, Sir Mungo of the Lea.'

4

DURING THE NEXT few weeks Mungo put in much
of his time confronting the unexpected, and coping with it
as well as he could. Quite small things could be disconcerting. Thus when, on the morning after the violent delights
of his first night in college, he put his head out of his
bedroom door, it was to have a glimpse of Ian (who fortunately didn't see him) dressed in a manner suggesting
the condition of a tramp in reduced circumstances.
Mungo dodged hastily back, scrambled out of his already
rather crumpled best suit, and vigorously insinuated his
person into his oldest jeans. As they made him feel a good
deal more at home, he told himself that his action hadn't
been a matter of craven conformity. But was he to go
and see his tutor—or the Provost or somebody like that—
in these informal if pleasingly virile garments? He would
have to ask Ian. He could foresee asking Ian as becoming
rather a bore.

Again, Pons de Beynac turned out to be one of Ian's
close friends; there had been some mysterious relationship between them at school. Pons, moreover, within
twenty-four hours of their fracas, was saluting Mungo
himself with civility in the quad, and very shortly after
that was even cultivating his acquaintance. For reasons
which were obscure to Mungo, Pons had decided to credit
him with an intimate knowledge of working-class life.
Pons was conscious that his future career in industry and
politics was going to confront him (although perhaps at
something of a remove) with the problems of proletarian

feeling, and he was anxious to obtain early bearings on the subject. Although rather stupid, Pons was a serious young man (superficially, at least, more serious than Ian); he would ascend to 4, 4, curl up comfortably on a window-seat in the mellowing autumn sun, and debate with Mungo on articles he had been conscientiously reading in *Crossbow* or *New Society*. Mungo, although pleased to be treated as a sage (particularly by a second-year man), sometimes wished himself livelier employment. He even had a hankering to see the meritorious Pons blind drunk again.

They didn't by any means—Ian and Mungo—live in each other's pockets: they were less intimate than might have been predicted on the strength of the agreeableness of their first diversions in common. They ignored one another for quite a lot of the time. But Mungo (who went in for analysing personal relationships) felt this to be a sign, if anything, of something established between them.

They shared some interests, but no associations. Ian owned a considerable ready-made acquaintance around the place, and was constantly having visitors; Mungo, at first, naturally had none at all. Ian's visitors took Mungo for granted, regarding him as one of the facts of contemporary life. They were entirely nice to him, but much of their conversation was unintelligible and they didn't try to haul him into it. He found that, on the whole, idle listening was the best means of coping with this situation. Reading would be unsociable; disappearing into his bedroom impossible; simply clearing out feasible only in moderation if Ian wasn't to be rendered unreasonably annoyed. Ian's sociabilities were effortlessly companionable affairs, since he and his friends had hand-picked each other long ago. On the other hand when Mungo started in on making acquaintances every second one was a fiasco or a misfire. This amused Ian to a tiresome extent. 'Exit another grey man,' he would say with satisfaction when some singularly flat coffee-drinking had come to an end.

Mungo had a great notion of joining clubs and societies around the university, and paid out numerous subscriptions in this interest: he had been instructed that these affairs made a large part of Oxford life. There were societies for celebrating William Burroughs, for promoting modernism in the Church, for combating modernism in the Church, for watching birds, for climbing rocks, for listening to Verdi, for boring other people with your poetry, and for a generous variety of political purposes. Mungo had a go at most of them, became vehemently enthusiastic about some, and had a gloomy feeling that he would be disillusioned with the whole lot before the term was over. All this, too, amused Ian, whose idea of a club (he told Mungo mockingly) was some chaps dining together, preferably in very special dress-clothes designed by their great-grandfathers, and then breaking all the windows in Surrey before being carried off to bed. This infuriated Mungo chiefly because he knew he was being baited; he felt there was something in Ian which didn't go with that kind of thing. Ian got infuriated only when Mungo declared that for him, Mungo, the college and the entire university of Oxford had been a wholly disillusioning experience. It was Ian's savage denunciation of what he called the callow posturing in this that told Mungo Ian rather liked him.

Mungo decided that the trouble was too much talk and too little action. One could only be relevant if one took up an activist position. And there seemed plenty of scope for this. Many of the *graffiti* which had so puzzled him on his first nocturnal wandering with Ian proved to have just such a slant. Some were urgent in-

junctions to smash things: not windows (which were what
some of Ian's friends had a kind of hereditary faith in
the propriety of chucking bottles through) but regimes
and ideologies and athletic occasions—many of which
appeared inconveniently far away for the purpose. Others
simply called for assembly in one place or another at such
and such a day and hour for the purpose of holding a
demo. For some time Mungo did several demos a week,
but they were commonly harangued by the same people,
and when there was any liveliness to them it was rather
in the style of what, in old-fashioned novels of varsity
life, was called a rag. This wasn't really much good, because although Mungo found some of the proceedings
funny it wasn't in fact fun that he was looking for. He
had a very vivid sense that *homo sapiens* was hard at
work smashing the world to bits, and he believed that
one's best reply was to get busy on one's own part of it.
Things being as bad as they were in South-East Asia
and Africa and Belfast, it seemed probable that they must
be pretty bad in Oxford as well, and indeed there were
some quite rational-seeming chaps convinced that the
university was virtually a little police state on its
own.

By the middle of term this line of thinking (or feeling)
took Mungo out of demos and into a sit-in. He didn't
know who had master-minded it, but the idea seemed
superb. The university was to be brought to a dead stop
by the simple means of paralysing its pay-roll. Occupy the
office from which the cheques went out, and in no time at
all the whole body of the dons would be queued up for
some sort of dole from the Department of Social Security.
It was a very well-organized sit-in, and with a strong
cultural flavour to it. People held discussions and gave
lectures, and some group or other came and did folk-songs
the simple airs of which were taken up as a whistle by

the policeman patiently wearing down the pavement
outside. Only it went on and on. It went on for days, and
Mungo—although he wouldn't have confessed it to anyone—began to find it a bit of a bind. Moreover it looked
as if it would result in his having to cut his tutorial at
the end of the week. This bothered him because his tutor,
although he didn't seem particularly useful, was an
amiable and conversible old gentleman to whom he didn't
want to be rude.

Then it was discovered they had occupied the wrong
office. This one didn't send the dons their cheques; it
administered university estates—and in so devious a manner that the total surcease of its operations would probably pass unremarked by anyone for several years. At
this the majority of the sitters-in produced their Oxford
University Pocket Diaries and discovered that they were
almost missing an important demo in Wolverhampton.
Two comfortably appointed motor-coaches came round,
and they departed to this fresh activity amid hilarity and
applause. The Thames Valley Constabulary also departed
upon other occasions. And Mungo, who had never heard
of Wolverhampton, returned to Howard 4, 4. When Ian
got back from casually sampling some well-reputed lec-
turer he found his room-mate gloomily learning Anglo-
Saxon verbs. Mungo learnt them quite fast, but to the
accompaniment of a great deal of cursing of this fatuous
aspect of the English School. Ian mocked his disaffection.
English literature was something civilized people picked
up as they went along, and as an academic subject it
needed to have something senseless and arid packaged
with it, so that the English dons—'ushers', Ian called them
—could hold up their heads among the others. About the
fiasco of the sit-in, on the other hand, Ian was tolerant,
even although his common line with people running that
sort of thing was to advise their taking a single ticket to

Haiti, Brazil, or any other locality in which there was something honestly to create about. But the fantasy of ushers on the dole tickled him.

Oxford's three terms—Michaelmas, Hilary, Trinity—astonish the hard-working outer world by each lasting eight weeks and no more. Subjectively, their temporal dimensions are conditioned by being poised—Michaelmas most of all—upon a turn of the year. To Mungo's hyperborean sense his own arrival had been into lingering summer: almost full summer by day, with only the vapoured evenings to draw autumn on. At noon the main quadrangle showed like a formal chamber, remotely roofed in a blue upon which some baroque artist had here and there whimsically sketched a fleecy cloud. Warmth still radiated from the north front; by hugging it you could pleasantly toast yourself on two sides at once, and pluck figs or grapes or peaches from imaginary espaliers on the grey stone. In the centre of the quad the fountain splashed ceaselessly into its great basin of dark green water, but without disconcerting the lazy silver and gold of the cruising fish. Mungo understood that people occasionally got chucked in; the fish were large enough to take quite a nibble at you, he thought, as you scrambled out amid the unfeeling laughter of your enemies or—more probably—your best friends. But these would be nocturnal occasions. By day the place sometimes contrived to be deserted, Chirico-like, with only perhaps a very old don, permitted by some random academic charitableness to linger on beyond his time, creeping like a dusty tortoise from his unfrequented lodging to the patchy sociability of a common room.

At first the afternoons too were almost for basking in. The Isis was restless with rowing; you could watch the sweaty spectacle as if it was a chunk of op art—the image flicking into reverse and the oars doing all the work, heaving the rowers to and fro like sacks of flour with red and furious faces on top. But the Cherwell was Kenneth Graham stuff: an inefficient fooling about in boats and punts—only by humans instead of animals—on a slow snagged stream upon which the leaves were slowly falling and drifting and turning like weightless guineas. The girls had rugs but the men had only shorts or jeans; it was possible today, might be possible tomorrow, and then would be folded away until an April as distant as the moon. The voices, the transistors would fade, the sun-flecked stream perhaps be frozen over by the unimaginable end of term. Caledonian Mungo—sandy-haired, freckled, long-limbed, on the raw-boned side—strode through these appearances with a ready grin for anybody prepared to notice him, at times not resisting an imbecile and exulting sense that he had arrived, that he owned it all, and at times very much wondering what he had landed himself with. It wasn't the world he had taught his senses to be vigilant before or his mind to respond to. He wondered whether he could ever assimilate it to the serious vague purposes that had come to hover before him when, with books in his rucksack, he had played truant first in the compassable wildness of Cluny Hill and later through the dark ridings of Darnaway with a wary eye for the keepers as he walked.

This was rather solemn. But solemnity faded at tea-time—either in a crowded J.C.R. or snugly in Howard, making his own and Ian's anchovy toast before the electric fire. The anchovy toast was something new, and so was the quality of the evening hours it introduced. This was in part simply an atmospheric phenomenon. Anywhere in the south of England, of course, dusk was a more rapid affair than in Moray, but it sometimes seemed to deepen in these quadrangles as rapidly as if it had walked

through the lodge with a casual nod to the man in the
bowler hat. The crepuscular hours from five to seven were
supposed to be a period for work. You were even quite
likely to have a tutorial at six, and there was a book of
rules saying that music must not be indulged in during
these hours. But this was little attended to. Music came
from all over the place, and surprisingly little of it was
mechanically produced. Through lighted and uncurtained
windows one saw—as well as men brushing their hair,
scrambling into shirts, gossiping with girls, or throwing
parties which were like a crowded ballet much involved
with glasses and bottles—pianists and fiddlers and flaut-
ists addressing themselves with wholesome confidence to
pieces often largely beyond their technique. Mungo found
this cultural manifestation more impressive than Ian
appeared to do, perhaps as being something that didn't
much happen in Forres.

At times the concert was muted, as if somebody had
pressed down a soft pedal on the whole performance.
The earlier dusk was increasingly bringing in with it
mists and vapours. They were sometimes dun and pervasive like a fog, sometimes white and wraith-like and
drifting—the ghosts of girls, Ian sombrely announced,
haunting the scene of their betrayal at Commem. balls
long ago. Mungo was ignorant of Commem. balls, but he
had read Pope and took the reference. It touched a theme
he hadn't much been thinking about, although he did
rather suppose that quite soon sex would be rearing its
ugly head. Things would be going badly wrong if it didn't.
There were a lot of girls about the place, and although
none ever came to Howard 4, 4 he suspected with a certain envy—or perhaps it was even jealousy—that Ian was
ahead of him in examining the general problem they
represented. What he was himself aware of was of having
entered a masculine and traditionally segregated society

which was now under threat: it was rather like Tennyson's *The Princess* in reverse. If by girls one meant young
women with approximately one's own brains and habits
and assumptions, then Oxford was a crackpot place in
which they were in criminally short supply. But if this
pushed up the energy and ingenuity put into luring them
inside, it didn't at all make them the less intruders in
terms of the obstinate lingering ethos of the place.

This was most apparent to Mungo in these evening
hours—both before dinner and after it. There would be
girls around until quite late—he hadn't at all gathered
what the regulations were—and correspondingly there
would be men out and around Oxford until as near dawn
as they pleased. But essentially in the evening, at the
violet hour, the place closed in upon itself, as did a score
of these grey stone honeycombs around Oxford. It became, to its own deeper sense, the kind of place a barracks
must be, or a public school. Bred into Mungo, and un-
disturbed until this his nineteenth year, was another
notion of the violet hour. As for the fisherman and the
typist in *The Waste Land*, it should be the signal for
going home.

For some weeks the violet hour tended to give Mungo
the blues.

But one doesn't sit back and think in such a fashion.
The Oxford full term has its velocity as well as its brevity,
and perhaps it was the consequent *carpe diem* feeling that,
about half way through, set Ian and Mungo talking to
each other a good deal. *Dum loquimur, fugerit invida
aetas,* Mungo was actually able to quote to his friend—
since his curious syllabus had turned out to embrace a
little Latin as well as Anglo-Saxon poetry. Except on
Mondays, when Ian wrote his weekly essay into the small
hours, and Thursdays, when Mungo did the same, they

talked pretty well every night. The great college bell banged out the hours across the quads; revellers returning from parties clattered up their staircases and went to bed; the two occupants of Howard 4, 4, each with his long limbs ingeniously curled up on his sofa, talked absorbedly on. If they paused, it was only to drink Ian's whisky and munch Mungo's biscuits. These respective adjuncts to debate represented a disparity in material resources that didn't trouble them in the least. At the start they had taken to each other more or less at a glance; for weeks they had been friendly with an element of wary reserve; now they had, so to speak, frankly signed one another on. They exchanged intellectual persuasions and somewhat edited sexual histories; and (as Ian's mother had predicted) pooled pretty well anything that came back from the wash. By day they stalked about the college together, and Ian taught Mungo to play squash. Mungo's tutor, having encountered them strolling in the Meadow one day, gracefully informed them that they were as twinned lambs that did frisk i'th'sun, and that what they changed was innocence for innocence. Mungo looked this up, and was obliged to give it poor marks as a felicitous pleasantry. Leontes and Polixenes hadn't exactly stayed chums.

An important event took place: Mungo wrote his first Oxford short story. It came to him as he lay soaking—all but most of his legs and thighs—in a very hot bath. Around him, through open doors and across perfunctory partitions, naked youths, either mud-bespattered still or fresh-washed and glinting, were talking loudly and boisterously about a rugger match. Inspiration up-welling in such banal surroundings must be too authentic to be put by, and Mungo clattered on his typewriter, regardless of Ian's slumbers, all through the night. He worked in a state of high excitement that didn't in the least impair

his conviction that here was something absolutely detached
and controlled at last. What had been revealed to
him in his bath was the innermost working of the psyche
of the old gentleman like a tortoise, a don after the style
of a past age. Like another such whom Mungo had read
about somewhere in E. M. Forster, the old don went in
tremendously for young men. In fact he made a full-time
job of sentimental but entirely high-minded and Freudi-
anly unaware relations with them. But now young men
had ceased at all to dig that kind of thing, and as a result
the old don was isolated and lonely. (You could divine
this, if you were sufficiently sensitive, just by watching
him as he crept from his unfrequented rambling set in
an obscure corner of the college to some arid senior common room.) He was an aged innocent, and about how
undergraduates behaved in Oxford today he just hadn't
a clue, so that when a group of them started being charming to him in the dear remembered fashion he was fatally
slow in discovering that all they wanted was the convenient solitude of his rooms to smoke pot in when their
owner wasn't around. Finally, the police came along with
a lot of dogs, and the dogs sniffed out a cache of pot behind a row of learned journals, and the unfortunate old
gentleman was put in gaol.

This sad little story, if not quite up to Henri Beyle *dit*
Stendhal, after all, was at least finished before breakfast.
Ian read it later in the morning, pronounced a favourable
verdict with gratifying conviction, and added casually
that the sentimentality was not exactly confined inside
the old don's head. Mungo received this qualification un-
resentfully, having a certain seriousness in these matters
which enabled him to accept truths when presented to
him. Anyway, he said, he would scrap the thing, since
he wasn't going to have future dons talking about his
juvenilia. At this Ian grabbed the story, locked it up in a

drawer of his own, and declared that he would get it published in *Isis* next term. Mungo, who had appeared in
print in his school magazine and been thereby baptized
in those dark waters of vanity which all authors know,
protested rather feebly. And that was that.

What Ian presently recurred to was less the story itself
than the how and why of its coming into existence. He
seemed almost alarmed.

'But it's perfectly natural,' Mungo said. 'Haven't you
ever written anything yourself?' And he added unwarily,
'Your mother says you have.'

'That's just bits of verse, which is entirely different.'
Ian had flushed swiftly. 'But concocting stories about
people is really extremely strange. Just look! You see
this perfectly actual old man pottering across the quad—
probably with the placid intention of taking a glass of
madeira and a biscuit with a crony. And then you make
a grab inside your head at something having nothing to
do with him: rot you've read in some paper about drug
addiction in the university. After that you take another
look around at this chap and that—a bit of Pons, say,
and a bit of me and half a dozen others—and turn us in
a perfectly arbitrary way into treacherous young clots.
And there's your story! I repeat it's frightfully good. But
that just makes the process—putting two and two together, and bringing out the answer as a triumphant forty
—all the odder.'

'And more dangerous?'

'Well, yes. It's in *Rasselas*, don't you remember?'
(*Rasselas* had quite clearly appeared as Ian's favourite
book—although it was not at all like *Bevis*.) '*The Dangerous Prevalence of Imagination*. That's what the chapter's
called. The astronomer gets fancying things. Pushing them
round inside his own head, just like you—only it's the
sun and the moon, instead of senile dons and junkie

undergraduates. Sends him off his rocker.'

'A professional risk.' A shaft of morning sunshine had sought out Howard 4, 4, and Mungo on a window-seat was trying to squeeze himself into it. 'You have to take them.'

'Are you saying you mean to be what they call a professional writer?'

'It sounds daft, put like that. But it's the only way I have of explaining myself to myself—to suppose something of the kind. Am I beautifully clear?' Mungo paused, and Ian at least didn't say he wasn't. 'And I suppose the real professional risk is not having quite enough bread and lard in your garret.'

'I think there are others—just in possessing that sort of mind. Always being agog to make things up.'

'Man, you're havering.' With Ian, Mungo now allowed himself an occasional plunge into the Doric. 'I think the first Cardowers must have been Covenanters. Sour first cousins of sour English Puritans. Believing that poets tell lies.'

'They were nothing of the sort.' Ian was amused. 'On the other hand, they haven't—not so far as I know—produced a professional fairy-tale merchant. Only I have to admit I'm not the only Cardower to cohabit with one. My uncle David does. Oh, damn!' The big college bell was banging out noon, and Ian had scrambled to his feet and was rummaging for his gown. (The sunshine having been pre-empted by Mungo, he had been toasting himself on the hearth-rug.) 'Bloody tute.'

'Ho, ho!' Mungo said lazily, and edged a bare chest into the November warmth. Although he had registered Ian as saying something odd, he was too drowsy to feel curious, and the door hadn't closed behind his room-mate before he was very comfortably asleep. Being Henri Beyle *dit* Stendhal through the small hours had quite taxed the energies even of six-foot two and eighteen years.

*   *   *

In the eighth week Ian finished his essay quite early—
not much after one a.m. Mungo hadn't gone to bed. Having grown tired of Stendhal, he was reading *L'Éducation
sentimentale* and wondering whether he would ever experience such an obsession as Frédéric Moreau's for
Mme Arnoux.

'I say,' Ian said, 'why not come home with me when we
go down? The house will fill up with relations for Christmas, but you could stay until just before then.'

'I'd have to be home myself by then, anyway. But a
few days would be very nice. Do you think your parents
would mind?'

'Of course not. You have their invitation already. But
probably you've forgotten. You got so frightfully tight.'

'I did nothing of the sort. I mean, they might find this
a bit prompt.'

'Rot. *Fugerit invida* whatever it is. As a matter of fact,
I've had a letter from my father suggesting I should invite you. But I was going to, anyway.'

'Then that will be fine.'

This uneffusive exchange seemed satisfactory to both,
nor was Mungo in the least displeased when Ian a little
unexpectedly added: 'Do you know? I think I'll ask old
Pons too.'

The plan having been settled, Ian carefully collated
his essay and secured it with a paper-clip: when you were
reading these things aloud it could be disconcerting if the
pages proved to be out of order. Mungo turned off the
fire: you paid for your own electricity. They made for
their bedrooms. It was rather their habit, however, to
pause with a hand on the door-knob and swop final remarks.

'I say,' Mungo said, 'do you dress for dinner at Stradlings?'

'Well, yes, as a matter of fact. Dinner jackets.'

'Hooray! I can wear mine. It's still all wrapped up in auntie's tissue-paper. She was quite clear it's essential to young Oxford life.'

'I sometimes don't believe in auntie. But you must let me meet her one day, if she does exist.'

'Agreed,' Mungo said—and added seriously: 'She'll put you in your place, my boy. You wait.'

5

TERM WAS OVER. Like a traveller hurtled across the globe in a jet, Mungo felt that only part of himself was going to arrive on schedule, leaving another part either staying put or struggling along behind. For there are psychological just as much as there are physical discontinuities to which the human frame simply does not stand up. Of course if you have been at a boarding school you are conditioned to them. But to be confronted for the first time, when virtually on the threshold of middle age, with the prospect of three years of schizophrenic existence is surely insupportable. Mungo—who was actually in high spirits—expatiated on this to Ian, and received in return practical advice on how to comport himself at the valedictory ceremony known as College Collections.

'Don't stand as if you were on parade,' Ian had said, 'and don't lounge, either. Keep your great paws out of those bloody pockets. Smile, if you like, but don't unleash that awful great grin. Say Thank you, Sir—particularly if he blows you sky-high—but smartly enough not to make it sound ingratiating or even grateful. And if you must bow, make it as near a straight nod as you can manage.'

'I suppose all that's what you call protocol. And it's nice of you to be so anxious about me. Not that you can know anything about it, anyway. It's just what you've been told by the bigger boys.'

'You'll see.'

Mungo saw. It must have been an occasion of awful solemnity once upon a time; indeed, it retained a trace of that now. But it had gone schizophrenic in its own way. Some people had put on their most formal clothes, while others had kept the appearance of being crept out of a dust-bin invented by Samuel Beckett. You were herded in batches into hall, and there at high table, just as if about to attack one of their gargantuan dinners, were the Provost and a squad of dons. Someone bellowed out your name, and you had to march up the whole length of the place, with your hobbledehoy footfalls coming back at you from the lofty raftered roof. When Mungo reached the Provost the old chap was consulting, or effecting to consult, an enormous Domesday-Book affair in which it was to be supposed that all one's sins were recorded. 'A good first term, Mr Lockhart,' the Provost said, cocking up a bird's nest of a beard in order to manage a glimpse of Mungo's chin. 'A very good first term.' And that was the whole of that particular goon show (whatever a goon show may have been). At a hasty gulping of coffee in the J.C.R. afterwards it became apparent that the hundred-odd freshmen had all scored a very good first term.

'It's called the psychotherapy of warm praise,' Ian said. 'We're supposed all to be wanting to tear the university to pieces. And gracious words are going to temper those bad devices and desires in our hearts.'

Elizabeth Cardower had driven over to Oxford in an estate car, which was divided into first and second class compartments by wire netting. Presumably the inferior passengers were commonly basset hounds and the like. But on the present occasion Ian and Mungo piled in their suitcases (Pons had to go to London, and was coming down to Stradlings by train a few days later) and Lady Robert drove across Oxford to the supermarket in Cowley. They shopped in such a big way that both young men had to push round capacious trolleys. Mungo liked this. Lady Robert was a good shopper; she had it all in her head, and reached out with quick decision to the shelves and into the frosty bins. When they had finished loading up, the estate car looked like a grocer's van. They drove back over Donnington bridge and turned south, and soon the towers of Oxford were no more than an improbable spectacle, rinsed in winter sunshine, floating into distance. They were unreal, scarcely to be held on to at all. Mungo looked back on his eight weeks as if they were a dream which he knew to have been vivid and coherent, but which was dissolving away and eluding him, all the same. Fortunately he had been wrong in supposing the change would be traumatic. He was going to learn all about life at Stradlings. And it was a gorgeous day.

Ian had said that his home was a farm-house, and added that it was rather like *Howard's End*. Mungo didn't remember much of the actual set-up in Forster's novel, except that there were pig's teeth in a tree and the book-cases were unsteady on their feet. Stradlings stood in a downland coomb, sheltered by beeches which were the only trees within sight. It was a low-roofed house, built round three sides of a courtyard in the middle of which was an old well. The centre part was in stone, and looked to Mungo like a small monastic building which had been knocked about in aid of non-monastic living. One wing was a black and white half-timbered structure of the *Life in Shakespeare's England* order, and the other was in fairly modern red brick.

'It's not my idea of a farm-house,' Mungo announced as they drove up.

'Perhaps it's God's idea of a farm-house.' Bringing the car to a halt, Elizabeth Cardower offered this reply in a

tone making it impossible to tell whether it was a pious
reflection or a joke. 'And there's Anne.'

'God's idea of a sister,' Ian said. 'But where's Mary?'

'Didn't I tell you? Mary has gone to stay with her
friend Polly Pope. She won't turn up until Christmas.'

'I hadn't heard. Well, all out.' Ian appeared disconcerted, as if his younger sister's absence had upset some
calculation. 'Anne, this is Mungo Lockhart.'

Anne Cardower shook hands briskly, and at once turned
to give a hand with the suitcases. She was tall and fair
like her brother, dressed in riding-breeches, and had come
out of the house followed by a lollop and slaver of
spaniels. Mungo told himself that it was all going by the
book—a pretty simple-minded book. But from the first
moment he was a good deal struck by Anne.

And she was interested in him. At first he thought it
was her father's kind of interest: a polite appearance of
setting more store by your opinions (or even non-opinions)
than was plausible. But he found that when Anne asked
questions she waited for answers. And more of her conversation was in the form of questions than would have
been approved by the superior school-mistresses who had
'finished' her. For Anne was obviously 'out'. (Mungo told
himself that to keep his chin above water at Stradlings he
would have to make heavy demands upon his knowledge
of the not-so-modern English novel.) She was also a
straight-glancing sort of person, rather as Ian was. Mungo
was instantly confident that he was going to get on well
with Anne Cardower.

'Do you know this part of the country?' she asked as
she handed him tea.

'No. I've never been here before.'

'Do you ride?'

'Yes. But I haven't brought anything to ride in.'

'The important thing is can we mount you. And I think

we can. You can borrow breeches from Ian. Are you older than Ian?'

'No—nine months younger. Do I look older?'

'Oh, yes. Or you look more responsible. A firm and formed character. You'll be good for Ian.'

'Ian runs me, as a matter of fact.' Mungo saw he was being made fun of. 'He knows all the ropes, and hands them to me at the right moment. He has an instinct for ropes—and for all the wheels and pulleys. I'm no good at them.'

'What are you good at?'

'Well, I know what I want to be good at. Not at manipulating the social structure, but just knowing—or feeling—how individuals tick.' Mungo was conscious that this must sound pretentious and half-baked, but at least he believed what he was saying.

'If you're nine months younger than Ian, then you're two years younger than me—and about ages with my sister Mary.'

'I see.' Mungo found these precise calculations disheartening. 'So we know where we are.'

'Oh, I hope not. That would be dull. We are almost completely unknown to each other. And that's much more interesting.'

'Finding out about other people,' Lord Robert said, 'is one of the major pleasures of life. But it should always happen at first hand, and through the medium of conversation, so that anybody who doesn't want to needn't play. And one mustn't treat the other fellow as if he were in the witness-box.' Lord Robert paused on this, a thing he didn't commonly do in mid-stream. Perhaps he was obliquely rebuking his daughter, or Mungo, or both, for going so baldly to work. 'Take Mungo, Anne. I hope to learn a great deal more about him. But it will be from himself, and without his being aware of the process.' Lord

Robert made another pause here, and Mungo was aware of a momentary regard more thoughtful than quite matched the lightness of this talk. 'Mungo, you see, will be too busy feeling that he is finding out something about me.'

'Mungo's own method is different,' Ian said. Ian was sprawled on a sofa, much as if he had been in Howard 4, 4. The Cardowers treated each other rather formally, Mungo had been noticing. But this effect of cool courtesy, such as one adopts with strangers, didn't, somehow, prevent the whole effect from being relaxed and easy. 'Mungo fires away with direct questions, just like Anne. It's part of his turn as the simple Scottish boy.'

'It's not a turn,' Mungo said.

'All right—it's not a turn. But the point is that the blunt demands for information are deceptive. What he really uses are antennae. That's why he's going to be a writer.'

'Why not a diplomat?' Lord Robert asked. 'My own career has been impeded precisely by the lack of such an endowment. Metternich owned antennae, and I'm inclined to think Talleyrand had them too. Mungo, what do you think?' He put down his cup, and moved towards the door; he seemed to have some occupation which prevented his being much around. 'Exactly!' he said—although Mungo, who was ignorant of nineteenth-century diplomatic history, had said nothing at all. 'I entirely agree with you.' And he drifted from the room.

'Now we can go on,' Anne said. 'Have you any brothers or sisters?'

'No. I missed out on any chance of them when my parents were drowned. They'd only had time to have me.'

'How were they drowned?'

'They were going to visit relations in Invergordon, and the ferry between Fort George and Fortrose went down.

It was probably a rotten old tub in those days. I ought to have been on it too, but I was left behind with my aunt because I had chickenpox. I've lived with her ever since.'

'Is she married?'

'No. She's a school-teacher. It was a great bit of luck.'

'The chickenpox?'

'Oh, no! It's not at all certain that one is lucky in being alive. Sophocles and a good many other—'

'Don't be pedantic, Mungo. This isn't a tute. *What* was a bit of luck?'

'My aunt, of course. If you *are* going to be alive—for more than half a century, quite probably—you do want to look around.'

'Survey mankind from China to Peru,' Ian said over his shoulder. He was following his mother from the room, so that Mungo and Anne were now alone. It didn't look as if the Cardowers were all that nervous, after all, about ineligible young men.

'There's your brother being pedantic too, and quoting Dr Johnson. He does it quite often. It's funny. Johnson usually appeals to people with a sombre temperament, and Ian certainly hasn't got that.'

'Hasn't he? I suppose the antennae must know. But go on.'

'Well, I wanted to survey at least a little more of mankind than would be possible from, say, behind the counter in a corn-merchant's office in Elgin. So it was lucky that my aunt had all the teaching of me until I was twelve. Latin included—although I don't think she'd ever had to teach anybody else Latin. I believe she got it up for the purpose.'

'It all sounds very Scottish.' Anne Cardower said this seriously, and it was seriously that she engaged Mungo's glance. 'And then?'

'I went to school in Forres. It was six miles on a bicycle.

There was no difficulty, except when there was heavy snow. It was a school on a shoe-string, but good in a frugal way. Rather brutal, perhaps. I don't know that I was worried by that.' Mungo's short sentences revealed an inward eye bent on already distant things. 'But philistine, too. I think that would be the word. By the time I was sixteen it had really run out on me. So I more or less went into opposition. That was a bit premature, because they could still leather me. It was rather an awkward time.'

'But it must have come straight, somehow. Because— well, here you are.' Anne seemed to feel that this might be misinterpreted. 'At Oxford, I mean.'

'Yes—but ought I to be? I find it hard to tell.' Mungo felt that he had been coaxed into talking about himself in a big way. But he went on, all the same. 'What happened was that I read a lot, and they came to notice that. And I can't have been hopeless at the school subjects, since the headmaster decided to shove me in for Oxford. I wouldn't have allowed him to, if I hadn't seen my aunt wanted it as well. Even so, he was suffering from delusions of grandeur about his school. When the papers came they were totally beyond me—or most of them were. They called for a critical patter that hadn't reached Moray. But there were two hours in which to write an essay on Landscape. Just like that: Landscape. It sounds idiotic. So I scribbled away—I think in a prose-poemish fashion —about the few square miles of the stuff I knew.'

'That sounds sensible to me. It wouldn't have been much good writing about Mont Blanc or the Bay of Naples.'

'Of course it was sensible. And what happened was that some don or other—I suppose it must have been my present tutor—took a fancy to this rhapsody, and as a result I got an interview. That's how it works, you know.

All the candidates write their examination papers at school, and then the possible ones are summoned to Oxford. There was a lot of resistance in me still to the whole idea. It seemed exotic and absurd. But when this summons came it bowled me over. I'd cleared one hurdle in an unexpected way, and I was damn well going to do my best to clear the next.'

'Good,' Anne Cardower said briefly.

'I expected a tremendous great oral examination—a kind of super *viva*. So I mugged away like stink—reading Dr Leavis, and Dr Tillyard, and God knows what.'

'Was it useful?'

'Absolutely not. When I got to Oxford all I found was a notice stuck up on a board saying I was to call on the Provost at eleven a.m. on the following day. And the next man was down for eleven-ten.'

'Depressing.'

'Well, I went along. He asked me, not very hopefully, if I'd ever read any of Scott's novels. I said I'd read quite a number. I think he felt from all the marks that I hadn't a hope, and was pretty cross with somebody for bringing me 500 miles on a fool's errand. At least I could see he was determined to cut short the agony, for he started asking me about *Anne of Geirstein*. Honest, Anne! The old ruffian did just that.'

'And Super-Mungo, the wonder boy, knew this obscure romance backwards.'

'Well, it did happen I'd read it.' Mungo took this sally in good part. 'And that seemed to me to make the Provost furious. My only sense was that I was drowning, swiftly but painfully. But when I surfaced at last it was to discover we'd been talking about Scott for nearly an hour. What happened to the eleven-ten chap and those following him, I never knew. Anyway, that was it. I was in.'

'Mungo, that was absolutely splendid!'

Mungo had the sense of coming to with a jerk. It was as if he had been drowning again—and this time had discovered on surfacing not an old gentleman with a bird's-nest beard but the girl of all his dreams. He told himself that this wouldn't do. Quite spontaneously, and after cheerful mockery, Anne Cardower had said something very nice and rather admiring. But that was no warrant for falling in love with her on the strength of half a day's acquaintance. Ian had invited him to Stradlings, and loyalty to Ian had to be the first thing. He mustn't have Ian cursing his stupidity in introducing the Forres loon into his home.

Mungo had these creditable feelings genuinely and quite strongly; he also had a clear enough head to wonder how long they could be made to last. Perhaps it rather depended on Anne.

The next day he and Anne went riding together on the downs. It was sunny and cold; the ground was firm but unfrozen beneath the horses' hoofs. Mungo had been afraid that English horses might not be like Scottish horses—or not like the Scottish horses he had ridden. But this anxiety proved to be without substance; he knew during their first canter that if he didn't ride elegantly he did ride confidently and well. And he found after their long gallop, when they had drawn rein and turned into the wind, that he was far from being too breathless for talk.

'We had me yesterday,' he said, 'so it's your turn now. To tell me about yourself, I mean. What sort of things do you like doing?'

'I like doing what I'm doing now: riding with a young man who tells me he's a shade taller than my brother.'

'You asked me if I was.'

'Did I? I don't remember. I must have been trying

hard to keep up a polite conversation.'

'You were doing nothing of the kind, Anne. What else do you like?'

'Fox-hunting. And coursing—but we do that only in Ireland.'

'What a blood-thirsty crowd you are.' Mungo kindled to what he knew was Anne Cardower's mockery again. 'Even Ian wouldn't come riding with us because he wanted to clean his gun—just to have something lethal in his hands.'

'As a matter of fact, you're on Ian's horse now.'

'I wondered if I was.' Mungo was abashed. 'I think perhaps we should go back and let him take over.'

'Don't be silly.'

'I'm not being silly. Come on.'

'Mungo, *please*. He'd be furious with me for telling you. He was frightfully bucked to have you go out on Ajax. You must have seen that in the stable yard.'

'Well, yes—I did. Your brother is always madly nice to me. Did you ever read Peacock's *Melincourt*?' Rather fatally, a bizarre analogy had come into Mungo's inventive mind.

'I've never even heard of it.'

'It's quite funny. There's a country gentleman in it who gets hold of an orang-utang in order to prove some theory or other. He grooms it carefully, and buys it a baronetcy—it's called Sir Oran Haut-ton—and a seat in the House of Commons. Sir Oran is a great success. I wonder if I'll be that once Ian has desegregated and integrated and assimilated me.'

'Mungo, I call that a stupid joke.' Anne was angry, and showed the fact by nudging her mount into motion. 'Or at least it is when offered to me. I suppose it might be all right as part of the rubbish you and Ian talk together. But my brother doesn't make friends because he has

designs upon them. He likes them for what they are, and
not for what they might be groomed into.'

'You're quite right.' Mungo's freckled face had flushed.
'Stupid things occur to me, and I come bang out with
them. I'm sorry.'

'Forget it, Mungo. And I promise to read *Melincourt*.'

It seemed to Mungo that this small *contretemps*, although it would dismay him in the watches of the night,
had in fact advanced his intimacy with Ian's sister.
There was no occasion to fall into discouraged silence.

'Do you know,' he said, 'something that puzzles me?
Your family seems to belong to my part of the world, and
yet I've hardly heard of them. Auldearn is near where I
live, and your grandfather is Lord Auldearn. But the
name as attached to a person rings only the faintest bell
with me.'

'My grandfather never goes near Scotland.'

'I suppose that's it. Is your father his heir?'

'Oh, no. The immediate heir is my uncle David.'

'You do seem to stick to more or less Scottish Christian
names, which is something not particularly fashionable
in the Scottish aristocracy. What's your uncle David
called?'

'Well, if you were inviting him to a party, what you'd
put on the envelope would be The Viscount Brightmony.'

'That's another place-name. But I've never heard of
him.'

'He does live in Scotland, as a matter of fact. But, as
far as that invitation goes, you might save your postage
stamp. Uncle David never goes anywhere. You might say
he lives in seclusion.'

'I see.' Mungo didn't pursue his enquiries about this
relation of Anne's, because he felt that people described
as living in seclusion are commonly lunatics. Instead, he
tried a spot of mockery himself. 'I'd like the Cardowers

to have romantic associations in my mind. But it seems no go.'

'The surname can hardly be called romantic—can it?' Anne was amused by this conversation. 'You know what a cardower is?'

'How very odd! I never thought of it. He's a chap who goes round mending old clothes.'

'Yes. The original Cardower, you see, rose from that lowly occupation to the honourable office of Court Tailor at Dunsinane. When Macbeth proposed to get out of his nightgown it was my ancestor who came forward with an appropriate pair of breeks.'

Mungo's condition was by now such that he judged this mildly funny nonsense to be brilliantly witty.

'Do you know,' he said, 'that only the king was allowed a nightgown? Poor old Banquo and the others are in their skin—and on a very dirty night. "When we have our naked frailties hid," Banquo says, "That suffer in exposure, let us meet." So the Elizabethans enjoyed nudity on the stage, just like us.'

Having discovered this ability to entertain each other, Mungo and Anne rode back to Stradlings in a highly companionable way. They had to stop at a level-crossing while a train went by, and Mungo had some difficulty with Ian's horse. He controlled the situation with an ease highly agreeable to the innocent vanity in his heart. *Women in Love* being his idea of the supremely good English novel (and so almost as good as *Le Rouge et le Noir*), this made him think of Gerald Crich in a similar situation. This in turn reminded him of how he and Ian had wrestled in the darkness on the deck of a college barge. He told Anne about this, only omitting one or two things which, in the heat of the fray, he had promised Ian to do to him. He was about to go on to the later events of that memorable night, including the splendid

drunkenness of Pons de Beynac. But he remembered that
Pons was coming to Stradlings, and a prudent instinct—
which his aunt would have called canniness—told him to
leave off. This was to prove extremely wise.

'I've thought of a Cardower you may have heard of,'
Anne said, when they were walking back to the house.
'The bad Lord Douglas.'

'Yes, I think I have heard of him—as a kind of legend.
He sounds as if he were in a Border ballad.'

'Well, he isn't. He was just my other uncle, and he
lived like his brother—my uncle David, that is—in Scotland. I don't remember him, because he died about fifteen
years ago. Probably I shouldn't have been allowed to see
him anyway, on account of his being so bad.'

'He must have been Lord Douglas Cardower, just as
your father is Lord Robert?'

'Of course.'

'How strange that he should be the only one of you I
ever heard of—before Ian and I got to know each other,
I mean. And that it should have been at a kind of folk
level. The bad Lord Douglas was just a bogey-man. It
never occurred to me he'd been real. And now he turns
out to have been your uncle. And here are you and I
talking about him.' Mungo was in high spirits, as he sometimes was when something had struck his imagination.
'I call that rather fun.'

'I don't think my father would call it that. Poor uncle
Douglas is distinctly tabu.'

'Too bad for words?'

'It isn't quite that—not quite simply that. At least, so
I feel.' Anne halted before the door of Stradlings, as if
anxious to get something clear before going inside. 'I
suspect that, in addition to being very bad, or before
being very bad, he was very lovable. I believe they all—

his parents, his brothers, everybody—adored him. And then there was some terrible disgrace, and they can't bear to think of it all.'

'Yes, I see,' Mungo said, and fell silent. It wouldn't be a good idea, he felt, to pursue this family skeleton further. People like the Cardowers, he supposed, were particularly sensitive to the stirring of anything of the sort in their cupboards. 'I'm going to find Ian,' he said, 'and have it out with him about that horse.'

6

IN THE COURSE of the next few days Anne Cardower
became the prompting occasion of everything that went
on inside Mungo's head. This didn't mean that he thought
of nothing and nobody else. When he was with her—as
she seemed pleased he should be for most of the time—
his talk was of shoes, ships, sealing wax, and the problem of whether pigs have wings. When he was away from
her he sometimes found these conversations continuing
silently and of their own momentum; at other times he
was showing himself notably in command of a variety of
striking situations of which she was a spectator; at yet
others she had retired into the wings in favour of one or
more of her relations. In these last fantasies Mungo's
maturity, breadth of view, and soundness of judgement
impressed more than favourably Anne's parents, her
grandfather Lord Auldearn, her uncle Lord Brightmony
(although he was mad) and even her other uncle the bad
Lord Douglas (which was surely the extreme of imaginative debauch, since the bad Lord Douglas was dead).
There were also times when Mungo quite forgot about
the Cardowers, Anne included, and found his inward
eye contemplating with amazement and awe the master-
pieces which he now knew he was going to write.

Al this mene I by love, he told himself satirically out
of Chaucer. But it was really no use affecting to be detached about himself. He had taken a header, and he
knew it.

His acquaintance with girls hadn't been extensive or

impressive, partly on account of the social persuasions of his aunt, Miss Guthrie. He could make Ian laugh with a scathing account of the class structure of a small Scottish town. But it was something quite real, and stiff enough to have to be counted as among the facts of life. He had hardly known a girl with whom he hadn't been at Sunday school. For every attendance at this institution you were given a little religious picture to stick in a scrapbook, so that his first experience of the commerce of the sexes had been a matter of swopping a Good Shepherd for a Lamb of God, or a Light of the World for a Wise Virgins. This hadn't led anywhere very much. And as they grew older it was only a minority of these girls who showed much promise of exciting the imagination or even the nervous system—and only a minority of these again who qualified for party-going status in Miss Guthrie's mind. Of course other regions existed, and Mungo hadn't been so unenterprising as not to explore them. He had gone sprunting with the farm lads—an activity reticently defined in Scots dictionaries as running among the stacks after the girls at night. It had proved—and even before turning what might be called definitive—not quite his thing. He found he couldn't certainly work out what kind of fastidiousness was responsible for this disappointing result. It didn't seem to be a straight sexual fastidiousness, nor a moral one either. Perhaps it was an aesthetic fastidiousness. Probably it was simply and shamefully snobbish. When young and silly, and given to reading of a romantic and chivalric order, he had been prone to dream that he dwelt in marble halls with vassals and serfs at his side. It might be some hang-over from that which was responsible for his not much taking to what Donne calls coarse country wenches.

So here he was—his aunt's nephew, precipitated into the society of a girl so remote from these as to be dis-

tinguishable from the minister's or the doctor's daughter
as well. Not that Miss Guthrie would much approve of
the Hon. Anne Cardower. Her attitude to the aristocracy
was not ambivalent, and Mungo had never detected her
as obtaining the smallest vicarious satisfaction from their
doings as reported in the popular press. She believed in
superiors, equals, and inferiors—and also in the wisdom of
keeping clear of either outside of the sandwich. At the
same time, and because she had a proper respect for his
talents, she was inclined to treat her nephew—although
cautiously—as a special case. She judged it right and
proper that the exceptionally endowed should rise in the
world, provided it was through strenuous efforts of their
own. This had been the basis of her uncompromising vote
for Oxford. She couldn't have foretold Mungo's tumbling
into a set of rooms with the grandson of an absentee Scottish landowner. But she certainly held an exaggerated idea
of the upper-crust flavour of the place as a whole.

Mungo wondered whether any of his excitement about
Anne had got through to Ian. He rather hoped not, and
he couldn't somehow see himself adding the precipitate
fact to the stock of confidences which he and Ian had
exchanged during the latter part of the Oxford term. He
might have done so—have baldly announced 'I'm terribly
in love with your sister'—if Ian hadn't in some way become for the time being rather a background figure. It
was as if being at home were drawing him back within a
family pattern. He had taken on some of his father's
gestures and intonations, and even his father's air of being
alert to be perfectly charming to absolutely anybody who
turned up.

Yet Ian's likeness to Lord Robert didn't seem to Mungo
more than superficial. Perhaps in character Ian skipped
his father and harked back to earlier generations of Cardowers about whom Mungo could only guess. Perhaps,

too, he was ambitious. Every now and then he would
disappear for hours on end, to turn up again with some
vague remark about having been helping the stable boy,
or carrying out one or another handy-man's job about
the place. Mungo thought that he might really have been
tackling the vacation reading which his tutor had no
doubt urged upon him. Mungo himself read hardly anything at all. He was too busy living his own dream.

Dreams commonly dissolve and fade. But sometimes
they are shattered—by a shake on the shoulder or a loud
noise in the street. It was a loud noise in the courtyard
of Stradlings that told Mungo of the arrival of Pons de
Beynac. Mungo had been out looking for a missing spaniel
—and in consequence of this simple commission feeling
rather like a son of the house—when the row drew him
round a corner and confronted him with a bright yellow
sports car which had come to a halt before the front door.
It had the sleek lines and hypertrophied snout of a really
classy specimen of its kind, and its provision of space
for mere human beings was so scanty that an effect of
surprise attended the unloading from it not only of Pons
himself but also of a good deal in the way of suitcases
and sporting impedimenta. The morning was frosty, and
only a diminutive windscreen had protected Pons from
a nipping air; in consequence he was as pink—Mungo
told himself—as a hunk of good quality salmon out of a
tin.

'Hullo, Mungo!' Pons shouted amiably. 'You here
still?'

'Hullo, Pons.' Mungo didn't see why he should positively confirm that he *was* here still. Indeed, the question
didn't please him a bit.

'I thought you might be gone.' Pons was struggling out
of an overcoat fabricated from dark leather and snowy

fleece. 'Glad you haven't. There are things I want you to tell me about. Shop stewards, for example.'

'I don't know anything about shop stewards. I've never met one.'

'I was reading rather a good thing in some rag or other.' Pons, whose references tended to be vague, ignored Mungo's disclaimer. 'It seems shop stewards are the real mischief. So I think they oughtn't to be allowed —not into the factories, I mean. That would solve the whole problem, it seems to me. But I want to know what you think.'

'Shop stewards work in factories.'

'That's it. That's what's wrong. I don't think they should be allowed into the industrial areas at all. Or not without permits, or something of that kind. You could take away the permit if one of them started a strike. Where's Anne?'

'I don't know.' The suddenness of this transition would have given a duller youth than Mungo a jolt. 'If you want to clock in, Elizabeth's writing letters in the drawing-room.'

'Then I'll go and pass the time of day.' Pons had looked sharply at Mungo, almost as if he were bright enough to glimpse some hinterland to so firm a suggestion. 'But I'll shove these things in my room first. Of course, I know which it is.'

'I'll lend you a hand.' Mungo heaved a suitcase and a gargantuan golf-bag out of the car. 'You ought to have a valet, Pons, to cope with all this.'

'A valet?' Pons, who was incapable of detecting irony, laughed loudly. 'My dear chap, taking a man around went out with George the Fifth and Bertie Wooster. Trouble with you is, you get everything out of books. Where's that awful man Cardower?'

'He'll turn up presently, and say he's been putting turnips through the chopping-machine, or grooming Ajax.'

'Good old Ajax! You wouldn't know—but he's a damned decent mount. I intend to borrow him shamelessly, even if it means leaving Ian by the fire, dozing over some dreary book about the Norman Conquest. It's a pity the Cardowers—this particular lot, I mean— haven't a bean. Makes one ashamed of merchant banking, and a father who's been Lord Mayor, and all that kind of thing. You're bloody lucky, Mungo, not to be in the mun. At least, I suppose you're not in the mun?'

'Not yet but who knows?' Mungo found himself unresentful of this innocent patronage. 'Do you know that an American publisher once offered a Victorian poet £5,000 for a poem of three stanzas?'

'Good Lord!' Perhaps for the first time in his life, Pons de Beynac was awed before the poetic character. 'Just think how much that would be now.'

'Yes,' Mungo said. 'Almost what you might call big money.'

But in what followed there was no fun. Pons and Anne turned out to have known each other from childhood— and so well that they scarcely needed to converse. This couldn't be called their fault, but nevertheless Mungo felt it to be unfair. Pons, although a decent enough oaf, was as thick as they come, so that if much in the way of intelligible speech *had* been required of him this near approach to idiocy would have appeared. As it was, he and Anne got along in terms of a code the mainstay of which appeared to be the more or less monosyllabic recall of former occasions. 'Hailstones,' Anne would say; Pons would reply 'Bunn's barn'; and both would laugh as if something extremely amusing had occurred. Or Pons would come out with 'Snuffle?' on an interrogative note; Anne would reply 'Snaffle, boy, snaffle'; and this imbecile exchange would again occasion merriment. They would

ride happily off together for a whole morning of this
ridiculous commerce, leaving Mungo to help Ian with
the turnips. This, it was true, was fair enough, since it
was Pons's turn for Ajax, a creature not to be treated as
if he were a bicycle built for two. And it couldn't be
said that Anne was flirting with Pons, any more than it
could be said that she had flirted with Mungo. She was
just seeming extremely pleased with the one in the precise fashion that she had seemed extremely pleased with
the other. In fact—Mungo told himself furiously—Anne
was devoted to the wholly social thing very much as
her father was; she put on a turn for whoever turned up.

There was a mournful comfort in this last reflection—
for as long, at least, as Mungo was able to maintain it to
himself. But after a day or two he was obliged to decide
—or imagine—that Anne and Pons were really a little
more in each other's pockets than that. And this seemed
confirmed by Ian with a casualness which betrayed him
as feeling on tricky ground.

'Never could understand what Anne sees in old Pons,'
he said. 'But she insists on my importing him every now
and then.'

'That's why you asked him this time?'

'Well, yes. And I'm sorry if it hasn't turned out too
well.' Ian, it seemed, had not been unobservant. 'Fact is,
I was relying on my other sister—Mary, that is—to show
you around. But she's gone off on some stupid visit. Mary's
said to be much prettier than Anne.'

Mungo naturally didn't find this last piece of information consoling or interesting in the least. He began to
hate Pons de Beynac. Even Pons's exotic name appeared
disgusting. And when Lord Robert pressed a further glass
of claret on Pons, or Lady Robert asked him about the
health of his aunts, Mungo told himself it was because
these Cardowers hadn't a bean, and Pons was a Lord

Mayor's son and absolutely rolling. Then he would see that this was nonsense, and become most depressingly ashamed of himself. But he did occasionally wish that Anne could see Pons sprawling dead drunk on the floor, or even just hear him talking drivel about the ready way to prevent strikes.

It didn't make things any better that Anne continued to be very nice to Mungo in the intervals of being very nice to Pons. She was doing it, he assured himself, as automatically as somebody with the correct manners turning now to the left and now to the right at a dinner-table. He himself had enough pride to talk to her on these occasions as gaily as before. But he kept on feeling that he was perhaps making a gauche fool of himself as he did so. Worse still, Anne seemed to be aware of his feeling, and to turn on a little extra niceness as a consequence. And what could be ghastlier than that?

This was the state of affairs at Stradlings when, at breakfast one morning, Ian opened a letter, read it, handed it to his father, and said darkly, 'It's a summons.'

7

FOR A MOMENT Mungo supposed that Ian had fallen
foul of the fuzz, and was to be up before a magistrate
for speeding or something of the kind. But then it turned
out that the summons had nothing to do with police
courts; it was an invitation to lunch from Ian's grandfather, Lord Auldearn. Among the Cardowers this
appeared to be equivalent to a royal command. Ian
evidently saw it this way.

'Your grandfather naturally expects a visit,' Lord Robert said. 'He still takes an interest in Oxford. In fact, he
went to a college gaudy last year, and made them a speech.
It appears to have been a little eccentric, but it was a
success, all the same. And it would be my guess that
he said a word about you to the Provost at the same time.
Not by way of edging you in unfairly, of course, but
simply as vouching for your character. And now it will
be nice for him to hear about a new generation of undergraduates. Ian, don't you agree?'

'I suppose so.' Ian spoke on something nearer an ungracious note than Mungo had yet heard at Stradlings.
He looked gloomily round the table, and it was almost as
if he momentarily caught his sister's eye. 'I'll tell you
what,' he said suddenly. 'I'll ring him up, and ask if I
can take Pons and Mungo over to Bamberton.'

'An excellent idea,' Lord Robert said briskly. 'I would
like Mungo to meet your grandfather.' Lord Robert had
suspended operations on a piece of toast—this in order
to direct upon Mungo what had lately become a thought-

ful as well as an amiable glance. Perhaps he had tumbled
to Mungo's feelings about Anne, and was benevolently
trying to think up any possible ground for viewing Ian's
low-born friend in an eligible light after all.

'Of course grandpapa has had Pons before,' Ian was
saying, 'and won't be much interested in him. But Mungo
is new. He could have a go at Mungo, and Pons and I
could play tennis.'

'Super idea,' Pons said amiably.

Mungo didn't feel that he agreed. He suspected Anne
of having signalled to her brother that she would be glad
of a quiet day to herself. Perhaps she was so bored with
him that she wanted a holiday even at the expense of
doing without Pons as well. Or perhaps—which was almost as discouraging—she was just tired of turning on
the niceness business for either of them. Again—and although he was always willing to extend his acquaintance
with men and their manners—he wasn't sure that he wanted to be had a go at by Ian's grandfather. And the
proposal that Ian and Pons should play tennis seemed
entirely odd. There was now snow on the ground at Stradlings. He didn't know where Bamberton was. But if it
was possible to go and lunch there it couldn't be climatic-
ally all that different.

Ian, however, put through the arrangement he had
suggested, and in the middle of the morning they piled
into his mini—a battered affair to which he was much
attached, and which he had been furious to discover he
couldn't keep in Oxford while still a freshman. Pons, because he didn't need so much leg room, was shoved in
the back—a relegation which he accepted quite cheerfully.
In fact they were all rather cheerful during the run, as
young men together tend to be when under nobody's
regard but their own.

'What about Ajax?' Mungo asked. 'Could you take *him*

up with you? He'd be much better fun than this stinking
little thing.'

'I don't know. Pons, could I take Ajax up?' Being in his
second year, Pons had to be deferred to in a matter like
this.

'You can hunt, if you want to.' Pons was cautious. 'But
I suppose Ajax would have to be at livery somewhere.
They wouldn't let you drive into Howard with one of
those transport affairs for horses.'

'There's a man who keeps a falcon,' Mungo said. 'So
why not a horse—or an elephant with a howdah, for that
matter? It wouldn't do anybody any harm.'

'There are a lot of statutes started in the middle ages,'
Pons said learnedly. 'They twist them to fit anything they
don't like. Rutherford-Brown had a sporting rifle an uncle
gave him for his twenty-first. His scout reported it—those
chaps are all spies, and nothing else—and a nervous and
teetering don told him it wouldn't do. R-B asked why not.
And the don produced some Latin rigmarole about pro-
hibiting bows and arrows.'

'I don't want to hear about Rutherford-Brown,' Mungo
said. 'What did he want with a rifle, anyway? A rifle isn't
like an elephant. It's no use at all. The man must be an
idiot. What I do want to hear about is Ian's grandfather.
And I want to know what you mean by saying he'll have
a go at me. I think it's probably a hoax, like those end-
of-term Collections. He'll just shake hands, and say I've
had a very good first week in civilized society. And I'll
remember to say Thank you, Sir—and give him more of
a nod than a bow.'

'Just you wait.' Ian's continuation of this nonsense sounded almost serious. 'I'd back him even against your
famous aunt, any day of the week.'

'Then you'd lose your money. You'll probably lose your
life, by the way, if you go on driving at this pace.'

'Rubbish.' Ian endeavoured further to depress the accelerator, but it was already down as far as it would go. As they were descending a hill, however, the mini built up to a startlingly good pace. 'Pons,' Ian shouted, 'sing us the Cambridge Boat Song. It may relax Mungo's strained nerves.'

So Pons sang—tunelessly but with vigour—an interminable obscene ditty. Mungo duly relaxed. They arrived surprisingly quickly at their destination.

'Christ!'

Mungo produced this pious ejaculation unaffectedly. He really was staggered by his first glimpse of Bamberton Court. Stradlings, although more roomy than any dwelling he had ever been in before, didn't propose itself as built for any other purpose than living in. You could imagine a large family filling it comfortably—and able to shout at one another from top to bottom and wing to wing. Bamberton had been built for ostentation, in some age that didn't understand either wealth or power unless they were expressed in outwardness and display. It was very much an architectural achievement, but it was a political and economic statement even more than that. Just as robes and wigs and all the archaic palaver of a law court existed to keep the vulgar in awe so did this monstrous pile exist to assert a vast remove from squires and merchants and parsons and all the people who are nowadays called middle or upper-middle class.

Mungo, who had developed a sharpened social consciousness as a consequence of his recent exposure to new influences and assumptions, saw this before he saw the aesthetic virtues of the place. Bamberton wasn't like a skyscraper or an air-terminal or a monstrous hotel. It did cunningly suggest, although baselessly, that it had preserved some sense of the normal human scale. You felt that you could at least drive a golf-ball from one end of it to the other, or a tennis-ball—if you were in the Wimbledon class—clean over any of its imposing façades into whatever courtyards lay beyond. You could comfortably perambulate its several terraces to the east before breakfast, its answering terraces to the west before dinner. It was a bit overwhelming—as it was meant to be—all the same.

'Round about 1710,' Ian said in a tone of self-conscious irony. 'Vanbrugh and Hawksmoor, in off-times when they weren't busy on Castle Howard.'

'Still a bit short on baths and loos,' Pons pronounced, 'but otherwise a very reasonable sort of house.'

'Don't be idiotic, Pons.' Ian spoke with a surprising snap. 'There's nothing reasonable about the place. Showy— that's the proper word for Bamberton. But it's one of the top things of its kind in England, all the same.'

Mungo wondered whether Ian, thus displaying a divided mind over Bamberton Court, would one day own the place. He retained, from some bit of talk or other, a vague notion that it was a possibility, but it wasn't a matter he had thought about. At the moment the house was like some monstrous toy on a turntable, for it seemed to be pivoting on them as the mini took a great curve of the beech-lined avenue.

'How many people live in it?' Mungo demanded.

'Just my grandfather. My grandmother died ages ago.'

'Nobody else?'

'No—except that he sometimes puts up what he calls a chum, meaning another old gentleman like himself.'

'But there must be somebody to look after him! Do you mean that he boils his own egg?'

'Of course there are servants.' Ian was amused. 'Far more than make sense, probably.'

'Is he a kind of recluse?'

'Oh, no. It's his eldest son, my uncle David, who is that. He's the one who lives in Scotland. I suppose he likes the morose temper of its inhabitants.'

'Mungo will probably emigrate permanently,' Pons said companionably from the back. 'We have to give it to him that he's one on whom cheerfulness sometimes breaks in.'

'Good Lord!' Mungo exclaimed, 'Pons has produced an echo from the great world of books.' Mungo had quite forgotten that he hated Pons de Bcynac. For the moment he had even forgotten Anne. He was only reflecting that one could be friends with two fundamentally remote young men, and explore in their company an archaic way of life which normally one would catch only a glimpse of by paying at the door. 'Do you know,' he said over his shoulder to Pons, 'what is called a great house in Scotland? Either a bogus little mediaeval castle, or a bogus little French chateau, or a decent four-square mansion by somebody with a name like Dreghorn or Gillespie. No wonder nobs like the Cardowers, when on the up-and-up, dig this sort of thing for all they are worth.'

Mungo found this chatter silly even as he uttered it, which meant that he must be feeling nervous. What was Bamberton's equivalent of the man wearing a bowler hat and sitting in a little glass box? It wouldn't be long before he knew, for they had now come to a halt before a flight of steps broad and high enough to have looked quite well if shunted off to the palace of King Minos at Knossos. Against it, it was now the mini's turn to look like a toy: a Dinkie toy or the kind you buy inside a matchbox. There was deep snow everywhere on the ground, but the steps had been swept clear of it as if for the passage of a platoon of grandees marching abreast. There didn't seem to be any way of entering Bamberton Court—at least if one belonged to, or was temporarily

affiliated with, the proprietary classes—other than by puffing one's way up to the top and being engulfed within an
enormous portico. In fact this imposing façade was on
such a scale that from ground level you couldn't see even
the top of the great dome which, from farther back,
showed itself as dominating the entire building.

'We're for it now, chaps,' Ian said. 'Pons, you great oaf,
mind your manners. And up we go.'

Ian had been right about the servants. The visitors'
mere arrival had produced two old men and several young
ones. The young ones, who were distinguished from their
seniors by wearing black and yellow striped waistcoats,
offended Mungo at once. Ancient servitors, pottering
round with trays, polishing silver, brushing clothes, or
doing any other appropriate thing you could think of,
were part of a picture vaguely hallowed by time. But that
youths of your own age—no older and no younger—
should step forward and deftly take your coat and scarf,
or precede you with an unnaturally soft and unresilient
step through the kind of marble mausoleum which the
inside of Bamberton seemed to resemble, was somehow
shameful all round. Not that he mustn't keep such feelings to himself. He'd accepted Ian as Ian had accepted
him—and along with the chap it was fair enough that
you should buy his *ambiance.*

In any case, this effect didn't last long. They were in
a great square hall, with marble goddesses in marble
niches staring at each other sightlessly, and overhead the
dome swimming pink and blue. Across the hall, framed
within tall columns, there was a glimpse of a further
large, ornate, and seemingly empty chamber. *Inexplicable
splendour of Ionian white and gold* Mungo not very ap-
positely quoted to himself. Then he was aware that, from
some hidden entrance near the end of this vista, an old

man had appeared and was coming towards them—sound-
lessly, because in carpet slippers which he scarcely raised
from the floor. The old man lifted an arm briefly in an
impatient gesture, and at this, almost as if a wand had
been waved over them, the servants vanished. So here was
Ian's grandfather. He was shrunken within ancient and
shapeless tweeds which he had no doubt reasonably filled
out decades before, so that the present effect was rather
of a dwarf who had been charitably accommodated from
the cast-off wardrobe of some person of normal stature.
He ought to have looked ridiculous, but was for some
reason quite far from doing so.

'Ian, Pons—and you are Lockhart.' With this economical greeting, delivered in a low voice which seemed at
once weary and alert, Lord Auldearn held out to Mungo
a hand the limpness of which suggested that he had determined upon the nullity of such gestures a long time
ago. But no impression of this sort attended his glance.
Some degenerative process of old age, indeed, had painfully everted his eyelids, so that his pale blue eyes looked
out from reddened circles and one had to wonder
whether he found it agonizing to blink. Yet this only enhanced the steely scrutiny of the regard he turned for a
long moment upon his grandson's new friend. Lord Auldearn followed this up with a curt nod which seemed
obscurely to suggest his having made up his mind about
something. Perhaps, Mungo thought, he had been thus instantly vetted and found presentable. At least Lord Auldearn now smiled. It was a curiously sweet smile, but not
in the least of the artificial sort that such a description
might convey. And you had scarcely received it before
it was gone. You then realized that this old man's habitual
mood was melancholic. He had made up his accounts,
you felt, and had concluded they didn't amount to much.
He was simply waiting to move on.

'You two go about your game. When Lockhart and I
have got to know each other we'll come and join you
before lunch.' With this, Lord Auldearn gave a slight
nod and walked away—so regardlessly that Mungo had
to be thumbed by Ian into following him. Mungo wondered, indeed, whether he ought literally to follow his
host or whether to draw abreast of him. He decided on
the second course, but this didn't result in conversation.
They walked silently side by side through Bamberton for
what Mungo began to reckon must be a quarter of a mile
or thereabout. Only when they were passing through
something that ought probably to be called a state apartment Lord Auldearn halted, touched Mungo's arm, and
silently faced him to a wall. He saw that what was
before him was a Titian—an out-size Titian. Actaeon was
having his dekko at Artemis, and was already sprouting
horns—a phenomenon which was adding to the conster-
nation of quite a number of naked nymphs. It was a tremendous Titian. Mungo gave it time, but uttered no
enthusiastic or other comment. Lord Auldearn grunted
and walked on. They passed through an enormous library,
clothed to the ceiling with imposing and no doubt informative books, and suddenly ended up in quite a small
room. Here there were a lot of books too—many of them
rather shabby ones. It was an untidy but comfortable
place. Mungo guessed that servants weren't often tolera-
ted in it. Lord Auldearn wagged a finger at a chair, went
over to a shelf, and rummaged. He turned round and
handed Mungo an open book.

'Read me that,' Lord Auldearn said, and sat down himself.

This was really startling. Not even Mungo's tutor would
issue so abrupt and arbitrary a command. Mungo looked
at the page, and saw that what was before him was Tennyson's 'Frater Ave atque Vale'. He opened his mouth to say

something, checked himself, and began to read the poem.
'*Row us out from Desenzano, to your Sirmione row!*'
Mungo began. He didn't dare to raise his eyes from the
print, but was aware that Lord Auldearn was as immobile
as something carved out of old ivory. At least it wasn't a
long poem, and Mungo got to the end of it. '*Sweet Catul-
lus's all-but-island, olive-silvery Sirmio,*' he concluded—
and closed the book, stood up, and handed it back to
Lord Auldearn. He had the good sense to do so without
saying anything at all.

'Do you know who I last heard read that poem?' the
old man asked in his weary voice.

'No, sir.'

'Tennyson,' Lord Auldearn said without emphasis.

This time, Mungo didn't have to tell himself to keep
his mouth shut. He had enough imagination to find the
information overwhelming.

'My parents were fond of that set: Tennyson himself,
Gladstone, Allingham, Jowett, the Duke of Argyll. George
Argyll, that would be.' Lord Auldearn had paused to
make sure of this point. 'When one was on a day's visit
to Aldworth, it was the thing to take one's children, so
that they might remember having had a glimpse of the
Laureate. I was quite old enough for that. I even remember being told that the poet had recently lost a son. That,
of course, was Lionel, a very promising fellow. I thought
it shocking and unnatural—a son's dying before his father.
I rather imagine I supposed it wasn't permitted.'

Lord Auldearn paused again, and this time his chin
sank a little on his chest, so that Mungo wondered what
he should do if the old man fell asleep. But he had merely
lapsed into a brooding abstraction, which Mungo now
instantly understood. Lord Auldearn, too, had lost a son
—and a son who had become a kind of peasant legend
as the bad Lord Douglas.

'Except in his grumpy moods'—Lord Auldearn was speaking quite unemotionally again—'Tennyson was fond of reading his poems aloud. And this is the one he read that afternoon. It had been written at Sirmione shortly after an earlier death in the family: that of one of his brothers, whose name escapes me.'

'Charles,' Mungo said. And having, as it were, broken his duck, he added: 'It doesn't seem a particularly suitable poem to read to a small boy.'

'It was to my parents that he was reading it. He entertained me after what he judged to be a more appropriate fashion. The bard got down on his hands and knees and barked like a dog. I was much too well brought up not to demonstrate satisfaction. So he put on his famous black cloak, and waved it around, and croaked like a raven. It was all extremely nice of him—but it was the poem I remembered, all the same. You are the first person I have let read it to me since that notable day.' Lord Auldearn paused yet again, and the momentary smile passed over his face. 'Mungo Lockhart of the Lea,' he added softly.

Mungo felt that he had been paid a fantastic compliment, and that its extravagance had been deftly redeemed by the hint of mockery in this last address. But he was startled as well.

'That's Ian's joke,' he said.

'Of course it is. I make Ian write me a monthly letter. It's an attention which the head of the family may properly exact. Do you agree?'

'Yes, of course.' Mungo was amused to have come upon the origin of one of Lord Robert Cardower's conversational mannerisms. 'And Ian has made quite a thing of me?'

'Not that, at all.' Lord Auldearn, who hadn't got the wave-length here, looked almost startled. 'Ian wouldn't dine out on you, my dear lad, or exhibit you as a scalp or trophy or witness to some egalitarian spirit he may be affecting for a time. The Cardowers—and you are sufficiently perceptive to have grasped this—have been too high up for too long to have any notion of snobbery. The concept just doesn't enter their heads.'

'If that's so, it's because of their disposition, and not their station.' Mungo was uncertain whether he was resenting the odd turn this talk had taken—but what he next said made it look as if he did. 'Proust's duchesses are as snobbish as anybody in his book.'

'They're not duchesses, you young donkey.' Lord Auldearn's smile came swiftly to the rescue of this outrageous apostrophe. 'In French they're *duchesses*, and six a penny. In any case, Proust was a Jew, and couldn't know what he was talking about.' The old man had produced this with a sudden snarl that didn't witness too well to the Cardowers' elevation above social prejudice. 'You might as well cite a Hottentot or an American.'

Mungo ought perhaps to have found this freshly revealed side of Lord Auldearn horrifying, or at least alienating. But in fact he thought it rather comical—with the result that he unleashed, whether inappropriately or not, that large grin against which Ian had warned him upon a previous occasion. Surprisingly, this went down well.

'I'm an addle-pated old man,' Lord Auldearn said, 'and express myself awkwardly. I only wanted to say that my grandson, if he makes a friend, will be wholly loyal to him. And he doesn't make friends easily.'

'I know about Ian and myself.' Mungo said this with a confidence that caught his own ear. 'But as for other friends—why, he has heaps of them. Pons, for instance.'

'Friendliness isn't friendship. It's a mere social acquirement. But I don't want to talk about Ian. I want to hear about yourself, and from the start. Your father, for

instance—what can you tell me about him? I believe he
interests me.'

'I don't quite see why he should.' Mungo had stiffened
before this hint of inquisition. 'My father died when I
was very young.'

'Not before he had you christened.' Lord Auldearn's
smile came and went again. 'Out of a favourite poem of
mine—and of his, Ian tells me. You remember what "Sir
Mungo Lockhart of the Lea" rhymes with?'

'Of course. With the refrain: *Timor mortis conturbat
me.*'

'It's my case.'

'Sir?' Mungo hadn't understood this.

'Otherwise I shouldn't be talking to you now, my dear
lad. I'd be in my grave, if death—or being dead—didn't
terrify me. Does it seem strange to you that a very old
man should feel like that?'

'I don't think it terribly strange. But perhaps it's unfortunate.' This was as good a reply as Mungo could manage. There was something about Ian's grandfather that
made his sudden dive into the confessional not as embarrassing as it might have been. Mungo didn't want
more of it, all the same, and it was perhaps because of
this that he presently found himself obeying the injunction to give some account of his life and circumstances.
It wasn't a subject in which his interest was negligible,
and in the drawer at home there reposed, after all, a
good many starts on autobiographical fiction upon the
memory of which he could now draw. Lord Auldearn, of
course, didn't want fiction; he wanted what might be
called raw Moray fact. In this interest Mungo faithfully
attempted to strip down, so to speak, the variously em-
bellished Mungo Lockharts wandering around inside his
own head. It was at least a stiff exercise, and at the end
of half an hour he had learnt something that was new

about the difficult enterprise of walking naked. Lord Auldearn was a good listener; attending upon the confessional didn't embarrass *him*. But he knew perfectly what was going on—as appeared in what he eventually said.

'Mungo'—there was a kind of deft timing, Mungo thought, in this first simple address by his name—'life is a formless and sprawling affair. And the artist—unless he throws up the sponge, as some seem to be doing now—has the cheek to shove it around until it makes a pattern. He is like a child before a tumble of building bricks. And that's you, the Lord help you. You are doomed to imagine about yourself all sorts of things that are not—and to see the whole world, for that matter, as what it isn't either. The result will be another couple of feet or so of novels and plays on the shelf. And now we'll go and find those two innocent young men at their tennis.'

'I don't see how they can be playing tennis in weather like this.'

'There's something called real tennis, Mungo. Just as there is, perhaps unfortunately, something that has to be called real life.'

'I know that. It's what I'm after, even if I am some sort of day-dreaming type.'

'In that case, good luck to you.' For a moment Lord Auldearn's exploratory scrutiny again played over Mungo's features, rather as his son Robert's had taken to doing from time to time. Then he got to his feet—his bones actually creaking as he did so, Mungo usefully noted—and led the way out of the room.

8

THE TENNIS COURT was a surprising place, having rather the appearance of a shanty-town, or even a chicken-farm, disposed round an enormous hall. The true, the monstrous, scale of Bamberton was given away by the fact that it could tuck away such a structure in some unnoticed corner. As for the game, Mungo didn't see much of it, since Lord Auldearn was not disposed to wait for his luncheon—the less so because he seemed to disapprove of Ian's and Pons's style of play. Probably they were making up their rules as they went along, or at least ignoring any they couldn't be bothered with. They were in T-shirts and shorts—and, even so, sweating hard—Pons in particular, Mungo thought, pretty well larding the lean earth as he pranced around. Racquets and squash racquets and ordinary tennis were compounded in the performance; and by constantly lamming, or trying to lam, the ball through apertures variously disposed round about—and beyond which one might imagine the wretched shanty-dwellers or chickens to be cowering—they emphasized the further influence of a kind of maniacal billiards. It was a perfectly idiotic game, Mungo told himself. But he would have liked to have a go at it, all the same.

'You two can't sit down in that state,' Lord Auldearn said grimly. 'You'll have a shower while Mungo and I have sherry.'

Mungo hadn't reckoned on a further conversation *tête-à-tête* with his host, and its opening was far from promising. Lord Auldearn appeared to have been put in a bad temper by watching bad tennis.

'I gather,' he said, 'that, until you met Ian, my family name was unknown to you?'

'Yes. If I'd heard it, it hadn't much registered.'

'And Auldearn was simply the name of a little town, and not of a marquisate?'

'That's so—and I don't think I'd have known what a marquisate is, either.'

'You'd never heard of my son David—Lord Bright-mony?'

'No.'

'Then you certainly won't have heard of his brother Douglas either.'

'As a matter of fact, sir—' Mungo had hesitated over this awkward point—but it was to find that Lord Auldearn had turned away and walked across the room. He returned with a silver-framed photograph in his hand, and now held it out before him.

'That was Douglas,' he said casually. 'At about eighteen, would you say? He was a well-grown lad—the tallest of the lot.' And then, before Mungo could do more than glance at the thing, he turned away and restored it to its place. 'I can't understand it,' he said as he came back. 'You must have been a very alert and intelligent boy. It's inconceivable that we shouldn't at least be gossiped about.'

'Not to me.' Mungo's displeasure before this patrician badgering was mounting. 'And not to my aunt either, I'd suppose.'

'Your aunt? A Miss Guthrie? With whom you live at Fintry?'

'Yes, sir.' Mungo was a little startled by these staccato questions. 'My aunt doesn't—'

'It's bad—very bad.' The old man was now glaring at Mungo as if he couldn't believe anything he said. But

behind this, Mungo suddenly perceived, was less bad temper than distress. 'We are declined indeed, Mungo, when
nobody so much as mentions our name. We don't own
what we did, and what we do own we leave it to others to
look after. A man's lands are no more than his stocks and
shares when he ceases to ride over them.'

'I don't see that *you* could reasonably be expected to do
that, sir. Not at your ... your advanced age.' If Mungo
said this awkwardly, it was out of a sudden feeling of
sympathy for Lord Auldearn's feudal view of the matter.
'Doesn't Lord Robert ever go to Scotland?'

'Robert has his career, Douglas is dead, poor David is
as he is. The duty remained mine, and I have failed in
it.'

'But Ian goes to Scotland sometimes. He goes shooting
on what I suppose are your family estates.' Mungo, who
didn't like this suddenly lugubrious Lord Auldearn, was
reaching about for cheer. 'And I'm going to take him to
Moray myself—to see, well, other aspects of the place.'

'That is strange—very strange.' Lord Auldearn seemed
quite to mean this. 'And I am glad to hear of it. Only I
could have wished that, when Ian first became known to
you, it had been as a member of a family already a little
existing'—Lord Auldearn's rare smile came—'in that
imagination of yours. There have been Cardowers not
undeserving of a place there. But, of course, long ago.'

Mungo told himself that this was a perfectly honest
piece of rather senile sentimentality; that from so very
old a man it was reasonable and proper enough. Nevertheless he felt uncomfortable. He was quite a new friend
of Ian's, even if a close one, and he happened to come
from a part of Scotland where Ian's family were great
lairds—and had once, perhaps, been lairds greater still.
These facts didn't seem to qualify him very adequately
as a recipient of the kind of talk he was now listening to.

And against it, moreover, something that might be called his political sense rebelled. Bamberton Court was doubtless, as Ian had said, one of the top things of its kind in England. It was a good guess that it had been what guidebooks call the principal seat of the Marquises of Auldearn for several generations. Whatever the origins of the family, and wherever the mysterious Lord Brightmony now lived, they had beaten it from a small, poor country —so small and poor that it had never recovered from Flodden Field—and done themselves pretty well elsewhere. So Lord Auldearn's tears—and he had seemed at least ready to weep from those permanently red-rimmed eyes—were crocodile's tears, and that was that.

But hadn't Mungo Lockhart—the simple Moray loon— lately opted for the same racket? It was perhaps this thought—or perhaps it was some simpler response to challenge—that elicited from Mungo what he heard himself saying now.

'Come with us, sir.'

'What's that?'

'I expect you've got a decent car?'

'A decent car?' The formidable Lord Auldearn appeared, for the moment, floored by this attack. 'I have a car made by Rolls and Royce, and am told it is thoroughly reliable.'

'We'll all go in that—and Ian can flog his mini and buy pea-nuts. Easy stages. We can put up in your sort of hotel—'

'My sort of hotel? I haven't been inside a hotel for fifty years.'

'Then you'll find them more comfortable now. We'll do Moray and Nairnshire. There will be plenty of old people who remember enough to doff their bonnets to you.' Haranguing Ian's grandfather in this way was rather going to Mungo's head. 'I'll introduce you to

my aunt. And generally show you what Scotland's like
today.'

'You'll show me—' Lord Auldearn controlled himself.
'Mungo, you make a handsome offer—but I shall never
visit Scotland again. I have my reasons. But do you know?
If anybody were to persuade me to go, it would be such
a lad as yourself. You remind me of ... of my own children, when after a month or two in the north they had
taken something of its colour on themselves.' Lord Auldearn set down his glass, took a step forward, and for a
moment touched Mungo on the arm. 'You may be a credit
to your country one day. Don't go wrong.' Then suddenly
he was furious. 'Half past one,' he said. 'Where the devil
are those boys?'

Lunch was a constrained occasion. The young footmen
were again in evidence, and Mungo was unreconciled to
them. At dinner in hall he had got used to being waited
on by the college scouts, but they were hardened characters who behaved more like kennel-men than domestic
servants, banging and snatching the dishes, and strongly
disapproving of a feeding-time in any degree prolonged
by conversation. The Bamberton automata in striped
waistcoats were another matter. Mungo would have liked
to know what they really thought of their job.

During most of the meal it was Pons, fortunately, who
made the running with their host. Pons must have guessed
he would be taken over to Bamberton during his visit to
Stradlings, since he had plainly been getting up a suitable topic, the pros and cons of reforming the House of
Lords. Ian's grandfather, it appeared, had once been Lord
Privy Seal, and thus the government's top man there.
But Mungo suspected he no longer took much interest
in the concern. He answered Pons's questions and listened
to Pons's views with a courtesy which only deepened

whenever Pons was particularly absurd, but always with a hint of fatigued abstraction. His inner mind was elsewhere. Perhaps across a shortening future he was meditating death, or being dead. Or perhaps his concern was with the past, and with wrongs committed or suffered. Mungo would have liked to get inside his head and make a few rapid observations of what was going on there. But how could it be done? How could he so much as glimpse the inner being of a man more than four times his own age, and belonging to a totally remote social set-up? Mungo remembered with shame brash things he had sometimes said about proposing to become an authority on how people tick. He had even said something of the kind to Anne.

This was an unfortunate thought. For Anne Cardower, thus invoked, at once annihilated the context she had bobbed up in. Mungo continued his meal—he had a dim impression of its being meagre although protracted—with only Anne in his head. Or only Anne plus a bit of Pons— the bit that was so imbecile that the thought of her conceivably being in love with him was an outrage. He reminded himself that he hated Pons. But he was also fond of him. He had laid Pons out on the floor of Howard 4, 4. And Pons, on some more sober future occasion, was quite capable of laying *him* out. Pons, in fact, was an acceptable feature of a complex, if immature, masculine society which Mungo, within a space of eight weeks, had quite fallen for. But this could be a disagreeable thought in itself. Perhaps he was doomed to endure years and years of being a kind of time-lagged public-school boy.

Mungo's gloom now answered Lord Auldearn's. Ian even glanced from one to the other curiously, as if wondering what his grandfather had been up to with his friend. Fortunately no gloom visited Pons. Encouraged by his host's inflexible appearance of attention, he had

moved on from the Lords to the mysterious region of
the Constitution and the Crown Prerogative.

The question of what the Queen, in given critical circumstances, could 'do' took Lord Auldearn and his young
guests as far as coffee. This was served not at table but in
a faded and indefinably feminine apartment which
Mungo imagined to have been the boudoir (if one really
used such a word) of Ian's grandmother. Lord Auldearn,
he decided, led a kind of peripatetic existence amid the
immensities of Bamberton, covering as much ground as
he could in the course of a day. The menservants presumably chased round after him, carrying bacon and
eggs, decanters of port, bath towels, or hot water bottles
according to the hour. For dinner Lord Auldearn changed
into a different pair of bedroom slippers. Did he still have
a nightgown, like Macbeth, or had he got round to
pyjamas? Mungo found that these foolish speculations a
little enlivened him. And he became aware that the conversation had at length got away from the grave issues
canvassed by Pons de Beynac.

'Ian,' Lord Auldearn was asking on a sharp intonation,
'when did you last see your uncle David?'

'A little over a year ago, sir.'

'You stayed at Mallachie?'

'No. I just dropped in to tea. I was staying with people
near Fochabers, who have marvellous fishing, and a bit
of shooting as well.'

'It would have been proper to stay at Mallachie.'

'I don't think that would have been exactly gay.'

'I'm not discussing occasions of gaiety.' Lord Auldearn
was suddenly at his most savage. 'I'm discussing what is
due within a family.'

'I'm very sorry, sir.' Ian wasn't taking his grandfather's
admonition very well, Mungo thought. The 'sir' business

surely showed that— and Ian had gone quite pale into the bargain.

'Acquaintances drop in on you for tea. Kinsmen put up with you for a few nights.'

'Very well. Next time I go north I'll put up with uncle David. It will be in both senses of the term.'

'That is an unbecoming witticism, Ian. But I let it pass. Mallachie is no doubt a depressing house for the young. But stay there, all the same, when you next have the opportunity. Mungo tells me that you think of going to Scotland together. He appears to believe that he can improve your mind there. Indeed, he believes he could improve mine. He blithely suggests we might all three go in the Rolls.'

'Well, sir, why not?' Ian wasn't going to let Mungo's notion be treated as bizarre.

'Super idea,' Pons said. Pons mightn't be quite clear what was going on, but he had an instinctive sense of when solidarity was the proper thing.

'It has its charm.' Lord Auldearn was now almost good-humoured again. 'But I have had to plead age and infirmity. When you do go, Ian, draw on me for your expenses if you want to. And take Mungo to Mallachie with you. I particularly desire that. It is important to me.'

'Very well—and thank you very much.' Ian looked puzzled by the command. 'There will certainly be room for both of us. But I don't honestly see why Mungo need—'

'If you are to meet his aunt, he should meet your kinsmen in those parts.'

'Absolutely right,' Pons said heartily. 'I think it's often frightfully interesting, meeting a chap's people. They can turn out so fearfully odd. Wouldn't you say, sir?'

This interposition met with no favour. Lord Auldearn responded only with a stony glance, and Ian with a scowl.

'Very well, sir,' Ian repeated, as if accepting orders. 'But you don't call Leonard a kinsman, do you?'

'There is a family connection. He and David didn't come together fortuitously. And Mungo should be interested in him'—Lord Auldearn added—'from a professional point of view.'

'Please, who is Leonard?' What had just been said suggested to Mungo something so extremely odd that he asked this question boldly and at once.

'He is a man called Leonard Sedley,' Lord Auldearn said. 'And he was regarded as a very promising novelist at one time.'

'But isn't he dead?' Mungo realized that this was a stupid question. 'But obviously not.'

'Obviously not.' Lord Auldearn was at his driest now. 'He has fallen silent, as they say. But you should read at least one book of his—*An Autumn in Umbria.*'

'But I have. It's in our rooms in college. Ian and I have even talked about it. But Ian didn't—'

'Claim a distant relationship? Well, that's his own affair. Do you think the book deserves its reputation?'

'Of course it does. It's a marvellous conversation novel. A bit sophisticated for me, really, but just as good as Norman Douglas's *South Wind.* I've vaguely known that Sedley was—is—rather a one-book man.'

'It's said that he continues to talk well.' Lord Auldearn stood up, clearly by way of bringing the visit to a close. 'So go and listen to him, and see what you think.'

Part Two

SCOTLAND

9

Ten days at Stradlings left Mungo with four weeks at home. He was obliged to break his journey in Edinburgh because he had to see—or rather be interrogated by—Mr Mackellar S.S.C. This lawyer had been an intermittent and mysterious power in Mungo's life for as long as he could remember. If he was even to have a bicycle, Mr Mackellar S.S.C. had to be written to. As he never heard the name uttered without these appended initials, he had at one time concluded that Mr Essessee would be a legitimate and more compendious form of address, and had even so employed it upon the only occasion of Mr Mackellar's appearing in Moray. Whereupon Mr Mackellar had explained to Mungo that he enjoyed the distinction of being a Solicitor before the Supreme Court. Mungo received this with proper awe (if also with a tincture of precocious religious scepticism), and it was some time before he could wholly free himself from the persuasion that Mr Mackellar was claiming to be an archangel. The general meaning of 'solicitation', which he managed to extract from a dictionary, supported on the whole this portentous view. Mungo had been required to spend considerable periods every Sunday listening, with properly screwed up eyes, to extended exercises in intercessory prayer, and it seemed conceivable to suppose that Mr Mackellar was privileged to engage in the same activity on a direct access basis— like the saints who cast down their golden crowns around the glassy sea. For the universe, after all, could have one supreme court only.

The prosaic truth about Mr Mackellar had emerged later. He controlled a small trust, vaguely intimated as of a charitable nature, which stumped up something towards the orphan Mungo's keep and education from time to time. Mungo now knew that such institutions were quite in order; at his own college, as he had recently discovered, there was a similar benefaction for such of its junior members as were 'ingenious, diligent, and of a godly conversation'. Roughly speaking, Mr Mackellar conceived it his duty to keep an eye on Mungo's rating in qualities of this sort; and this was the purpose of the present interview. Mungo didn't pretend to himself that he wasn't ingenious; his having scrambled into Oxford must count as diligence, at least for a term or two; and as for godly conversation—well, he wasn't likely to chuck at Mr Mackellar's bald head the sort of words and images that so agreeably adorned Pons's Cambridge Boat Song. So with luck Mr Mackellar should just be a bit of routine.

Mungo left his bags at the station and climbed to windy George Street. He knew quite a lot about George Street. It contained more than the office of Mr Mackellar—which was as dingy as a lawyer's office in Dickens, and filled with a metaphysical Calvinistic gloom almost as palpable as the superbly metaphorical fog in *Bleak House*. (Mungo was rather pleased with this; it wasn't quite right, but it would work up.) In George Street Shelley and Harriet had lodged on their wedding-journey—about the time when Scott, a stone's throw away, was thinking of getting busy on *Waverley*. Next to Frederick Street Peacock had stayed; and at the end of the vista, in St Andrew Square, had lived Peacock's butt, Lord Brougham, and David Hume who had apparently been the Bertrand Russell of the eighteenth century. Even Kenneth Graham, who had thought up Toad and Ratty, had managed to get himself born in George Street; and from George Street had issued the number of *Blackwood's* that had attacked Keats.

Mungo Lockhart, Oxford undergraduate, quickened his pace (an operation easy enough to one with his length of leg). He hurried forward, if not like a guilty thing, at least like one who has made an ass of himself by selling out of a sound investment. It is the penalty of being ingenious to be susceptible to such awkward feelings. But as he mounted Mr Mackellar's staircase he cheered up. He could have done without the coming inspection. But mild comedy was probably to be extracted from it.

So he entered the lawyer's room confidently, remembering not to trip on the holes in the carpet, and rather taking to the smell of mouldering leather that issued from the ranked volumes of *Scots Law Reports* on the shelves. There was an attractively weird picture on the wall. It showed a hundred or more legal characters (no doubt including Mr Mackellar's father) assembled in an imposing hall, and its oddity consisted in its being a fake photograph—a *collage*, in fact, fabricated from individual portraits ranked with a rough and ready attempt at linear perspective. Mungo kept his eye away from this, having recalled that on a previous occasion the philosophic problem posed by this Assembly-that-Never-Was had distracted his attention from the admonitions of his paymaster.

'Let me hear about you,' Mr Mackellar said briefly.

Mungo gave an account of himself—neither too bleak (he thought) nor too spirited, and certainly with a tight rein on the fancy. Mr Mackellar heard him out in silence. And when Mr Mackellar attacked (as it were) it was from an unexpected angle.

'I seem,' he said, 'to detect a considerable alteration in your speech.'

'Sir?' As he produced this, Mungo realized that it was itself such an alteration; ten weeks before, he would have

produced half a dozen words instead of this economical
challenge.

'Your accent has been influenced by your new environ-
ment to a degree which I judge remarkable in a mere two
months.'

'I didn't know. I haven't intended anything of the sort.
I'm assimilative, I suppose. And in more important things,
too.'

'You would make a very tolerable advocate.' Mr Mackellar, who, in a general way, could in the matter of grimness have given points to Lord Auldearn himself,
distinguishably smiled at Mungo for the first time in
their acquaintance. 'A change in speech habits is inoffen-
sive if involuntary; it is instantly resented if an element
of intention or pretension appears.'

'Well, that gets me clear.' Mungo, encouraged by the
smile, responded with his hit-or-miss grin. 'And I don't
much mind what noises I make. I'm not going to be an
actor.'

'You certainly are not.' Mr Mackellar, all Scottish
thistle again, gave this a mandatory emphasis which
Mungo didn't quite like. 'So let us talk sense. If you were
to be called to the Scottish bar, Mungo, you would not
derive any advantage from having come to speak what is
called received standard English. Before the Senators of
the College of Justice the point would be immaterial. It
might not be so when pleading before a Scottish jury.'

'I suppose not.' Mungo wondered what was going on.

'Several young advocates who were sent to English
schools have made the point to me.'

'I can imagine they have something there,' Mungo
said colloquially. He was a good deal startled by a new
and unsuspected Mungo Lockhart who appeared to exist
in Mr Mackellar's eye. He had always supposed himself
to be receiving, from this trust or whatever, assistance

designed to place him, at the most, on some respectable office stool. This wasn't his own idea of himself, and it hadn't troubled him that it might be other people's. He'd make his own way, he believed, when the time came. Mackellar had always treated him—not particularly offensively—as a plebeian on some sort of dole. Of course it was natural that this business of going to Oxford should a little alter the lawyer's view. But that the old chap should be planning for him a career as a fellow legal shark was something of a facer. At the moment, it might be a good idea if diversionary tactics were applied. 'About my work,' Mungo said virtuously. 'It looks as if I ought to tell you that I'll be requiring a good many books. Not just out of libraries, I mean. You see—'

'There will be no difficulty.' Mr Mackellar had raised an authoritative hand. 'Any reasonable disbursement by you in that regard will be honoured by me. And waste no time about it. Your tutor writes to me that vacation study is regarded as of the highest importance.'

'Yes, of course.' Mungo wasn't too pleased at the revelation of this correspondence. For a moment, indeed, his indignation was such that he resolved to tell his tutor off about it at his next tute. Then he reflected that the poor man was probably obliged to reply to enquiries from properly accredited persons. And anybody who pays you money out of some fund or other certainly regards himself as that. 'I've got a course of reading mapped out,' Mungo added, as with a consciousness of modest worth.

'I am glad to hear it—the more so in that I observe some part of your vacation to be already elapsed.'

'Oh, yes. I went to stay with a friend.'

'Ah.' Mr Mackellar didn't give this an overtly interrogative intonation. He paused on it, all the same.

'A man called Ian Cardower. He's in my own year, and reading History.'

'Cardower, did you say?'

'Yes. I found myself sharing rooms with him, which is how we got to know each other. His people live at a place called Stradlings, which is where I've been staying. It's rather a nice house.'

'Very pleasant,' Mr Mackellar said. 'Most agreeable.' He was regarding Mungo curiously, and appeared moment-arily at a loss. 'Did you happen to discover if your friend is any relation of the well-known Scottish family of the same name?'

'I'm afraid I don't know, sir.' At this point, Mungo allowed himself to look beautifully vague. 'Perhaps there are several well-known families called Cardower? Ian's grandfather is a Lord Auldearn. We went to see him at a house called Bamberton Court. I don't know whether you'll have heard of him.'

'Of course I have heard of the Marquis of Auldearn.' Mr Mackellar was now looking at Mungo hard. 'He has had a most distinguished public career. But he must be a very old man now.'

'Oh, yes. His clothes don't fit him any more, and he wears carpet slippers all the time. Only, in the evening he changes into tartan ones.' Mungo was unable to resist this single flight of fancy in the midst of so much per-fectly veridical, if mischievously slanted, reporting. But he added hastily, 'But he's awfully impressive, all the same. He reminded me of Cicero's *cum dignitate otium.*'

It would have been hard to tell whether Mr Mackellar was impressed—and, if so, whether it was by this young Oxford scholar's Latinity or his rapid progression into aris-tocratic circles. But he certainly had the appearance of a man confronted by a problem. As to what it might be, Mungo hadn't a clue—until Mr Mackellar looked at his watch and stood up behind his desk.

'I judge, Mungo, that our business is concluded.' And

then—as Mungo prepared to make himself scarce, with suitable expressions of gratitude—he added, 'If your departure-time admits of it, I should be happy if you would lunch with me in my club.'

'Thank you. I'd like to, very much.'

Mungo got out this social prevarication with commendable expertness. He didn't dislike Mr Mackellar, but he did dislike their relationship. This business of being periodically paraded as a charity boy was something he couldn't even give Ian a burlesque account of. No doubt the old man was constrained by the terms of the trust to hold these interviews, and he did so quite decently, according to his lights. But Mungo thought they were now a bit out of time, as well as a shocking waste of the trust's money on railway tickets. He had resolved to write Mackellar a letter or two over the next year which would be both a civil report on himself and a hint that these confrontations were a bore to somebody who was now quite grown up. And here was this invitation, which suddenly set the relationship on a new basis.

They left the office, walked down Hanover Street side by side, and turned into Princes Street. But Edinburgh's east wind was now blowing so strongly and freezingly that any words they uttered would either have been whirled away in the direction of Glasgow or simply congealed on their lips. Mungo employed the resulting silence in telling himself that he mustn't be obtuse. A rocky old person like Mackellar S.S.C. was unlikely to be a guileless snob, or to have changed gear simply because the youth from Forres had been hob-nobbing with the nobility. He was merely effecting what might be called a necessary transition in rather an abrupt way. And it was quite possible that this lunch was going to be a valedictory occasion.

Mr Mackellar's club was in Princes Street; it appeared to be one of the few remaining islets of dignified repose

among the increasingly commonplace shops. Pausing in
its portico, and being thus a little sheltered from the blast,
Mr Mackellar animadverted unfavourably upon the in-
cursions of modern commerce—controlled, he pointed out,
by people in London, who were themselves controlled by
people in New York. He named august establishments,
all with good Scottish names, now departed from the
scene. Could his mother, he declared, be set down at one
end of this historic thoroughfare today she would undoubtedly walk to its other extremity without remarking
anything that warranted purchase. Mungo, although he
judged this to be an exaggerated view of the matter,
began to feel there was more to be said for Mr Mackellar
than he had hitherto been prepared to admit. Scotland for
the Scots was one of the few political persuasions with
which he had equipped himself.

He had never been in a club—except, indeed, for a for-
lorn and crumbling affair tenuously maintained in Oxford
by undergraduates of Ian's sort. So he prepared to make
useful observations. There was, for a start, a man in a glass
box, just as in college. He hadn't a bowler hat, however,
and he was dressed in a kind of muted uniform which
somehow suggested to Mungo the sort of character who
locks and unlocks the gates of a gaol. This effect was
enhanced by the fact that he was plainly keeping a vigilant
eye on two elderly gentlemen who, although obviously
of considerable consequence, were huddled on an uncomfortable bench close to the door. Mungo divined that the
wretches were guests who had arrived in advance of their
hosts, and must remain under close surveillance until
these chose to turn up. Mungo himself, being beneath
Mr Mackellar's wing, was quite in the clear, although
Mr Mackellar had to hasten to inscribe his name in an
enormous book. It must all be rather like this, Mungo

thought, when one visits somebody in a top security prison.

Apart from these appearances, there was nothing on view that could be at all unexpected to a reader of English novels. The somnolent silence, the enormous leather chairs, the barricades of newspapers and journals behind which sundry members were sheltering from any possibility of social intercourse, etc., etc.—all these were duly on parade. Mungo became aware that he was a good deal less observant than simply hungry. As he stood in a vast bay window overlooking the street and the gardens and the Castle, and consumed a glass of sherry while Mr Mackellar discoursed on the history of the Leith wine trade, he was hoping that all these old men didn't diet themselves in their club on the same frugal scale that he remembered at Bamberton.

Two or three drably attired characters—perhaps they were fellow S.S.C.'s—passed the time of day with Mr Mackellar, and Mr Mackellar gravely introduced Mungo to them as a client of his, Mr Lockhart, now at Oxford. But this didn't exactly start any ball rolling, and Mungo was presently led off to the dining-room. It had never occurred to him that he was a client of Mackellar's, and he doubted whether it had ever previously occurred to Mackellar either. It was all part of this business of rather sudden promotion. He felt distrustful of it, but that didn't spoil his lunch. At least as a nosh-house, the club got high marks, and in addition to the eats he was provided with a little decanter holding a third of a bottle of claret. Under the influence of this he talked to Mackellar quite a lot, for his head was still as light as Ian had once discovered it to be. He retained enough sense, however, to decline a glass of port with his cheese and before his coffee. It was just as well, after all, to continue to chalk up a good mark with the old chap every now and then. Moreover he had

become aware—perhaps it was a matter of the antennae—
that something more was brewing. Mackellar had a surprise up his sleeve—or perhaps to get off his chest. There
were several preliminary hums and haws that came to
nothing. It was only when the old boy had returned from
a desk where he had been signing his bill, and the moment
to turn Mungo out had patently arrived, that he uttered.

'My dear Mungo, this is the moment to say a further
word about your affairs. I have to inform you that, upon
the occasion of your coming of age, I shall have a communication to make to you.'

'A communication?' It was pretty blankly that Mungo
repeated this.

'Precisely. A communication. You must understand,
however, that nothing more is to be said about it now.'

'But I *have* come of age. There's a new law, isn't there?
And I'm over eighteen.'

'Ah, yes. And you are undoubtedly of mature years.' As
he said this, Mackellar smiled—and in a way that Mungo
quite liked. 'But I have expressed myself loosely. The instructions I hold explicitly designate the twenty-first
anniversary of your birth—unless, indeed, a certain event,
which I am not at liberty to explain to you, should take
place before that date. In that event, and in that event
only, I should be at liberty to use my discretion. And
there we must let the matter rest at present.' Mackellar
made a weighty pause; he seemed absolutely to enjoy this
idiotic mystery-mongering. 'Although I think I may go so
far as to say that there is nothing portentous about it,
or that will effect any marked change in your circumstances. So, for the present, you may dismiss it from your
mind. Shall I have them call a taxi to get you to the
station?'

'No, thank you. I've time to walk. But I don't see—'
Something obscure but powerful in Mungo made him

break off. Conceivably it was pride. 'Thank you very much,' he said—formally and in what might have been called his most Stradlings manner. 'It was a splendid lunch. Should you ever be in Oxford, I hope you'll allow me to show you round. Good-bye.'

Mungo shook hands with Mackellar S.S.C.—this rather than let Mackellar S.S.C. shake hands with him—and tumbled himself out of the club and into Princes Street. A howling gale from somewhere off Norway assisted his progress towards the railway station.

10

WITHOUT MUCH DIFFICULTY, Mungo found himself a corner seat in one of the refrigerated chambers which, on this particular wintry afternoon, the Scottish Region was passing off as a railway train. Warmth would begin to seep in somewhere in the neighbourhood of Pitlochry or Blair Atholl. Before that, one's only hope lay in a fug, and it didn't look as if there were going to be enough passengers to generate one. The Scots don't do much travelling at Christmas. Their family get-togethers happen at the New Year. Mungo saw not much prospect of cheer during his journey, except from the mere names of the places he would be passing through. Dunkeld, Killiecrankie, Dalnaspidal, Kingussie, Aviemore: these decidedly had the edge on Chipping Sodbury and Goole and Stoke and Jump. It was true that in Caithness there was a Slickly, and also what appeared to be a gent's residence called Glutt Lodge. These rather let down the side. But could it any longer be called *his* side? Wasn't he just another scuttling Scot—as much so, in his small way, as all those well-heeled Cardowers who had beaten it to their Bambertons and Stradlings?

Being told that he was beginning to speak Oxford English, or whatever it was to be called, had a good deal shaken him—much more, he told himself energetically, than had Mackellar's solemn talk of a communication to be made to him when he was twenty-one. The notion of sophisticating his native tongue, whether by design or not, was obscurely disconcerting—perhaps, he thought, as seeing to ally him with those pitifully timid of God's creatures, like the ptarmigan or Alpine hare, who change their colour with the seasons. You could write a short story called 'The Turncoat' about a chap who—

Mungo was distracted from this creative thought by the train's starting to clatter its way through the alarmingly archaic cantilevers of the Forth Bridge. He looked up the Firth, where the contrasting elegance of the road bridge was silhouetted against the declining sun. *The old order changeth, yielding place to new.* He might be destined to live until the road bridge was as much a collector's piece as the railway bridge was now. What made this an appalling thought was the extent to which each of these future decades would be almost totally unplanned and undirected affairs. How far ahead had he looked when he'd let himself be booked in for Oxford? Hardly as far, even, as this first return home. For instance, there was his closest school-friend, Roderick McLeod. *We twa hae run about the braes and pu'd the gowans fine.* Roddy, now articled to a lawyer in Eglin, would certainly be disconcerted by somebody who had taken to saying 'awf' when he meant 'off'. (Not, Mungo was sure, that he had come to *that*.) And how could he tell Roddy that he'd rapidly made an equally close friend of the son of a lord?

This extremely self-conscious meditation lasted Mungo quite some time. A man came along the corridor, banging the doors open and shut, bellowing into empty compartments that afternoon tea was now being served. Mungo almost took refuge in it. But it would cost the moon, and he'd had that big lunch. So he dug out his next Great Novel, which was *The Idiot*. Dostoyevsky, it seemed, had produced eight versions of the story. In one of them the idiot was to be like Christ, and in another he was to be like Iago; and in the face of the fantastic confusion thus created the novelist had pretty well gone mad. Gloomily, Mungo plunged into this desperate but accredited masterpiece.

The Grampians were under snow; there was snow in great drifts against the snow-screens; beyond the dark forest of Dail-na-Mine the summit of Beinn Dearg—the red mountain—was flushed to rose. Snow was falling as the train toiled up the Pass of Drumochter; the great diesel brute dragging it still had untaxed energies stacked in its guts, but you couldn't help feeling it was about to expire. Dusk deepened. The snow-flakes, although falling faster, faded slowly into invisibility, as if in some vast theatre at the turn of a rheostat. But they still sploshed wetly on the window close to Mungo's nose; they even formed small snowdrifts in the window-corners. Mungo was alone in the compartment, and beset by a great melancholy. But at least the temperature was mounting rapidly. The engine's note, its rhythm, suddenly changed; at this moment it was the most exalted engine in the British Isles; it gave a cry, a wail of triumph and agony, like an athlete going through the pain barrier; and then it was lolloping on its downward course. Uninformed travellers would feel that it was spurting for the tape, and that in no time their journey would be over. Mungo knew better: there were still a couple of hours to go. He became drowsy. For a brief space he heard things not possible to hear from the interior of this chunking and rattling monster: the sound of mountain torrents, of peewits high in air, of wind in dry heather. He fell asleep.

He was walking endlessly through the corridors and enormous intercommunicating apartments of Bamberton Court. It was an exhausting occupation, and as he walked he explained to himself why this was so. The house was not really Bamberton Court. It was the Deserted Palace, infinite in extension, which is familiar to drug-addicts, and which gained symbolic status—although he couldn't think what symbolic status—in the period which some-body—but he couldn't think who—had named the Ro-mantic Agony. Yet it *was* Bamberton Court, and he was its owner—or rather it owned him. And this was so be-cause he was the Marquis of Auldearn, obscurely com-pelled thus to perambulate for ever and ever in carpet slippers.

Ian was walking beside him. He explained to Ian how reasonable all this was. He strove to dissipate in Ian's mind the notion that there was anything illogical in Mungo being the Marquis of Auldearn, and the Marquis of Auldearn being Mungo. That it was impossible was merely the popular view of the matter. Persons of superior intelligence, of up-to-date scientific knowledge, would see no difficulty whatever. Mungo-Auldearn's measured argu-ments had their weight with Ian. Ian nevertheless ad-vanced some objections which Mungo-Auldearn was able to refute. But Ian's attention was now being distracted from this grave and consequential matter. The endless corridors, the concatenated state apartments, were lined with pictures crammed with naked goddesses, nymphs, stripling youths. Ian was taking a great deal of interest in these—particularly as all the thronging nudities were beginning to cavort in a lively manner within their frames. Mungo-Auldearn didn't understand this phenomenon, and didn't care for it either. It was now Ian's turn to adduce reasoned argument. The Lord High Chamberlain, a relation of Ian's—or was it of Mungo-Auldearn's?—had been obliged to shut up shop. Nudes no longer had to stay immobile in order to remain officially decent. They could now wriggle as they chose. Like *that* one, Ian said —and came to a sudden, a transfixed halt.

Mungo woke up. The train had jerked to a standstill,

and through the window there was a blaze of lights. But such an appearance was impossible in the middle of the Cairngorms. He must be on the wrong train, and have arrived he didn't know where—Blackpool, perhaps, or a place like that. Before this vexatious mistake he felt a panic so disproportionately deep as to puzzle him, and he had a fleeting sense that it must have accompanied him out of his dream. Then he saw that this was all nonsense. The train had simply stopped at Aviemore, which had been a decent little straggle of a village only a few years before, and now had been turned into a glittering winter sports centre. Mungo stared at the lit-up posh hotels and whatever in a glum and unreasoning resentment. He'd never gone to sleep on a train before, and supposed it to be a sign of advancing years. Moreover—what was a very odd thing—his dream had frightened him.

The train drew out of Aviemore, and Mungo had another go at his novel. Prince Leo Nikolayevich Myshkin —the idiot, that was—was making an uncomfortable railway journey too. The Warsaw train was approaching Petersburg.

At Forres (which was not at all like Petersburg, except in being colder than was agreeable) Mungo was met by his aunt. Miss Guthrie's car, which he was accustomed to think of as about the same age as himself, had a fabric hood and uncertainly fitting side-screens of discoloured celluloid. It couldn't have been called made for comfort. But it did seem to be made to last, since nothing ever went wrong with it. It took Miss Guthrie—Aunt Elspeth—in and out of Forres every day of her school term. Mungo piled his possessions into the back (from which an antediluvian contraption called a dicky-seat had been removed), and they drove off into the darkness. Only a very light snow was falling. The climate of Forres is officially 'mild', and Mungo had remembered just in time not to commit the solecism of commenting unfavourably upon the temperature.

'And you saw Mr Mackellar,' Aunt Elspeth said interrogatively. When this question elicited only a simple affirmative she added, 'And what did he have to say to you?'

'He said I could buy any books I reasonably needed, and that he'd pay up.'

'You should have written ahead about it. Books take time to obtain in Elgin or Inverness. And here's a good part of your holiday gone, Mungo.'

'That's just what Mackellar said. He did some heavy *in loco parentis* stuff.' Mungo retained a naïve faith in employing a little elegant Latinity when addressing those who had been responsible for his education. 'But it's all right about the books. I took a chance, and bought them anyway.'

'You're a rash laddie. Where would you have been if Mr Mackellar hadn't agreed to pay?'

'Not ruined—only furious. I've more than eighty pounds in the post office.'

'And a credit to you it is.' Aunt Elspeth was a just woman. 'But how do you find the other students, Mungo? Your letters are good ones of their kind, but too full of your fancies to be relied upon.'

'I find them very nice. Some of the freshmen from small places say nobody bothers or takes up with them. But I haven't found that at all.'

'I can believe that.' Aunt Elspeth didn't offer this comment in any distinguishably approbatory tone. 'But are they serious, the ones you take up with? This Ian Cardower, you've been staying with—what about him? He comes from a very frivolous class of society, it seems.'

'Ian is quite as serious as I am.' Mungo had resigned himself to the prospect of stiff inquisition. Being very

fond of his aunt, he didn't resent it in the least. But there
was quite a lot that he wasn't likely to make clear to her,
since he was far from any comprehensive clarity himself.
'Ian has been a great thing for me,' he said firmly. 'Far
more than I can be for him.'

'He's certainly taken you among grand people.'

'He's taken me among very civilized people.'

'And you've felt at home with them at once?' The
note of curiosity in which she had asked this seemed to
strike Miss Guthrie as contrary to her principles, for she
answered her own question without a pause. 'And no great
wonder if you have. For you'll be a man of solid cultiva-
tion one day, Mungo Lockhart. And you're a braw lad now.'

Mungo was silent—and glad that he was able to scowl
into the darkness unseen. Aunt Elspeth made him uncomfortable when she was taking pride in him. He liked
her best in her most astringent mood. Possibly a consciousness of this informed her next remarks.

'From what you say, the two of you seem to be ever
talking. Do you keep to your book when you should, in
this room you share?'

'Well, not really. It's hardly the idea, exactly. Of course
you're expected to browse on the fodder in the library
enough to scratch up your essay. But I believe your tutor
actually hopes you're spending quite a lot of time talking
about this and that in a general way. Mine is always
saying that the vacations are the time for systematic and
substantial reading.'

'And so they are, I don't doubt. And so, Mungo, here
you are.'

'Well, yes.' Mungo was able to pause here, because they
were turning off the main Nairn road into a lane requiring careful manoeuvring on the driver's part.

'Yes?' Aunt Elspeth echoed, when this hazard was behind her.

'There's really quite a big problem. I've discovered I don't properly know what sort of person I am. And even if I work that out, there's still the question of just how I should spend these three years. What to go for.'

'What would you be thinking to go for, Mungo, except First Class Honours from your professors?'

'Well, of course it's silly to talk contemptuously about the rat race, and turn bloody idle. But—'

'Mungo!'

'Sorry. Turn idle. But not everybody's made for what you might call the straight academic grind.'

'You've gone from a small school to a great university. If you feel a little overborne for a time, it's natural.'

'I don't feel overborne.' Mungo was surprised by the ease and confidence with which he tossed these words into the darkness. 'There are men in my year who are far cleverer than I am. The two Open Scholars reading English, for instance. They're from big English grammar schools, and were born able, and have been fearfully well taught. They're clear and logical, and they can look right ahead and know how their argument's going to develop. They're the sort of people, I suppose, who get Firsts, and that kind of thing. They've got an awful lot that I haven't got. But if what *I've* got is something *they* haven't got, I might be going all wrong in competing with them on their own ground.' Mungo paused, and there was a silence. 'They're consecutive men,' he added, suddenly remembering a helpful remark by Keats.

'Is your friend Ian Cardower a consecutive man?'

'I think Ian is something quite different again. But I'm not sure what. Ian's a dark horse.'

'I'd like to meet him.'

'You shall. I'm going to bring him here. But not these holidays.'

'Mungo, I think I know what you're telling me about

these holidays. You're going to read a little of what you've been told to read, and a lot that you haven't. But you'll spend most of your time mooning around the countryside, talking aloud when you think there's anybody watching you, and coming home to clatter at that typewriter—even between your porridge and your egg. Is that right, Mungo Lockhart?'

'It's about right.' Mungo didn't resent the small precise barb included in this package, since it was disinfected by its truth. 'But I'm not going to go to extremes, and disgrace you before the dons. I'm not moving into opposition, as I did in that bad year at school.'

'I nearly took you away. They hadn't an idea in their heads except to thrash it out of you.'

'The treatment had its points,' Mungo said judicially. 'It was better than playing upon my good conceit of myself, or even than just not bothering with me. Talking of conceit, I haven't told you everything about Mackellar S.S.C.'

'Mr Mackellar has a wee touch of self-importance, perhaps. But I don't think, Mungo, you should call him conceited.'

'It wasn't that. Mackellar ministered to *my* conceit. He gave me lunch in his club on Princes Street. I was duly overwhelmed. *Sublimi feriam sidera vertice.*'

'I wonder.' Miss Guthrie, aware that her nephew had been received at the board of the ancient nobility of her country, was unable to accept this profession as other than ironically intended. 'Mr Mackellar has always taken a keen interest in you, Mungo. You mustn't mock him.'

'Yes, he has. But always as if I belonged to the good poor. So this wasn't the same thing.'

'It was a very proper attention to an undergraduate at a famous Oxford college.'

'I don't know about that. But it was a very proper lunch.

Incidentally, he said something rather odd at the end of it.' Mungo had decided to have a go at this in the remaining few minutes before they reached home. 'He said he would have a communication for me—that was his word —on my twenty-first birthday. Can you tell me what it's going to be?'

'No, I can't.' Miss Guthrie had been silent for a moment, and then spoken sharply. 'It might be something about money.'

'He said it wouldn't be portentous—and that sounded a bit portentous in itself. And he said it wouldn't bring about any marked change in my circumstances.'

'That certainly sounds as if it were about money. I expect your bursary includes some small lump sum to help set you up. Just a final payment rather larger than the ordinary ones.'

'Perhaps we could ask somebody who has had a bursary from this fund before. I mean, about what happened at the end. Do you know anybody else who has been whatever it should be called—a beneficiary?'

'No, I don't.'

'Do you know how it was first fixed up for me?'

'It was arranged by the last minister, Mr Bonallo. He's dead.' Miss Guthrie drew the car to a halt. 'I'm afraid you'll have to get out and open the gate,' she said.

Mungo did as he was told. The drive, no longer than a cricket-pitch, and oddly overshadowed by an ash, an elm, an oak and a beech, ended in a semicircle of gravel before the grey four-square house. Under the very moderate illumination from the car's headlights the snow made blue shadows, glinted in minute diamonds. It was a Christmas-card scene of an unpretending order. All Mungo's life had been here, and the place's quiet seemed to rebuke him for badgering his aunt about nothing, or at least about matters long passed out of mind. A flicker of light from his own bedroom window told him that she had lit a fire by way of welcome. He decided that, with his aunt at least, he would drop Mackellar's small mystery. Probably he ought to keep it small, even inside his own head.

Mungo pushed back the gate. Because sagging on its hinges, it cut a crisp arc in the snow. The old car jerked into motion again, and passed through.

EASTER FINTRY AND Wester Fintry were adjoining
hillside farms. The farm-houses, both facing bleakly
north, lay within two hundred yards of each other. Origin-
ally each farm had comprised approximately the same
modest acreage, and the houses must have been almost
identical, like the labourers' cottages which were disposed
at a respectful distance from them. Nowadays all the
land went with Wester Fintry, and Wester Fintry had
in consequence taken over Easter Fintry's byres and sted-
dings. Conversely, Easter Fintry's farm-house had been
enlarged by building on at the back, so that it was now a
fairly commodious dwelling, surrounded on three sides
by somebody else's cattle and hay and implements. This,
although it didn't make for elegance, had been to the
advantage of Mungo (who might have been facetiously
described as the young laird of Easter Fintry). Throughout his childhood there had always been something going
on, and acquaintances to make, more or less outside the
windows.

In those days both the Fintrys had been in the occupation of Guthries, although apparently they hadn't been
related to each other. But the Wester Fintry Guthries
had departed long ago. Mungo had never asked how the
Easter Fintry house had come into the possession of his
aunt, or when it had shed its land, enlarged itself, and so
become the rather indeterminate place it was. This wasn't
at all because he had an unenquiring mind; it was because he had early discovered that such questions elicited

replies which were much less interesting than answers he could make up for himself. At least the changes must have happened quite long ago, since the new bits of the house now looked as old as any other part of it.

Just across the road, and now Wester Fintry property, were the traces of an artificially levelled patch of ground which had clearly once been a tennis-court. This surviving token of leisured life had all the air of an antiquity, and it, too, Mungo preserved in his mind as a small enigma. He peopled it with gentlemen in straw hats and ladies in bustles and trailing skirts playing a kind of pit-pat game across a drooping net. What was commonly to be viewed there now was a tethered Wester Fintry goat.

Mungo's was a large attic room, with dormer windows at each end. To the south he looked across the Muckle Burn (extravagantly so named, although it grew a little larger before joining the Findhorn) and straight into Darnaway Forest, an enormous darkness of fir trees fading to the horizon. To the north was the abandoned tennis-court (particularly ghostly by moonlight, which made even the bustles eerie), and then Hardmuir. As Hardmuir was nothing less than Macbeth's blasted heath itself, any ordinary vista would have been proud to close on it. But Mungo's stretched further. First there was the Culbin Forest—which had slowly and magically raised itself, seemingly out of the sea, in the course of his childhood. There was, of course, a prosaic explanation: the Culbin Sands had been afforested. But the Culbin Sands were themselves magical. They had simply appeared—thousands of acres of them—during a stormy night in the year 1694. Beyond the Culbins lay the sea: first the Moray Firth and then, between guarding promontories which were seldom more than pencilled delicately on a faint horizon, the narrow passage to the sister Firth of Cromarty. On two or three days in the year, perhaps, this re-

mote prospect extended itself to Mount Morven in Caithness. More distant than that there was only the North
Pole. And this was why, round about midsummer, the
small Mungo had been able to read his book until he
dropped asleep in the small hours, without the customary
necessity of hiding an electric torch in the bedclothes.

Such was Mungo's kingdom or habitat. It comprised
almost everything he was thinking of when he had once
told Ian there were things he could hardly bear to leave
behind him on coming to Oxford. But when he awoke to
their repossession on the freezing morning of his return
he didn't manage to leap out of bed and embrace them.
Instead, he drew the eiderdown up to his nose and medi-
tated his divided condition. He missed the respectable
old person who, at Stradlings, had brought him a cup of
tea; he even missed the college scout who would burst in,
let up the blind with a bang, and offer an unnecessary
appraisal of the weather. But these were only symbols of
what he'd broken away to. Even Oxford itself, although
he supposed it to be the most beautiful work of man he
had yet encountered, was no more than such a symbol, an
uncertain correlative to what, gazing through his school-
room window at a sensuously meagre and unfurnished
scene, he had cloudily but sometimes fiercely known he
must go for or perish entirely.

Mungo continued to lie in bed for a time, elaborating
this solemn line of thought, fishing around for words for
it, even trying out a cadence or two on his inward ear.
He wasn't too confident about the whole spiel as authentic
Mungo Lockhart. Too much had rubbed off on it from
Stephen Dedalus. Yet why not? In previous ages plenty
of people had worked themselves out in terms of Byron's
Childe Harold or Goethe's Werther. (Or was it Goethe's
Wilhelm Meister? He hadn't yet got round to German Lit.

There was too much English Lit. and French Lit. to make it practicable.) Every age needed its clarifying myth.

Having reached this satisfactorily large conclusion, Mungo got up and shaved with the electric razor that had come to him on his eighteenth birthday. It was beginning to have a gratifying amount of work to do.

After breakfast he wrote the proper letter to Ian's mother. *Dear Lady Robert.* It looked odd on the page, but he didn't suppose he could start *Dear Elizabeth.* Following this he thought he'd write a Christmas letter to Ian. It turned out to be a high-speed, enormously long affair, and although about everything it had too much impetus to be called rambling. He had never written anything like so long a letter before, and he wondered whether he was addressing it to Ian simply because he couldn't very well address it to Anne. For a moment he entertained the startling notion that brother and sister weren't all that distinct in his head. But this wasn't so. And with Ian, he told himself inconsequently, he was one up on Stephen Dedalus, who made whetstones of his friends. Ian definitely wasn't a whetstone.

Getting these letters into the post was like making sure of his lines of communication. He spent the rest of the day in a relaxed pottering around, arranging books and notebooks, doing odd jobs that pleased his aunt. The next morning he began his reading, and it wasn't until tea-time that he got restless. He mustn't be a recluse, he thought; and it was time he renewed a few contacts outside the Fintry ring-fence. So he went to the telephone, rang up the lawyer's office in Elgin, and boldly asked to speak to Mr McLeod. There was a short delay, and Mr McLeod was produced.

'Roddy—it's Mungo. I'm back.'

'Aye.' Mr McLeod seemed reluctantly to be admitting that this must be so.

'Have you still got the motor-bike?'

'Aye.'

'Then come over to supper. Will you?'

'It's a long road, and maybe it'll be a dirty night.'

'Och awa', Roddy! The main road's fine. Only mind our brae. There may be just a bittock of ice on it.'

'I'll come. Only don't talk in that daft way, Mungo Lockhart. I've no mind to take supper, or anything else, with Harry Lauder.'

'Then that's splendid.' Mungo was abashed. 'Come as soon as you can.'

'I'll come as soon as I get clear of my coloured knittings.'

'Of your what?'

'What you call red tape in the south. I tie up people's deeds and wills with it. I'll make you a will, Mungo, if you like.'

'I don't like. But I won't say I shan't consult you.'

'I shan't say I won't consult you.'

'What's that?'

'You must be careful of your wills and shalls north of the border.'

'Idiot! And just you hurry up.'

Mungo put down the receiver, pleased but frowning. He had almost forgotten how much he liked Roddy McLeod. And that sort of forgetfulness wouldn't do at all.

Miss Guthrie, too, was fond of Roddy. Mungo regarded him as clever, and she regarded him as steady. He therefore ranked fairly high in her list of good influences upon her nephew. This fondness was reflected in the quality, and indeed quantity, of the supper, and in the general agreeableness of the conversation following it. It was quite late before the young men got away to Mungo's attic, so that Roddy was soon talking of taking the road again.

'Roddy—do you know?' It was on one of his sudden impulses that Mungo took this plunge. 'I believe I'm like Tom Jones.'

'Lecherous but good-hearted.' It was among Roddy McLeod's qualifications for Mungo's society that, although not of a literary turn of mind, he had perused a surprising number of the novelists.

'Not that—or at least not. both.' Mungo grinned happily, and then was serious again. 'A foundling.'

'A foundling?' Not unnaturally, Roddy stared at his friend. 'Tom Jones wasn't a foundling, exactly. He turned out not to be, anyway. And just what blatherskite are you talking?'

'Harry Lauder!'

'Then what nonsense is this?'

'Well, I don't really know that I had any parents—'

'You must be dotty. Are you imagining you're the Second Coming or something?'

'Don't be profane, Roderick McLeod. You know what I mean, perfectly well. I don't remember my parents, and so I have to take people's word about them.'

'I suppose you've heard of the General Register House? And I suppose you possess a birth certificate?'

'I have a birth certificate, all right. It's not all that informative.'

'It's as informative as the law deems expedient.' Roddy said this with gravity. And it was with gravity that he went on. 'Mungo, I don't like this. What has put it in your head, man?'

'I get money from what pretends to be some charitable trust, but nobody has ever heard of it. And on my twenty-first birthday a communication is to be made to me. By the S.S.C. I've told you of—Mackellar. What do you make of *that*?'

'It sounds to me something to be let alone. And certainly not anything for you to build one of your fairy-tales on.'

'I see.' For a moment Mungo was checked by this. 'But that's exactly it!' he then went on triumphantly. 'I just want to know the plain truth, and then I can forget about it. For instance, I'd like to know when my parents were married.'

'Then, for the Lord's sake, why don't you ask your auntie? She's probably got your mother's marriage lines shoved away in a drawer.'

'I don't like to. There's a kind of reticence between us on such things. And that's significant in itself, wouldn't you say? Could you find out for me, Roddy?'

'Of course I could. There's no need to send to Edin-burgh. It must be in one of the parish registers here-about. And I'm set to go poking about in them often enough. It's a change from addressing the envelopes and licking the stamps.'

'And tying up the coloured knittings.'

'That too. But I think you're just havering, Mungo. And it's a bad thing to be imagining not decently about your parents.'

'One ought to know these things.' Mungo was obstinate. 'And Scottish marriages can be very queer, can't they? A man and a woman can just stand up and say they're married—and married they are.'

'I don't think it's quite like that now.' Roddy, who was going to make a good lawyer, was at once cautious before his own ignorance. 'There was surely a new law came in a good many years back. You must be living with a woman a long time, and the neighbours calling you man and wife, before there's what's called an irregular marriage. And even then, you need a decree of declarator—what-ever that may be, Lord save us—from the Court of Session itself. But I'll find you what you want, if it's only to stop

your silly gob. And I know your birthday, anyway. Do
you mind your tenth, Mungo? I brought you ten cigarettes for it. And we were both sick in this very room.'
    'Then that's fine.'
    'It's no such thing.' Roddy was almost angry. 'You're
in an unco confused state of mind, man. And if that's all
England can do for you, you'd be better coming home
again.' Roddy stood up. 'And now I'll be on my road,'
he said.

    Mungo went to bed thoroughly unhappy about him-
self. As he bloody well deserved to be, he thought. He
couldn't see that what he was after was indecent, although Roddy plainly thought it was. It was just that
Roddy's parents were alive, whereas his own had, in a
sense, never been alive at all. They were mere intellectual
constructs to him. For some moments Mungo, a slave to
words, took comfort from this idiotic expression. Then he
returned to swearing at himself. It was true that he knew
surprisingly little about his parents, and that his aunt had
always been undeviatingly silent about them, the bare
facts of their accidental death apart. So he had been conscious for quite a long time of something which could be
called a mystery, and Mackellar S.S.C. had given that
consciousness a fresh nudge. But all this was no reason
for turning his oldest friend into a kind of private enquiry agent. What would emerge, he now knew intuitively,
would be some small circumstance of an embarrassing
sort, such as most families have the good sense to tuck
away and forget about.
    The intuition was confirmed a few days later, when a
note came from Roddy. It stated, bleakly and without
comment, that Mungo's parents had been married in
Forres just five months before he was born. That Roddy
still thought poorly of having been made the instrument

of this not very significant discovery appeared in the fact
that he made no suggestion for his and Mungo's getting
together again before Mungo went south.

And now all this left Mungo bewildered over what
could possibly have been happening to him. Mackellar's
mysterious trust, even if it was an *ad hoc* affair established for Mungo's benefit alone, could perfectly well have
been set up by some wealthy person of a charitable disposition, who had been touched by the story of an infant
suddenly bereft of both parents, and who had the habit
of doing good by stealth. Very probably what was to come
to Mungo at twenty-one would be some such recital as
this. And what he had made Roddy dig out was irrelevant.

Having got so far, Mungo now went all the way with
Roddy in censuring his own curiosity. It *is* possible to
commit an impiety even towards parents you have never
seen. He'd done just that. But at least he'd never do it
again.

Mungo locked up his typewriter—viewing it, for the
moment, as a symbol of the perils of the imagination as
Ian had extracted them from *Rasselas*. He then plunged
furiously into his vacation work. Since at Oxford he was
reading English, this plunge was almost entirely into the
reckless imaginings of other people. But it was too late to
consider whether this constituted a wholesome education.
In three weeks he had read quite enough to surprise his
tutor.

Part Three

ENGLAND AND ITALY

12

WHEN MUNGO WAS writing to Ian from Fintry Ian was writing to Mungo from Stradlings. The letters crossed. And so too did two further letters which each fired off at the other. For no very clear reason, Mungo was surprised that Ian should write long letters during the vac. Mungo was inclined to think of epistolary correspondence, when not of a purely business order, as being engaged in solely by persons of literary inclination—something that Ian stoutly professed himself not to be. Mungo's own letters, moreover, were composed (even if at breakneck speed) in the potent if not very clearly formulated persuasion that they would one day occupy the early pages of *The Collected Letters of M. G. Lockhart*. As a consequence they were inclined to show off, and their progress was as random as a domestic firework display in a back garden. Ian's letters were quite different: serious rather than exuberant; much more sparing of wit; and confined, in the main, to two or three topics which were really exercising their writer's mind. This made them better letters than Mungo's were, and Mungo, whose intermittent power of self-criticism was considerable, several times condemned his own performances as thoroughly meretricious—although not quite in the root sense of that ugly word. When he addressed himself to another letter, however, it turned out not very different from the one preceding it.

In face of such a world as lay around one now, what on earth was one to do? This was Ian's largest question, not exactly a novel one, which he posed—very honestly, Mungo thought—more or less from within the tradition in which he had been brought up. His father would like him to enter the Diplomatic Service. But what use were career diplomats in an age in which politicians went charging round and round the globe in jets, irritating or confusing each other whenever they met? Whistle-stop diplomacy wasn't much of a life to aspire to tag on to. There were relations who could shove him into banking, industry, shipping, stockbroking, and what have you. All he would have to do was to buy himself an umbrella and a bloody bowler. But none of these activities looked like cutting much of a figure in an England or a Europe when on the brink of the twenty-first century. Perhaps by that date he could be in politics—in a fashion that did a little count—if he started off at something else. He supposed he had sufficient brains to be called to the bar, and even practice in some obscure branch of the law, until an opportunity came along. But it did look—Mungo when he had visited Mallachie would see that it did look—as if the title would come to him one day. In which case—but this must sound terribly silly—he wasn't at all sure that he'd want to renounce it in exchange for the privilege of continuing to scrap away in the House of Commons. So what did Mungo think?

Mungo wasn't able to think anything, except that he mustn't deliver himself of a purely jocular reply. That Ian was almost certainly going to be Marquis of Auldearn was something he had really known already, although it made rather more impact now that he realized Ian's way of looking at it. He remembered Ian's promptly squashing Pons about Bamberton Court: it mightn't be a reasonable sort of house, but it was one of the few of its kind in England, all the same. When it came to the crunch, Ian would stand up and be counted as an aristocrat—and as a nobleman if he became one. Firm and disdainful on the scaffold. All that.

Ian's other main topic was sex. This astonished Mungo. He had supposed Ian to be the sort of person who wraps sex up in several distinct and tidy packages: (1) practical exploration of the subject in its several branches (2) bawdy talk and bawdy song (3) private feelings about the thing's larger challenges and possibilities. But there was nothing tidy about Ian's mind here. He wrote so gropingly that it was very odd he should write at all. There seemed to be a great deal about himself that Ian didn't know; that he felt to be obscure and wanted to be clear about. He even wanted to know—bang in the middle of this context—why he and Mungo had become friends more or less at the drop of the handkerchief. It wasn't, almost to a puzzling degree it wasn't, a matter of their having got interested in the colour of each other's eyes. So when you had something that wasn't a sex-thing, just what was it that you had?

Mungo got the point, but again didn't find himself coming up with an answer. He was a little aggrieved that such problems should be more urgent in the consciousness of Ian, who was going to be a man of action, than in his own, which was to be dedicated to a more than Dostoyevsky-like plumbing of the mind of man. He remembered that it had been Ian who had shouted 'Rupert!' and he who had understood and answered 'Gerald!' at the crazy climax of their fight on the barge. It had been nothing but extremely funny. Yet here was Ian suggesting the same sort of analysing of their straightforward relationship as occupied a good part of the energy of the lavishly enigmatic Birkin and Crich in Lawrence's novel. Mungo didn't find this too strange, but it strengthened his sense of there being a lot in Ian that he hadn't got hold of.

Once they were back in Howard these matters vanished

from their agenda. It was Ian, on the whole, who seemed most disposed to forget them for a while. And this happened, too, with Mungo's dive into his parentage. When he told Ian as much as he had told Roddy about that, Ian's reaction was much what Roddy's had been. He listened, but disapproved of the whole enquiry. It seemed not very decent, for instance, to dig up the fact that one may have been the consequence of a shotgun marriage. Mungo couldn't really disagree, and the subject dropped dead. For one thing, something else turned up that had a good deal of awkwardness to it. One day Ian announced, baldly but with a certain embarrassment, that Anne was engaged.

'One up to Pons,' Mungo said stoutly, although the news was a terrific shock. 'And good luck to them.'

'Pons? Good heavens, Anne isn't going to marry Pons! What on earth should put that in your head?'

'Just that they seemed pretty thick.' Mungo was so puzzled that he could only mumble. 'Weren't they?'

'Anne has always liked having old Pons around—just in a kids-together way. But of course she wouldn't get *married* to him. It would be absurd.'

'I don't see why.' Mungo's confusion of mind was now such that he almost felt injured that Pons should be held a self-evident impossibility in this context.

'Well, it's just not happening. So that's that.' Ian simply declined argument. 'Anne's marrying somebody who's only been in the running for six months or so—quite a decent chap, five years older than she is, with some kind of job in the City.'

'And an umbrella and bowler.'

'I suppose so.' Ian hesitated. 'Mungo, I'm bloody sorry about that.'

'Bloody sorry about what?' Mungo demanded furiously. But that wouldn't do, for his incomprehension was insincere and his fury, if not spurious, at least shameful. 'I'm sorry,' he said. 'Cancel that. It's just that—although I thought you probably didn't notice—I spent some days falling in love with Anne. But of course there couldn't have been anything in it.'

'Why couldn't there be anything in it?' It was now Ian who seemed angry.

'She's two years older than I am, for one thing. And it will obviously be years before I earn a bean: that's another. Don't think I hadn't an atom of sense about it. I had.' Mungo managed a smile. 'I can even see it now as just one of those adolescent things.'

'Of course what Anne's doing now is what's called suitable.' Ian continued to be troubled. 'As I've said, he's five years older than she is, and no doubt quite a breadwinner in his way. Besides, she's in love with him. She was, months before you came to Stradlings. She'd be horrified at the suggestion she'd done anything—'

'I'm quite clear she didn't. Didn't, I mean, intend to lead me an inch up any garden path.' Mungo felt it desperately important to get all this right. 'You see, I'm not a socially experienced person. Let's forget it, for Christ's sake. You're not fated to make a brother-in-law of your faithful old college chum.'

'It would be a bit of a strain, I agree.' Ian frowned, as if judging this swing towards routine facetiousness all wrong. 'I'm sorry Mary wasn't at home. She *is* your age, and I think you'd like her very much.'

'It will be nice to meet her one day,' Mungo said. He was conscious of speaking not coldly exactly, but more conventionally than was admissible in Howard 4, 4. He remembered Ian's mentioning his younger sister in just this way at Stradlings, when he had perhaps guessed that Mungo was expecting a little more from Anne than he was going to get. It was, somehow, disconcerting that Ian should have been laying benevolent plans for him—perhaps thinking of his old college chum as a brother-in-law after all. And Mungo was—wrong-headedly, no doubt —certain that he was never going to fall in love with Anne's sister, however pretty and otherwise delightful she might prove to be. It would be an infidelity, and possibly a disastrous one. Wordsworth—or was it Coleridge?—had got tied up with the wrong sister. And so, surely, had Dickens. It looked to be just another of those professional risks of authorship which he was always hearing about.

With this fairly characteristic mingling of nonsense and sense, Mungo placed at least a large question-mark against the name of the Hon. Mary Cardower. Ian didn't mention her again, except to say vaguely one day that she might be visiting Oxford towards the end of the term. Harmony reigned in Howard 4, 4. Lord Robert, who had predicted that if Ian and Mungo became intimates they would certainly quarrel, might have been judged very wide of the mark indeed. And then—not exactly suddenly, but with a final acceleration to the brink of catastrophe—trouble appeared. It was girl-trouble, and of a different sort from that which had been satisfactorily ironed out.

Ian's early proposal that he and Mungo should range the countryside in quest of unsullied virginal beauty had not fulfilled itself, and had indeed clearly not been meant as other than an extravagance. Hunting in couples was perhaps something they were both too fastidious for. During his first term Mungo hadn't managed more than a few blameless encounters with unexciting young women of the lecture-attending or society-joining sort. When he came back from the vacation he still had Anne too much in his system to bear to be thinking of girls at all. He was aware it wasn't so with Ian. Ian would disappear (rather as he used to do at Stradlings, but for longer periods), and when he turned up again was not disposed to deny Mungo's conviction—advanced banteringly at first—that some amatorious occasion had been involved. He was rather secretive, all the same—more than Mungo expected, considering the large frankness existing between them. He was also quite often in a bad temper, or at least in a wicked one. When he said anything relevant, it was in a mock-Byronic vein. The curse of the Cardowers was upon him, he would declare. And he drank rather more whisky than his mother would have approved of. Mungo wondered whether he was indulging in what aunt Elspeth would have called low pleasures, and not getting too much change out of them. Certainly he never produced a presentable-looking girl—or, for that matter, any girl at all. Until about mid-term Howard 4, 4 was monkishly monosexual. And then, one wet afternoon, Ian marched in with a girl he perfunctorily introduced as Vera.

There could soon be no doubt about Vera. She was as fully Ian's girl-friend as she could possibly be. Mungo was too much a child of his age to disapprove, either with his head or his heart, of his best friend's having a mistress. It was their affair, and bless them. This didn't mean that he liked either Vera herself or Ian's having settled for laying her. He couldn't think that she was a particularly nice person, although there was no arguing against her as a bedfellow on a short-term basis. She was pretty in a bold way; she was also, and quite staggeringly, what he supposed was meant by the word seductive. Mungo didn't gather where she came from. He supposed it must be from one of the women's colleges. But she was something so far outside his social experience that he couldn't really give a guess.

The Vera business began to go really bad when Ian took

—it was the only possible word—to flaunting the girl. With Mungo in the room, he'd bundle her into his bedroom, and that was that. He turned her over his knee and spanked her under Mungo's eyes. Probably she damn well deserved it. But the excitement that this caused in Mungo was something he didn't care for a bit. And it wasn't in aid of anything. Obscurely but pretty massively, Mungo came to feel that, for Ian, Vera was for some reason just wrong.

He said so, and there was a scene—a theatrical scene with Ian in the role of the bold bad patrician that was in some way incredibly bogus. Mungo was horrified. He just couldn't get at the reason for the falseness of the turn. He told himself in bewilderment that Ian must absolutely hate sex. And then Ian did a crazy thing. He had Vera in for a night.

This—or rather being discovered as contriving this—seemed to be about the one thing you couldn't with impunity do. If you managed to be found out in such an idiocy—it seemed to be the dons' view—you were too stupid for the blessings of higher education. Moreover you were upsetting people who had come to Oxford to work and had the right to be protected from the distractions of the brothel. Mungo found this limited judgment fair enough.

Ian had found a large unused cupboard on the staircase of Howard 4, and in the morning he was going to shove the girl into it until the hour (which was noon) when it was legal for women to be around. Mungo thought this a revolting rather than an amusing idea. It would be all right in low comedy—or, for that matter, in very refined comedy of a vaguely Restoration sort. Putting it into practice in real life ought just not to be on. It was like a kid hastily hiding a dirty postcard in his desk. Mungo thought well enough of this comparison (which was perhaps not quite a fair one) to fire it at Ian as the climax of an injurious speech. Ian was furious. They had quite a rumpus.

Mungo regretted having gone to town about the thing. He didn't believe it could really happen, because he didn't believe even Vera would stand for it. He proved wrong. It all went off without a hitch. One consequence was that Mungo, just on the other side of not much of a partition, didn't have a very good night. He turned on the light and tried to read about Prince Myshkin. The chunk of Indian temple sculpture in the photograph eyed the attempt sardonically. Dawn found Mungo in a humiliated condition.

He and Ian avoided each other during the rest of that day. When they met in the evening Ian failed to suggest the satisfied lover who has brought off something more or less out of the *Decameron*. He was in a black temper.

'I don't see what call you have to create about it,' he snapped. 'It's not your affair.'

'It's not a matter of what *you* don't see—or of what *I* didn't see, either.' Mungo, having something pithy to say, gave a deftly illogical twist to Ian's speech. 'I didn't apply myself to the keyhole. I'm not a *voyeur*. But if there's such a thing as an *écouteur*, then I damned well had a front seat in the stalls. And I'll tell you what it sounded like. All the nasty little manuals on the subject rolled into one.' Having discharged himself of that one, Mungo's fury (for he was as furious as Ian) suddenly left him. 'I don't really know what I want to say,' he finished. 'So I'd better shut up.'

'I don't want you to shut up.' Ian said this spontaneously and oddly. 'Get it clearer. I'm listening.'

'Well, don't get me wrong. I'm all for harmless pleasure. But I think you're kidding yourself somehow, Ian Cardower.' Mungo paused, this manner of address having put quite a new idea into his head. 'Have the Cardowers ever been thorough-going Calvinists?'

'Of course not.' Ian managed to find this notion entertaining. 'Or not since I took any interest in them.'

'Perhaps these things are deeply ancestral.'

'Perhaps—but it sounds pretty far-fetched.'

'Guilt and so on—a sense of sin—can be powerful even when unconscious.'

'Rubbish.'

'Yes, it can. And it can result in joyless exhibitionism —bedwise, I mean. Byron, for instance.'

'All right—Byron.' Ian was accustomed to Mungo's resources in literary biography. 'But "joyless" is a bit steep.'

'So it is—but I think there's something in the general idea.'

'Could be. Anyway, I grant you the exhibitionism. Sorry about it. I won't manage such things just that way again. Get out the bottle, Sir Mungo.'

In this manner amity was restored. Mungo felt that he had acquitted himself with credit as a plain-dealing friend. Unfortunately there was a tumble in front of him.

The Vera affair continued, but with more regard to decency. Every now and then Vera would turn up of an afternoon in Howard, and Ian would promptly march her off to destinations unknown. On these flying visits Mungo spoke to her, and eyed her, frankly enough. He felt he had a vicarious knowledge of her person—and this, if it wasn't very nice, was intriguing. He rather thought her breasts were growing larger. Once, when Ian was late, he gave her a cup of tea and two chocolate biscuits. She remained totally strange, and he was without a clue as to the feelings operative at her end of the affair. Perhaps she was in love with Ian. Perhaps she thought it clever to have landed a

Hon., and went round bragging about it. Or perhaps she was presently going to do a walk-out on her current boy friend. It was impossible to tell.

Nor was it possible to tell whether Ian on his side was getting tired of the affair. Mungo had a robust faith in his own empathic power; it was going to be, after all, his chief stock in trade as a writer. Hadn't he, for instance, got himself perfectly inside the skin of that tortoise-like old don in his short story? It ought to be much easier to get inside the skin of Ian, who was his closest friend. And so he did, in a way. But not to the extent of knowing for how long Ian was likely to consider a girl like Vera any sort of good buy. Mungo had to admit to himself that here he lacked a necessary basis in analogous experience. He'd never been in Ian's position—if it might be put that way—or anywhere near it.

Ian was certainly becoming cavalier with Vera. At least in the brief periods when Mungo saw them together, his manner towards her was a displeasing mixture of familiarity and contempt. Of course Ian was by disposition fastidious and rather intolerant: these were not readily apparent truths about him which Mungo had now got a secure hold of. But if he had nothing except these qualities to direct upon this wretched girl he just shouldn't be continuing to go to bed with her. It would be more honest to let her find a truer admirer. And there were times when Ian seemed to have had enough. This was how Mungo interpreted his abruptly announcing one Saturday morning that he was going home for the week-end. Mungo watched him pitch a few things into a bag. It was plainly a spur-of-the-moment decision.

'Have you got leave from the Dean to go down?' Mungo asked.

'Bugger the Dean. You just get a summons from him, and you go along and make a polite apology. He fines you a quid, and asks you to drinks a couple of evenings on.'

'You do know all the ropes, don't you? I remember telling Anne you did. Give her my love.'

'O.K. And you can finish the whisky.' On this brotherly note Ian departed.

Mungo decided on a long reading day. Instead of going into hall he lunched agreeably on bottled beer and digestive biscuits. He was in the last chapter of *The Idiot*—it was a marvellous novel—when there was a perfunctory knock at the door, and Vera walked in.

'Where's Ian?' She had taken a rapid look round the room. 'Is he going to keep me waiting again?'

'Yes, he is until Monday morning.' Mungo had stood up politely, which he felt gave an extra edge to this not very kind reply. 'And I don't remember he left you a message.'

'You're not very civil, Mungo.' Vera showed no sign of withdrawing; instead, she surveyed Ian's disapproving friend at more leisure than he recalled her ever allowing herself before. 'Have you got any cigarettes?' she asked.

'No, I'm afraid not.'

'It doesn't matter.' Vera said this quite vaguely, rather as if she had forgotten her own question. She sat down on Mungo's sofa, made some self-conscious gesture of propriety with regard to her skirt, and looked at Mungo in renewed speculation. 'Say something,' she said. 'Say something that could reasonably be called nice. I'm rather tired of bad manners in this room.'

Mungo failed to say anything. He wanted to get shut of Vera quickly. His breathing had gone slightly odd, and he wasn't fool enough not to know why.

'Or do something, if you're dumb. You're big enough to do something quite dramatic, if you try.'

'Only digestives left.' Mungo had done something, although it wasn't dramatic. He had picked up the biscuit

tin and was holding it out to Vera. He meant the action to
be faintly derisory, but it didn't work out like that. She
took a biscuit, nibbled it, stood up, strolled to the window, and turned round. Something hit Mungo sharply on
the cheek. She had chucked the biscuit at him, and hadn't
missed.

'You are very *odd*,' Vera said, and began dancing round
the room.

Mungo watched her in what he supposed for a moment
to be deep dismay. His heart was now behaving in a fantastic manner, only to be described in the most horrible
literary clichés. Hammering in his chest. Pounding
against his ribs. That sort of thing. All this had built up
very quickly. There hadn't been time to think. It had been
like rounding a bend on a tranquil river and becoming
aware of uncontrollable rapids dead ahead.

'Is your bedroom just the same as Ian's?' Vera asked.
She had halted before the fireplace, and was looking from
one bedroom door to the other.

'Yes, it's exactly the same.' Mungo wondered just how
strange his voice sounded. 'Except that there's a stuffed
badger.'

'I know all about his.' Vera seemed to think she was
putting on a seduction act of the utmost subtlety. 'So I'm
going to have a look at yours.' She walked over to Mungo's
door and opened it. 'I think perhaps it's nicer,' she said,
and went inside. The door swung to behind her. There
was a long pause—so long that Mungo knew just what
must be happening. He found that he was trembling all
over.

'Mungo, there's a funny picture here. I can't work it
out. Come and explain it to me.'

Some observer—but an impotent observer—deep inside
Mungo was saying that Ian's Vera was even more of a drab
than he'd supposed. All the same, he was crossing the

room. And another voice—again his own, and more audible to his inner ear—was repeating the Greek alphabet. Because he didn't know it very well, there was a small mental effort in finding each next letter. He wasn't experienced in situations like the present, but he was well-read in them. This tip must have come out of a novel. Timing was the whole thing.

'Vera was here on Saturday. We made love.'

It was Monday morning, and Mungo said this the instant the returning Ian was in the room. Laying your best friend's girl was the worst sin you could commit. He had spent Sunday feeling that the end of the world had come.

'Good God!' There was chiefly astonishment in Ian's glance. 'Did she let you kiss her?'

'You heard what I said, didn't you? And you know your own language? We made love. It's the accepted expression—although it's a bloody bad one.'

'You *had* her?' Ian put down his suitcase. He seemed completely bewildered. 'It must have been Vera,' he said slowly, 'who had you.'

Being bad at lying, Mungo failed to deny this promptly. He had a muzzy notion that it was his duty to say he'd pretty well raped the girl. But perhaps, in such a context, 'duty' was a bogus substitute for 'vanity'. When he'd entered his bedroom Vera had been without a stitch. She'd known it would work. She'd known she could escape a boring afternoon by taking on a blundering boy. But—just at the moment—Mungo felt he'd rather die than get this explicitly across to Ian. It was bad enough that Ian *knew*. Which he certainly did. Through Mungo's head there floated the notion that they'd have to go to the bursar and ask for a change of rooms. For Ian and all the fun they'd had was now just part of his past. If only—

'I don't mind,' he heard Ian say. Ian had crossed the

room and sat down on his sofa. And Ian repeated, as if he hadn't heard himself, 'I don't mind.'

It was now Mungo who was bewildered. He knew about complacent husbands—fiction was full of them—and he supposed that there could be complacent lovers too. Perhaps Ian was going to suggest going shares in Vera as the convenient thing. In *L'Éducation Sentimentale*, he remembered, Arnoux and Frédéric had pretty well shared Rosanette for a time. But then Arnoux was a vulgarian, and Frédéric—although the hero—decidedly wet.

From this useless literary excursion Mungo's mind came back to a realization of just how Ian had produced that reiterated 'I don't mind'. There had been nothing cynical or relaxed about it. He had said something with which he had surprised himself. And perhaps troubled himself, as well. Just this appeared in the next thing Ian said. For although Ian used every word in the language he did so more sparingly than most.

'Because I don't give a fuck for her,' Ian said. He was staring at Mungo in dismay. 'Not a fuck.'

'I'd have thought it was just about what you did give. And me too.' Mungo sat down on his own sofa. This wasn't working out as the confrontation it ought to be. Perhaps it was something more complicated. 'Ian, are we making a joint effort to ditch Vera?'

'I don't know.' Of the two young men, Ian now appeared to be the more perplexed. 'Do you?'

'It's like one of those queer Renaissance—'

'Oh, not that gen, for goodness sake.' Ian smiled faintly.

'But yes—it's rather relevant.' This recourse to his own stuff almost cheered Mungo up. '*The Two Gentlemen of Verona* kind of thing. Chaps with high-flown notions of romantic friendship saying "After you" as they hand the heroine around.'

'I don't remember *The Two Gentlemen of Verona* as

quite showing that.' Ian said this as if he were playing for time. He was like a man groping for the facts of the case. 'Anyway, Vera isn't a heroine.'

Mungo, who was going to say 'She's a bitch', checked himself—partly as not knowing how Ian would take it, but mostly because he felt it a shabby thing to say about any girl you'd been in bed with a couple of days before. It was a sense of what was due to Vera that produced his next speech.

'I do think you ought to feel I've done something pretty bad.'

'Oh—I can manage resentment, if you require it. You've shown me up to myself, I rather think—and naturally one resents that.' Ian's smile came back, faint but wicked. ' "Ay me! but yet thou mightst my seat forbear." More Shakespeare.'

Mungo was scandalized to find himself laughing at this joke. He still wanted to be serious.

'Ian,' he said, 'be sensible. Where do we go from here? It might be—well, a recurrent situation.'

'I don't think so.' Ian seemed to be gaining confidence. 'And if it is, we'll play it by ear.'

'But we have to be fair to the girl. It wouldn't—'

'Never mind about Vera.' Ian paused. He might have been a comedian, counting a calculated three or four to his next gag. 'She'll take anything that comes.'

So their relationship was unchanged, or if not unchanged, unimpaired. Mungo felt, and guessed Ian felt, that there had been something rather shaming in the strain upon it having proved no greater than it had. If they'd parted for ever, or even had a fight, it would have spoken a little for a maturity which, in the actual event, had been decidedly missing from the affair. Mungo, despite his talent for finding first-aid in fiction, and Ian, despite his for clearing the air with the right bawdy joke, for some time intermittently looked at each other, if not misdoubtingly, yet in a decent embarrassment.

As for Vera, she was not seen again. Later on, enquiry elicited the rumour that she had set up in a relationship of the most sternly monogamous character with an inorganic chemist in the most obscure of the thirty-seven constituent colleges of the University of Oxford. Ian, whether seriously or not, declared that all had been for the best, and that her experiences in Howard had mercifully pulled her up on the brink of an ignoble promiscuity.

Hilary is the tricky term at Oxford, the term in which unsatisfactory things tend to happen. Mungo and Ian had experienced this fatality of the place. The trouble was that there remained something unresolved in the affair. It had, of course, been discreditable all round. And it had, undoubtedly, been more discreditable to Mungo than to Ian, since the incontinence of Mungo had involved an element of treachery absent from the incontinence of Ian. Yet it was Ian who had been more marked by the episode. Mungo, as soon as he was assured that Vera had cleared out and that Ian was his friend still, let his natural resilience take charge. He continued to go round with a grin for anybody who would respond to it, and in fact found himself becoming popular. Pons invited him to the annual dinner of a club dedicated to the defence of Church and King, and even third-year men conversed with him in the J.C.R.

Almost at the end of term, Mary Cardower appeared briefly in Oxford, as Ian had said she would. It turned out that she was a little younger than Mungo, had just left school, and was presenting herself for some sort of interview at Somerville. She came to tea in Howard, but with a train to catch not much more than an hour later. Mungo, the yet faithful lover of the betrothed Anne, found this

162   MUNGO'S DREAM

flying visit upsetting. He quite saw the point of admiring
Mary. She was ravishingly beautiful, she was clever, she
was friendly, she was mocking, she was joyous and gay.
It was the complete Zuleika Dobson effect—except that
Max Beerbohm's heroine was a bitch and Ian's younger
sister was dead nice every way on. She seemed to have
heard a good deal about Mungo, and to take it for granted
that he was the chief exhibit around the place. Mungo
stood up to this, and to Ian's artless satisfaction in having
contrived the meeting, as well as he could. When Mary had
to depart for the railway station Ian declared that, left
to herself, the feather-headed creature would infallibly
get on the wrong train. Unfortunately he was resolved
to attend an evening lecture which promised to be of ab-
sorbing interest, so Mungo was to take charge of the
concluding stage of her visit.

So they sat on top of a Number One bus, and Mungo
talked sixteen to the dozen. It was either that or stricken
silence, he felt, and putting on a turn was the less embarrassing alternative. He got back to college resolved
to denounce Ian's Pandarus-like behaviour. But he found
Ian so pleased with what he had contrived that he hadn't
the heart to make a portentous speech about it. And Ian
wasn't getting pleasure out of many things during this
fag-end of term. Except for Mungo's companionship, upon
which he asserted an absolute claim on demand, he had
fallen into a solitary habit. The casual but constant
sociability taken for granted by his school-fellows seemed
in particular to irk him.

Mungo knew that it was still the Vera business that
was responsible. It had confronted Ian with perplexities
which he, Mungo, hadn't the key to. He knew that he
mustn't fumble at it to Ian's knowledge. He just wondered
when the key would turn in the lock.

It was to be in Scotland that this was to happen.

13

BUT THE PLAN for a combined operation in Scotland, as distinct from Mungo's dutiful return to Fintry, was left over to a vaguely envisaged Long Vacation. During one's second term at Oxford the end of one's third seems astronomically far off.

So at Easter Mungo and Ian went to Italy in the mini. They were assured that Italian youth hostels were without any particular dedication to the virtues of long-distance pedestrianism, and would see no reason to exclude persons arriving in a mechanically-propelled vehicle. But they had a diminutive tent as well, and proposed to use it whenever they could. Although neither said so, they envisaged these three weeks hard up against each other as a clear assertion of their old relationship. And it did turn out that way.

Mungo had never been abroad, a species of insularity which a young writer finds it peculiarly embarrassing to admit. He was therefore unperturbed that the trip looked like costing him his savings. In fact it didn't quite do this. The college, which was said to have amassed over the centuries far more money than it knew what to do with, proved to have a travel fund out of which its junior members were assisted to improve their knowledge of men and manners in foreign parts. Moreover in a controlled way—mainly connected with the buying of wine—Mungo sponged on the rather more affluent Ian. This was a symbolical matter; a token that they were (as Mungo would have said if trying to impress Mr Mackellar) *Arcades ambo*.

They decided to make for Gubbio—this for the reason that they were amused by the sound of it, and that Ian declared it to be the ancestral home of Gub-Gub, a creature in the *entourage* of Dr Dolittle, and so familiar to both of them in the nursery. Italy turned out to be attainable only through a tunnel, so they had to abandon the proposal to drink champagne when picnicking on the summit of some tremendous Alpine pass. But the tunnel was impressive in itself, and they emerged from it into a clear warm sunshine which they innocently concluded to obtain throughout the year in this southern land.

Italy did its best to send Mungo off his head. Gubbio (although it was a bit chilly, after all) was alone worth their money; it seemed particularly so, somehow, because, until this trip was proposed, he had never so much as heard of the place. Moreover Gubbio was no distance from Sansepolcro, where he *had* known that there hung the greatest picture in the world; and Sansepolcro no dis-tance—although over the icy Apennine—from Urbino it-self, that grammar-school of courtesies, that windy hill. Mungo spouted Yeats and a great deal else. Because of his upbringing in a remote and lowly situation, there was as yet little of the *avant-garde* about his literary taste. He could describe Arezzo out of Browning or Ravenna out of Byron—or Venice out of Byron and out of Ruskin as well. (It was this old-world quality that kept him, although not notably docile or industrious, substantially in his tutor's good books.) Ian was indulgent to his companion's naïve behaviour, and at the same time appeared to draw satisfaction—even a sense of security—from the impunity with which he could pepper it, nevertheless, with injurious remarks. He said that Mungo was behaving like an ex-cited American schoolmarm; he said (with recourse to

Pope again) that he was raving, reciting and maddening round the land. Mungo accepted these and similar gibes in good part.

Perhaps it was true (as Ian also, and more seriously, averred) that he would have seen more of the actual Italy of today if he hadn't been so constantly popping on and peering through the spectacles of Englishmen either outmoded or dead and gone. Did he suppose it really likely, Ian demanded, that Poggibonsi or San Gimignano had consented to staying put as the Monteriano of Morgan Forster's *Where Angels Fear to Tread*? Or that Florence teemed with knife-brandishing desperadoes and comical Dickensian cabmen as in *A Room with a View*? Or that the Abruzzi were a haunt of cave-men of the kind Lawrence had dumped there in *The Lost Girl*? Or that there lurked on off-shore islands the picturesque anachronisms of *South Wind*, or in Perugia the loquacious expatriates that poor old Leonard Sedley had pinched from Henry James and paraded in *An Autumn in Umbria*?

Mungo was accustomed to Ian's spirited travesties of sacred books, and he wouldn't have much attended to this particular tirade but for its mention of the last specimen. He had been struck by Lord Auldearn's revelation that Leonard Sedley was distantly related to the Cardowers and lived with Ian's reclusive uncle, Lord Brightmony. Mungo had never met a famous writer, so that possessing this information had made him feel as close to a literary scene as he had come. Even to his own mind this was an ingenuous feeling, particularly as Sedley, although he possessed his niche and his acclaim, in the end had rather noticeably not come off. Mungo had refrained, therefore, from confiding the liveliness of his interest to Ian. But he had brought his copy of *An Autumn in Umbria* with him to Italy. He remembered that on first reading it he had been as much bewildered as impressed.

When they had exhausted Gubbio and its environs,
where it couldn't be asserted that a great deal went on,
they had driven to Perugia and established themselves
there. It was in a precariously terraced little garden, with
the *Prefettura* behind him and the valley of the Tiber
swimming in spring sunshine a thousand feet below, that
Mungo reread Leonard Sedley's notable work. Ian had
gone off on his own. To sit down in Perugia, he said,
and there read a novel set in and around that city, was
just another schoolmistressy turn. Mungo didn't apologize. He had noticed before that Sedley's name moved
Ian to one or another rather acrid comment. Mungo, perhaps because he was always making things up, felt that
there was the tip of a mystery in this.

Perugia lives on chocolate but was nurtured on
blood. As late as 1859—Mungo's guide-book told him—
'the papal Swiss Guards occupied the city after an in-
discriminate massacre', and much the same sort of thing
seemed to have been going on in the place, at least intermittently, since round about 300 B.C. Mungo doubted
whether, walking the streets unprompted, he would have
been conscious of what Yeats called odour of blood on
the ancestral stair. But it was present in Sedley's book. It
was present not oppressively, as in some laboured his-
torical romance, but unassertively in low-keyed descriptions which yet took a lurid colouring through the spare
and deft employment of apposite imagery. Mungo's first
fresh discovery in *An Autumn in Umbria* was how securely
the novelist commanded the spirit of place. And it was
all done very much without showing-off—a term which
Mungo often had to import into his critical vocabulary
when overhauling his own work.

And then there was the conversation. Mungo fairly
goggled—just as he had done on a first reading—before

its dry speed, its copiousness which yet never seemed to be without a passionate relevance. But a relevance to what? It wasn't that the talk, as it flashed and flickered around, served very obviously to differentiate the several characters engaged in it. The characters were there—or at least they were confidently stated to be there. But, perhaps to some aesthetic end Mungo hadn't yet got the hang of, they were all much of a muchness in the manner of their talk. One didn't find in tone and cadence, in vocabulary, range of allusion, and what not, anything that carried one to the individual contours of their minds. So far as these things went, they were all flattened to their creator's idiosyncratic palette.

But everything Sedley's subtle and intellectually athletic people so resourcefully said did have a relevance, relevance to a plot. If one remembered *An Autumn in Umbria* as a constantly talkative book (a conversation novel, as Mungo had called it out of some text book on such matters), that was merely because of the general brilliance of dialogue which was in fact driving narrative forward all the time. It was almost like a play of Ibsen's, Mungo thought, in this moving like an arrow to its catastrophe. And to pretty pervasive catastrophe. The whole action took place within a restricted circle of wealthy and cosmopolitan people whose villas were—a shade imaginatively, perhaps—sited amid and against a landscape Mungo could glance up at as he read. It was all drawing-rooms and gardens and polite entertaining of a sort that must have seemed pretty archaic even when the book was first published. One couldn't point to a stroke of overt violence from cover to cover. Yet nobody (or nobody except a lady who served more or less as the villain of the piece) was left unprecipitated into disaster—here dire, and there ironically trivial. There was a wonderful manipulating of events and relationships in the interest

of this sad state of affairs. You never heard a
creak—nor, for that matter, a tear fall. The swift speed of
the performance allowed nothing to a pausing sympathy.
There was almost an effect of malice—a kind of dry electric
crackle of it—in this unintermitted continence.

Of course Sedley's story wasn't, as might be the case in a
thriller or a romance, constantly present on the very surface of the page. As you read, you had to dig for this,
reach out for that; inferences, implications, momentary
pointers, hints lightly dropped: all these had to be
marked. Still, Mungo was puzzled that so basic an aspect
of *An Autumn in Umbria* should not have remained
more firmly in his memory. Perhaps this, in some paradoxical way, was because Sedley had been more in love
with his own contrivance than with the characters he was
enmeshing in its intricacies. Nobody remembers a yarn
through which you shove people you don't give a damn
for.

The practice of literary criticism had as yet made no
great appeal to Mungo, and he didn't for long persevere
with it in regard to *An Autumn in Umbria*. He was content to conclude that he still admired the book very much,
and in particular that it stood up wonderfully to being
read *in situ*. And about its writer he felt an even livelier
interest than before. What sort of a person was Leonard
Sedley? Why had he almost stopped writing? (It seemed
a very dreadful thing to do.) And how had a man who
seemed so in love with Italy settled down to living in a
remote and seemingly little-frequented Scottish country
house? Ian must know. And Ian must tell him.

14

'MY MOTHER'S IN Rome with Mary,' Ian said. He had been to the *poste restante* and picked up some letters. 'Let's go and collect a meal and a night's lodging off them. It's no distance.'

'Why not?' Mungo said at once. But he wasn't sure that he meant it. This was the first he'd heard of Lady Robert and her younger daughter being in Italy, and for some reason he found the news disturbing. It was as if he had discovered that Ian was under surveillance, and had to clock in and report to his family in Rome. That, of course, was wholly irrational. The Cardowers were very much the sort of people who went here and there, and mother and daughter were probably in Rome without giving Ian a thought. They might be finding somewhere for Mary to live and learn Italian in the interval between leaving school and coming up to Somerville. In which case it was natural enough that Ian should suggest looking in on them. But Mungo felt that he and Ian were doing very well as things stood; and that, in any case, Rome obviously wasn't a city it would be satisfactory to bob in and out of.

What Mungo was really feeling, as he very well knew, was that he didn't quite trust himself with Mary Cardower—and still less (he found) did he trust Ian's impulse to throw them together. It was no doubt nice of Ian, but not too sensible. That he had enjoyed a brief madness over Anne was not perhaps quite the insurance against falling in love with Mary that he was romantically disposed to believe. And everything that was prudent in

Mungo told him by just how much that wouldn't do.
The Robert Cardowers, he knew from Pons, weren't a bit
wealthy. Mary's husband would have to support her from
the moment they'd finished having their photograph taken
outside St Margaret's Westminster, or wherever else the
Cardowers had the habit of getting married. Mungo had
no dreams of wealth, and only distant prospects of earn-
ing anything at all. Mary wasn't a girl he could conceive
of having an impermanent affair with, and Ian obviously
wouldn't envisage such a thing for a moment. So Ian was
being more benevolent than clear-headed in rather insis-
tently bringing his friend and younger sister together.
Mungo decided he had better say something to this effect
now.

'There's no difficulty,' Ian was saying. 'We don't even
have to leave early if we're to be in Rome in time for
lunch.'

'But we can't batten on your mother. At least I can't.'

'Rubbish. She's been lent an apartment in something
called the Via Torino. Oceans of room.'

'All right. But what I really feel is that it's a little
tagging after Mary. You chuck us together on a bus. And
now—'

'You have the most imbecile notions!' Ian was angry
and uncomfortable. 'And, what's more, you invite the
most grossly sentimental remarks. Aren't we each other's
best friend?'

'It's beginning to look like it, I agree.'

'Well, then—isn't it natural I should want you and my
sisters to see each other and get to like each other?'

'You know I fell in love with Anne in the most absurd
and useless way. And now you seem—'

'Oh, stow it, Mungo! You're getting a one-track mind.
You're treating me like an old match-making dowager.
Can't you just enjoy—'

'All right, all right.' Mungo realized he was on untenable ground, even although he wasn't quite confident that Ian was being wholly ingenuous. 'I'm an ungracious ass, and we'll leave for Rome in the morning. Now let's go and get something to eat.'

This brief conversation had taken place beside their tent, which they had by now contrived to use on a number of occasions. Italy is not a country in which it is easy to find a patch of ground secluded from the view of somebody with proprictory feelings about it. But it was much more interesting to try than to let oneself be shoved into a *campeggio* and the society of solemn German and Scandinavian students. Negotiation was rendered difficult by the fact that they hadn't a dozen words of Italian between them. Mungo was ashamed of this, and was forming nebulous plans for acquiring an advanced familiarity with the language before coming back next year. Ian maintained that French was the only language that an Englishman need be ashamed of not employing with facility. When it came to confronting a voluble farmer Ian believed in producing 500 lire, and Mungo in shaking hands. They had lately concluded that both these operations could with advantage be performed simultaneously.

Here, just outside Perugia, they had done rather well, the 500 lire being evidently regarded as gaining them the lease of a sufficient territory for as long as they chose to remain, and a moderate daily sum securing the further convenience of a small boy prepared to guard their property whenever they were away from it. They walked, or rather climbed, back to the city now, and did themselves extremely well on the strength of being likely to enjoy a free dinner on the following evening. The wrongfulness of battening on Elizabeth Cardower had quite gone out of Mungo's head.

*   *   *

It was dark when they returned. Mungo, who had Boy
Scouting in his past, fussed contentedly over a vapour
lamp; Ian, with recent memories of absurd J.T.C. camps,
loosened guy-ropes. The tent was so small that they agreed
they might as well have planned to sleep in the boot of
the mini. But they enjoyed its narrow room, and enjoyed
cursing each other as clumsy restless angular louts. Insinuated into their sleeping-bags, and with a flap of the
tent left open while they smoked a last vile Italian cigarette, they sometimes fell asleep so rapidly as to be in
danger of burning to death, and sometimes started a des-
ultory conversation that went on for hours. There was
something very luxurious about the isolation in which
these talks were conducted.

'Do you ever try to account for yourself,' Mungo demanded, 'in terms of heredity?'

'You've fired that one off before. And why should I
try accounting for myself at all? I'm a prosaic fact. And
I don't go in for morbid artistic introspection.'

'You think about yourself quite a lot. Anybody can see
you do. I can tell it even in the dark. I lie here and suddenly I can say to myself "There's Ian Cardower started
chewing over Ian Cardower".'

'Talk sense, Mungo, or go to sleep.'

'Well, the heredity business *must* be interesting. Incidentally, it's one of the differences between us, isn't it?
You have a heredity and I haven't. I'm a *filius terrae*, so I
can't play.'

'Those silly Latin tags are growing on you. As for heredity in any scientific sense, it's very complicated. Genes
and so on. Has to be worked out with mice or rabbits.'

'That's primitive, like doing your computing with
match sticks. The depth of the thing can only be got at
intuitively. Do you feel you're like your father? You do
have some of his tricks.'

'I didn't know my father went in for tricks.'

'Mannerisms, then. And drop that silly aristocratic reserve. Do you?'

'I suppose he and I share a lot of assumptions. But, no—I don't think I do. And I don't think I'm particularly like my mother, either. Are you like your auntie?'

'What about your grandfather?' Mungo had ignored Ian's question. 'Would you say you were like him?'

'Yes—in a way. Sixty years ago, he may have been quite like me now. And sixty years on, I may be quite like him now. This is a very academic conversation.'

'I don't think it is. As a matter of fact, I'm beginning a short psycho-analytical investigation—no end beneficent, too—free, gratis and for nothing.' Having offered Ian this absurdity, Mungo took a last acrid puff at his cigarette, and chucked it accurately through the opening in the tent. It vanished into the darkness in a brief parabola of tiny sparks. 'What about your uncles? Lord Brightmony—David, isn't he?—must be older than your father. But there was the one that died. Was he older too?'

'Yes. I think Douglas was born within a couple of years of David. I don't know much about him. He died when I was quite a small boy.'

'Just when?'

'Just when?' Ian sounded surprised. 'I think it was 1955.'

'Anne told me he was very wicked. And I believe I've heard of him as a legend among the folk. Is that right?'

'Yes, it is. I think your psycho-analysis is very boring.'

'No, it isn't. You'll see. Because I've got a theory about you.'

'How dare you have a theory about me, you beastly youth!' Ian sounded entirely serious. 'Just drop it into the rubbish-bin of your mind, or I'll turf you out of this bloody tent.'

'We'll be fighting till dawn, my child, if you try.'

This was probably true, but not significant. They both knew that no fight was going to take place. The Gerald and Rupert business again, far from being uproariously funny, would be embarrassing and stupid. So there was silence for some moments, during which first Ian and then Mungo largely yawned. A few frogs were monotonously croaking near at hand, and from farther away came the growl and grind of some vast articulated lorry toiling up to the city.

'Is there a fee?' Ian asked humorously and by way of making peace.

'Not just at the moment. Consultation free, cure guaranteed.'

'*The Doctor's Dilemma.*'

'Quite right. I do like a well-educated infant. But back to the bad Lord Douglas. What's the charge? Did he stain the family honour by passing bad cheques, or was he simply a large-scale voluptuary?'

'What an idiotic word. But, yes—I gather he was that. There wasn't a girl in Moray who was safe from him, and when he went to stay at Bamberton it was impossible to keep a maidservant in the house. But it doesn't seem to have been just as a seducer of innocent girls that he was attractive. Everybody liked him, including his much-tried family. Now ask me if I feel I'm a second Douglas.'

'No. Instead of that, I'll tell you something. You wonder.'

There was another silence. Ian stirred in the darkness. He was so close that Mungo thought he could hear or sense the beating of his heart.

'Precisely what do I wonder?' Ian asked.

'Just a moment.' There was a fumble and a scrape, and Mungo had lit another cigarette. It spluttered for a moment in minute sulphurous explosions, so that his face came and went in a blueish light, and then became steadily outlined in a dim red glow. 'Listen, Ian. I have a serious idea—honestly. That bad-hat Douglas Cardower—'

'Steady on!' Ian's voice in the darkness was suddenly sharp and mocking. 'I can do a spot of psycho-analysis too. Did you ever hear of the Myth of the Birth of the Hero?'

'What the hell do you mean by that?'

'Not a girl in Moray was safe from him. Don't you remember? And Mungo Lockhart with ready-made notions about being a foundling. So I can tell you one fantasy *your* brain's been nurturing. That we may be first cousins— with your romantic self on the wrong side of the blanket.'

'The blanket makes quite a difference.' Mungo was staggered for a moment by what struck him as an uncanny diagnosis. It was true that his imagination had exercised itself from time to time with just this novelettish-seeming notion. But now he recovered confidence. 'You can be as frivolous as you like,' he said severely. 'I want to be serious.'

'Sorry. It's not a nice joke when one peers into it. Go on.'

'Right! As a small boy you heard a lot about your recently deceased uncle Douglas. He probably wasn't talked about before you by the family. But there was the tattle of nurses and servants, and all that.'

'You have the most idiotic notions of what's called upper class life. But continue.'

'It was traumatic—all this about your frightfully wicked uncle. And when you'd learnt a bit more about *how*—'

'All right. I grasp the argument. I was horrified.'

'Yes—and fascinated as well. One part of you would like to measure up to Douglas. Not a girl in Wiltshire, or between Oxford and Bablockhythe—'

'Don't be so clever about it, for Jesus' sake. Just finish.'

'On the whole, horror and revulsion win. You put a brave face on it, and all that. But really you nourish an almost mediaeval sense of the sinfulness of sexuality.' Mungo, whether trying to be clever or not, was pleased with this; he had a vague memory it was something somebody had said about Donne. 'And that's how it was with poor old Vera.'

'Poor old Vera?'

'Well, you used her as a kind of demonstration model. A tremendous bit of showing off. Think of the turn you put on on the other side of that matchboard partition.'

'It was a bit low, I suppose. By the way, I don't apologize for things twice.'

'And then off you went home that Saturday morning, and in Vera popped that Saturday afternoon. I think you really *intended*—'

'Stop a bit.' Ian spoke so quietly that it was surprising Mungo did stop. 'I'm still not clear whether you think you're just turning on an entertainment—a nightpiece confessedly in the highly imaginative Mungo Lockhart manner. So I'd better tell you I'm taking you seriously. In fact, I think there's a good deal in what you say.'

'Oh.' Very illogically, Mungo was brought up short. 'Well, when I said I had a serious idea, I meant it. But perhaps we'd better sleep on the thing. And wake up not remembering it.'

'I think that if there's more of the serious idea we'd better have it now.'

'All right, then. There's your uncle David too.'

Through a silence which succeeded upon this Mungo decided that he was hearing not frogs but the cicada and dry grass singing—a much more poetical phenomenon. Ian was still saying nothing.

'There's your uncle David,' Mungo repeated rather

obstinately. 'Who's still alive, and lives with Leonard Sedley. We're going to visit them, I gather. I want to know about him.'

'You seem to want to know a great deal about my family.' Ian said this with a sudden irritability. 'When they were born, and when they died, and what the parson said about them. I can't think why.'

'It's in the interest of the analysis.'

'Of some fairy-tale, you mean.'

'Well, I'll tell you what I think about uncle David. I think he sounds a bit of a hush-hush job too.'

'Your talents are wasted as an undergraduate, Mungo Lockhart. You ought to be a reporter sniffing out scandals for some low rag.'

'Apologize for *that*, please.'

'All right—I do. But you have those romantic notions about old families. Tremendously aware of kinship, and oppressed by a weight of tradition, and so forth. You want to drag me free of the tyrannous shadow of my uncles. That's what you mean by blethering about heredity and your precious analysis. I'm not saying you haven't got an idea. In fact, I also take back that you're just constructing fairy-tales.'

'Well, then—what *about* uncle David? How am I to behave, for instance, when we go to Mallachie?'

'My advice would be to veil your charms.' Ian's laugh came suddenly and harshly through the darkness. 'It's pretty obvious, isn't it? I've told you that when uncle Douglas was at Bamberton my grandparents couldn't keep maidservants. When uncle David was there they couldn't keep footmen.'

'An even greater hardship, no doubt.' Mungo, determined not to have this small disclosure exhibit itself in a dramatic light, perhaps overplayed a negligent note. 'At least you explain why you don't find Mallachie gay, and

don't much want to go there. But when your grandfather
wants you to go, and even to take friends to the place,
it's my guess he's right.'

'I know he's right. He alarms me—but I've more faith
in his judgement than in that of anybody else I know.'

'There goes the family constellation again.'

'No doubt. But Mungo—do you know?—I'm not sure
you won't be runner-up.'

There was quite a long silence—Mungo having the
grace to be rather overwhelmed by this. He knew that it
wasn't very seriously that Ian regularly denounced him
as practically a zany. But of what he'd just heard he'd
not had a notion. And he much doubted whether his
talk of the past half-hour deserved to be called judicious.
But at least it had been honest, or had owned an honest
aim.

'But,' Ian went on, 'you must have got on the right
wavelength about uncle David without my tuning you in
like this?'

'Well, yes—I suppose so. Somehow, it looked a fair
guess.'

'And I can see how it rates in your blessed analysis,
so you needn't give yourself the trouble of wrapping it
up nicely in all that kindly humour. Uncle Douglas casts
a shadow of sin and guilt over going to bed with a girl;
going to bed with a girl therefore doesn't feel quite as
the books say; and so up bobs uncle David and asks if it
isn't because I have quite a dollop of *him* in my constitution. That's the diagnosis. And the treatment is to
shake and bump and rattle the sufferer free from the spell
of all avuncular ghosts, living or dead. Isn't it?'

'I don't know about ghosts being living or dead. But,
yes—that's roughly it.'

'Well, well! Who knows?' Ian stirred in his sleeping-
bag in a manner suggesting a relaxation of his whole six-

foot-two. 'And now we can go to sleep. Rome tomorrow.'

'O.K. But, Ian, one thing. Leonard Sedley. Do you gather that he and your uncle David—?'

'Lord, Lord—who knows? Or cares a damn? They're just two old men who are obviously dependent on each other, and as to how they first came together I haven't a clue. And as to your own virtue, I don't suppose you need really tremble for it. Everything's fearfully proper at Mallachie nowadays. That's part of the dreariness of the place. Uncle David is excessively religious.'

'Religious? How odd! But, no—I suppose it's not. What kind of religion?'

'Spiky and High Church. He has a private chapel and a personal chaplain. Father Somebody, who wears a soutane and a biretta. It's a terrible scandal.'

'I should think so!' Mungo considered this curious information for a moment. 'Does Sedley join in their devotions?'

He got no reply. Ian had turned over once more, and fallen instantly asleep.

But Mungo himself lay awake for some time. Or perhaps it was only half-awake, for he was seeing some of those vivid evanescent pictures which often accompanied him over the threshold of sleep. He was seeing Robert Cardower, suddenly startled by a simple topographical statement. He was seeing Lord Auldearn looking at him, Lord Auldearn giving a sudden nod, Lord Auldearn so casually handing him a framed photograph of his favourite son, Douglas Cardower. 'A well-grown lad—the tallest of the lot,' he heard Lord Auldearn say.

When Mungo woke up next morning it was to the conviction that he was in the possession, after all, of something other than a fantasy of his own devising. He was in possession of hard knowledge. But fortunately it was knowledge which could have no practical repercussions in the world. It wasn't a thing to make public. And Ian still didn't know—or he surely wouldn't have come up with the possibility as no more than a drowsy and idle joke. Perhaps he'd have to know. But Mungo wasn't at all sure he wanted him to. For weren't they—the two of them—just right as they were?

They packed up and drove to Rome—where Elizabeth Cardower was charming and Mary Cardower enchanting. But the enchantment told Mungo only one thing. Anne Cardower hadn't, as he'd told himself, been a brief madness. It was the romantic reading of the matter that was right. He was in love with Anne still.

Part Four

SCOTLAND

15

MALLACHIE CASTLE STOOD in the middle of a
wooded park of 1200 acres, and the park in the middle of
Mallachie Forest, which was many times larger than
that. Apart from Mallachie Mains and the cottages attached to it, the nearest building was a ruined priory,
and the nearest after that an abandoned railway station.
The Castle itself retained no appearance of being a place
of strength, although substantial remains of the fifteenth-
century Tower of Mallachie were entombed in the middle
of it. It was a large low white-washed mansion, in the
construction of which its nineteenth-century architect
had been held on a tight rein so far as embellishments of
the Balmoral order were concerned. From every window
in the house the view ended, whether at a farther or a
nearer remove, in dark and densely-marshalled hosts of
fir and pine. And because Lord Brightmony retained in
his seclusion some interest in arboriculture, and because
his factor obstinately resisted the pursuit of this on other
parts of the estate, small plantations of one sort or another were constantly creeping across the park and towards the house, like the vanguard of an encircling army.
It might have been said that Birnam wood was coming
to Dunsinane.

Nothing, Mungo thought, could be more of a contrast
to Stradlings, where in every direction the eye was drawn
through casual colonnades of beech trees to the rolling
vistas of the down. And if Mallachie in its outward appearance suggested immurement on a heroic scale, everything

in its interior was equally claustral in effect—including
the monkish proprietor of the place, whom it was almost
impossible to conceive as having emerged from the same
womb as his brother, Robert Cardower.

Mungo had never in his life before been inside a great
Scottish mansion, but he couldn't believe that many were
like this. Wherever there was stone to uncover, it had
been uncovered and whitewashed to match the exterior of
the building. Tons of plaster and panelling must have
been bashed and ripped away to achieve this effect. There
seemed not to be a carpet or a rug in the house; where the
floors weren't again bare stone they were raw scrubbed
wood, with here and there a strip of rush matting of a
dismal pseudo-mediaeval sort. The pictures all had religious subjects. But whereas some of them one might
have met at Bamberton (including Murillos, Riberas, and
Zurbarans which testified to a lively eye in some Cardower who had followed Wellington around Spain),
others were hideous modern colour-prints of the kind to
be bought in ecclesiastical knick-knack shops. Mungo's
own room displayed, opposite the bed in a position much
corresponding to that labour of Indian piety in Howard
4, 4 which had interested Vera, one of those well-groomed
and pomaded Christs, himself faintly luminous like a
deep-sea fish, who points to a supernumerary and radio-
active heart pinned over his chest. Some of the pictures
in the more public rooms (not that there *was* a public)
had little lights burning in front of them.

Through this scene of things Ian's uncle David restlessly wandered for a good part of the day, muttering
out of a missal or breviary held before him. Sometimes—
and this could be quite startling—he produced a loud
pious ejaculation. At other times he could be heard in
his chapel, droning his way through penitential psalms.
According to Ian, the chaplain, Father Balietti, was not

only at his wit's end in devising penances; he was also required to reinforce his ghostly counsels with vigorous performances as a flagellator. Mungo, although as a psychiatrist he admitted the *a priori* likelihood of this, didn't really believe it. It appeared that, some years before, Ian had insisted to his father that uncle David was mad; his father had passed on the persuasion to Lord Auldearn; Lord Auldearn had somehow contrived to insinuate a couple of eminent mad doctors (as he called them) into Mallachie; and the mad doctors had pronounced Lord Brightmony to be not only sane but a man of notably interesting conversation as well. As a consequence, the heir to the marquisate of Auldearn retained the agreeable status of an aristocratic eccentric.

But there could be no doubt that somewhere inside Ian's skull his uncle David roamed as a disturbing presence. Lord Auldearn had probably known this when he had pretty well commanded his grandson not to dodge the duty of presenting himself at Mallachie in due season. Mungo had known it when he had pitched at Ian in the darkness outside Perugia the analysis which had become known between them as the theory of uncle-eclipse. (Lord Robert, Mungo considered, was too light-weight a character to eclipse anyone, which explained Ian's whoring after two disastrous uncles to stand in on the job. But this highly scientific embroidery of his case Mungo didn't pass on to his friend.) Ian himself knew it. It accounted for extravagances like the flagellation story, and one or two others so outrageous that Mungo, not easily distasted, had simply had to tell Ian to shut up.

Mungo himself was disturbed by Lord Brightmony. He had never met religious mania before, and it was uncomfortable in itself, although probably harmless enough. But what chiefly troubled him about Ian's uncle was the manner in which he seemed to exemplify the protean nature of family resemblances. Robert Cardower and his son Ian were remarkably like each other; Robert was not in the least like his brother David; but there were times when David revealed a startling likeness to Ian or vice-versa. Whether Ian himself was aware of this or not, Mungo didn't know. In any case, it was like a tantalizing piece of bad logic.

There was something more. Lord Brightmony—tall, dark, and cadaverous—had an eye as glittering as the Ancient Mariner's. But after a day or two in his company (and Lord Brightmony was punctilious and correct in the entertainment of his young guests) Mungo realized that he possessed no more than what had to be called a sideways knowledge of this. Apart from the one or two occasions upon which civility absolutely required it, Lord Brightmony had never looked at him. If he conversed indoors, that piercing gaze was fixed upon the floor, the ceiling, or the nearest edifying picture; if in the open air, upon the ground, the heavens, or the middle distance. Mostly it was downwards, which is what prudency prescribes. Mungo supposed that in this Lord Brightmony was acting under the instructions of his spiritual adviser, and it was with a jolt that its implication came to him. He might have been suddenly meeting the Baron de Charlus out of Proust.

Father Balietti was all silver crucifix and bulging belly, rusty skirts and supple speeches. Mungo didn't take to him at all. According to Ian, Balietti's hold over uncle David didn't prevent uncle David's leading him a dog's life. At seasons of special sanctity he was banished from the table at which uncle David and Leonard Sedley dined, and had to stand at a lectern and read theological works aloud: afterwards, a cold cutlet would be sent up to his room. Perhaps Father Balietti had hopes of a milder re-

gime at Mallachie in his declining years. He treated Ian
with obsequious respect, and Mungo with an only slightly
modified version of the same thing. The poor chap hadn't
much of a hope, Mungo thought. However it might be
with Lord Robert, when Ian became sixth marquis (which
seemed to be what the book of rules for these matters pre-
scribed) poor old Balietti would be out on his ear.

But if Ian hated Balietti, he also hated the whole thing
—hated it so much that Mungo was inclined to call morbid
the sense of family duty that had brought him to the
place. Perhaps without Mungo he wouldn't have come at
all. Perhaps this was one reason why Ian's grandfather
had rather oddly said that he particularly wanted Mungo
to be taken to Mallachie. But Mungo could now tell himself that there had been a more substantial reason as well.

So here they were. It was the first week of August, and
they had arrived after spending nearly a fortnight at
Fintry. The summer term had ended with Mungo's obtaining (to his professed utter astonishment, but not quite
so much astonishment as that in his secret heart) a First
Class in something called English Moderations. Ian, whose
History course didn't involve such a test at this stage,
had treated the achievement pretty well as his own, and
caused its celebration in a considerable quantity of champagne. The success was having a bad effect on Mungo's
studies. He concluded that, having rung that sort of
dons' bell early and once, there was no great point in
striving to ring it again two years later. So he had shoved
aside his books and begun to write a novel. At Fintry
much of Ian's energies had gone loyally into the effort
of persuading Miss Guthrie that this was a rational and
laudable course of conduct. Ian and Mungo's aunt had
taken to each other. But there wasn't much on which
they agreed.

The first few days at Mallachie were perhaps the more

difficult because Leonard Sedley was away. He was making one of his very rare visits to London. Ian said that he disliked Sedley as much as he disliked Balietti, but that he was at least conversable, and would have kept up some reasonable chit-chat at meals if he'd been around. As it was, these occasions were far from gay. But as Sedley had been one of the proposed exhibits, he supposed that they'd better remain at Mallachie until he turned up again. He himself could at least do a bit of fishing, although the river was some way off. And Mungo could either come and sit on the bank, or remain at Mallachie and get on with his book.

In fact, things fell out a little differently. Lord Brightmony, however withdrawn upon his peculiar devotional life, was sensitive to what was going on inside the heads of young men. This appeared in a proposal he made at lunch on their third day.

'Ian,' he asked, 'am I right in thinking that your plans, and Mungo's as well, are fluid so far as the rest of your vacation is concerned?'

'Yes—but, although we've got nothing fixed, there's quite a lot that we can do.'

'No doubt there is.' Lord Brightmony's gaze dropped to the floor. 'Still in each other's company, I suppose?'

'Quite probably.' Ian had stiffened, and there was a small silence in which Father Balietti could be distinguished as engaged in prayer.

'We keep each other out of mischief, you see.' Mungo struck in with this under some impulse to import a note of cheer into the talk.

'You would both be most welcome so to do while remaining at Mallachie.' Lord Brightmony gave Mungo one of his rare direct glances, and at this Father Balietti signed himself rapidly with the cross. 'But I am conscious that our manner of life here is not well accommodated to the entertainment of lads of your age. I am sorry that Leonard is away. You must at least stop until his return in a couple of days' time. Mungo, with his interest in literary pursuits, would enjoy meeting him. However, I have a further proposal to make. I think, Ian, that you would appreciate as much time on the water as possible.' Lord Brightmony actually smiled faintly. 'Until the fatal first of September arrives.'

'Well, yes.' Ian—rather absurdly to Mungo's sense— had brightened at once. 'But one can have a go at the partridges after that.'

'While waiting for the pheasants,' Father Balietti said smoothly.

'Yes, indeed.' Lord Brightmony never let a remark by his chaplain pass unacknowledged. 'But let me tell you what I have in mind. You remember the water-bailiff's cottage, Ian? Recently it has been in the occupation of the reeve at that end of the estate. But Urquhart came in this morning—'

'Mr Urquhart,' Balietti explained to Mungo in a courteous aside, 'is Lord Brightmony's factor.'

'—and told me that the man has left us, so that the cottage is vacant. It is a pleasant little place and, I am told, very reasonably fitted up. Would you and Mungo care to take it over for as long as you please? It is splendidly situated for the salmon. And at the same time'—on this occasion Lord Brightmony didn't glance at Mungo— 'it enjoys the seclusion which I understand writers to prize.'

'That would be extremely nice,' Ian said—with a formality signalling caution.

'It would, of course, be pleasant if you came over to dine with us. I am sure it would give Leonard particular enjoyment.'

'It sounds splendid,' Mungo said. He could see that the

fisherman in Ian was all for the idea. And he himself
did want an opportunity of meeting Leonard Sedley, and
discovering what a real writer was like.

So Mungo's verdict settled the matter. After lunch he
and Ian went into the garden to talk about it.

'Do you know'—Mungo said when they had got some
details settled—'it seems to me that those two worthies
have a very odd notion of us?'

'I think they have.' Ian didn't seem to be so amused as
Mungo. 'Meanwhile, what shall we do this afternoon? I
think I'd rather like a bathe.'

'In the river?'

'No. We'll make a dash for the sea.'

'Good!' Mungo's spirits rose, for there was undeniably
something claustrophobic about life within the curtilage
of Mallachie Castle. 'We'll hit it at Nairn. That's where I
used to be chucked in as a kid. You'll find it freezing.
And I bet I'll stay in longer than you.'

16

'MUNGO, DO YOU identify with the salmon, or with the fisherman? I believe "identify" is the word.' Leonard Sedley regularly made a small humorous business of being distrustful of modern terminologies.

'I don't know. It's exciting, I suppose.' Mungo paused on this, and looked at Ian waist-deep in the rapid river. In the presence of a professional writer, he was chary of making any claim to special sensibility. 'But I don't think I identify with either.'

'Oh, but surely you must. This combat has been going on for twenty minutes. It will probably be Ian's biggest catch of the season. And you have been watching intently.' As Leonard Sedley said this, he didn't himself cease intently to watch the spectacle in the tumbling brown water.

'Very well. I think I identify with the fish. I certainly feel that hook in my throat. And I'm wriggling.'

'Wriggling?'

'No. Worms wriggle—and perhaps belly-dancers.' Mungo was like a child being corrected and prompted in school. 'It's convulsive, or a kind of flailing. Or what you'd do if somebody was sending electric shocks through you for kicks.'

'Ah, for kicks. There's some virtue in that expression.'

Sedley was sitting on a tree-trunk in the sun. He wore Lovat tweed, and some of Ian's big salmon-flies were stuck in his cap. Yet he somehow wasn't altogether congruous with the scene. Perhaps it was merely that the soft pastel shirt, the considered tie, faintly belonged elsewhere. That was as it should be, perhaps. For he *had* an elsewhere, after all: that niche in the history of the English novel from which he had so unaccountably stood down.

'But what about Ian?' Sedley went on. 'It's a tremendous struggle. Isn't your body at play with his?' Sedley paused. 'Almost imperceptibly of course. Empathy works like that.'

'It couldn't work like that if one was trying out a bit of empathy with a billiard ball.' Mungo didn't yet know whether he liked the eminent novelist who had taken so flatteringly to conversing with him, but he did enjoy these bursts of talking to him on equal terms. 'Didn't somebody say he knew what it's like to be a billiard ball?'

'Then he was saying quite something.' Sedley smiled, as if signalling that he had consciously used a quaint figure of speech. 'But take a tortoise, Mungo. A tortoise is not so remote as a billiard ball, but it is very tolerably remote, all the same. Yet one knows, doesn't one, what it's like to be a tortoise? There are dreams in which one has to move in just that clogged and painful way.'

'That's atavistic. It's a stirring, in sleep, of some incredibly ancient racial memory. We struggled out of the sea millions of years ago. Like shelled turtles, pink and defenceless.

'It's a wonderful picture.' Sedley laughed agreeably. He did seem to find Mungo worth talking to. Almost every afternoon he made the quite long trek to the cottage by the river, and the two chatted together while they watched Ian fishing. 'Ian will be doing some struggling out of the flood himself, if he's not careful. Getting these queer waterproof breeches full of water isn't funny. And he almost went over now.'

'Oh, Ian will be all right. He has this ritualized slaughter all taped. Perfect timing of the wretched creature's

movements, and all that. Show-business without an audience, really.'

'But we're an audience. And he's certainly exciting to
watch, as you said.'

Mungo didn't think he had said quite this. And with
Sedley it seemed important to get things exactly right.
Sedley had told him, seriously although not pontifically,
that if he didn't think and conclude precisely he would
never come near writing precisely. So now he didn't pass
this point by.

'I only meant I can *see* it's exciting,' he said. 'When I
feel something's exciting I generally want to have a go at
it. But I don't want to catch fish, any more than I want
to shoot birds. Their life's their own affair—so why mess
it up? In any case, it's obvious that fishing is pretty boring
for most of the time.'

'Ian certainly isn't bored at this moment. Will you admit you are rather jealous of that salmon, Mungo, just
because Ian is so completely and absorbedly alone with it?'

'Oh, I hope not!' Mungo's grin felt a little awkward on
his face. He couldn't believe that Sedley nourished the
erroneous idea about Ian and himself that Lord Brightmony and his chaplain had to be suspected of indulging.
Sedley, with all the talent for understanding people that
his writing revealed, must be immune from going so far
astray. But there was an element of penetration in his
question, all the same, and Mungo tried to respond to it.
'But perhaps you're right. Ian and I have become friends,
but we're from totally different backgrounds. And sometimes—'

'It's what so interests me,' Sedley said softly. 'But I
beg your pardon. Go on.'

For a moment Mungo didn't go on. He had been
startled—both by the tone of Sedley's voice and by something enigmatical in the manner of his glancing from

Mungo beside him to Ian in the river and back again.
The novelist might almost have been trying to match
them in some way, to bring them together in his imagination—not in terms of any indecent fantasy, Mungo
quickly told himself, but rather as a producer, a choreo-
grapher might do. Or an out-of-work puppet-master,
Mungo brilliantly added—and became aware of this un-
governed imagination as being responsible for an awkward
pause.

'I'm sorry. I was saying that Ian and I have those different backgrounds. There have been times when Ian's background has stepped forward and nobbled him for a time
in a perfectly natural way, and then I *have* felt a childish
kind of jealousy. But that's not happening now. I just
hope he'll net that unfortunate salmon before tea-time.'

'And he has!' Sedley stood up and pointed dramatically.
He owned a pleasing ability to turn on a spontaneous
gaiety of a kind which, at Mallachie, was otherwise in lam-
entably short supply. 'And we've been so idle that we've
forgotten to put on the kettle. My dear lad, remedy that
now.'

They had tea at a rough table which Ian planted before
Sedley where he sat. Mungo brought forward a bench,
and he and Ian sat down side by side facing the novelist.

'How sad that I don't operate a camera,' Sedley said.
'It would be pleasant to have a photograph of the two of
you as you are now, simply as a reminder of this very
interesting holiday of yours. But we are all cameras ourselves, I suppose; only some more efficient than others.
Mine isn't bad, and I think I shall retain this picture
fairly well.' Sedley made these remarks the occasion of
holding each young man in turn in a considering, and
perhaps faintly puzzled gaze. 'Yes,' he continued, 'you
will certainly flash upon that inward eye which is the

bliss of solitude. Dear me! What a hackneyed quotation.'

'I don't much care for being photographed,' Ian said rather coldly. 'Not after any fashion.'

'Then I put my camera away at once.' Sedley gave no sign of having registered Ian's tone. 'How much you two must be learning from one another! I wonder which of you is the more curious of the two? The more inquisitive, that is to say.' He paused, but neither of the young men offered a reply. 'But there seem to be limits to the profitable exchange. Mungo, for instance, refuses to learn salmon-fishing from you, Ian. On moral grounds, I gather. Mungo, would you take up the same position if trout-fishing were in question?'

'I suppose so—if it's to be called a position. Catching salmon and catching trout are more or less the same thing, I suppose.'

'But not at all!' There was amusement in Sedley's voice. 'Ian will put you right on that at once. When he goes after trout, he places himself in quite a different relationship to his victims.' Sedley paused, as if expecting Ian to join in. When Ian was silent he stooped, picked up his cap from the ground, and tossed it on the table in front of him. 'Observation, Mungo! Always observation! What have you to say about Ian's salmon-flies?'

'They're rich and gaudy.'

'Quite so. Have you ever seen their like in real life?'

'I'm sure I haven't. I think you'd have to go to the tropics for them.'

'And trout-flies? You must often have looked at trout-flies; even if you have never angled with them.'

'They're shocking little miracles of deception. They've got fancy names, like roses: Wickham's Fancy and Greenwell's Glory. But they're as like real insects of one sort or another as can be made.' Mungo paused, frowning. 'Salmon don't feed in fresh water.'

'Exactly! The trout snaps at Ian's trout-fly because it believes it *is* a fly, and wants to eat it. But the salmon snaps at Ian's salmon-fly because it is annoyed by something unaccountable invading its territory. So trout-fishing has the beauty of being pure treachery. Salmon-fishing is more like a bull fight.'

'Except, I suppose,' Ian said, 'that there's no danger to matador or picador.'

'Perfectly true.' It struck Mungo that Leonard Sedley's complexion was registering an odd flush as of pleasure, at Ian's thus having been drawn into the talk. 'Except, I suppose, that you can get drowned. I was pointing out that possibility to Mungo. I've heard of it happening on the Spey.'

'Well, I'm going to put myself at risk for another hour after tea.' Ian appeared to have turned civil again. But at once he added, 'Is pure treachery all that beautiful?'

'It can be made so by art. Are you still fond of Pope? Think of the angler in *Windsor Forest*.' Sedley turned from Ian to Mungo, and his voice underwent some subtle change as he did so. Defensively, Mungo called this the great man's *cher confrère* manner—but he found it slightly intoxicating, all the same. 'Aren't some of the greatest novels in the world about betrayal? Think, Mungo! *The Wings of the Dove, The Golden Bowl, Under Western Eyes.*'

'They're not mere exhibitions of it, or gloatings over it.' Mungo didn't know quite why he said this. 'It's made the occasion for a rising up of other things: endurance, fidelity, repentance—all that.'

'As Ian's father would say, Mungo—how perfectly I agree with you.' Sedley shot a glance at Ian, as if to see how he was disposed to take this just and harmless family joke. 'In a last analysis, the interest of treachery lies in the response to its challenge which rare spirits can achieve.

"Commend me to my kind lord: O farewell!" One scarcely ventures to speak of such heights. But, at another level, treachery holds a perennial fascination for the writer. It is the sheer technical fascination of rendering it as at once visible and invisible, plausible yet startling. Nothing can be more beguiling. "Pleasure and action make the hours seem short"—as one connoisseur in deception rightly says.'

'I rather like the look of the water in this light,' Ian broke in. He had stood up suddenly, and it was clear that his remark was to be taken in a practical and not an aesthetic sense. He picked up his rod, and strode back towards the river.

'It's a mania with the dear lad at present,' Sedley said indulgently. 'But a fortunate one for David and myself if it makes him contented with Mallachie for a while. We are two elderly men who have come to live too much in solitude, so there is something heartening about a stir of young life around the place. But how is it with the junior bachelor *ménage*? You're not finding cottage life dull?'

'Not in the least. Ian doesn't fish all day, and we've been doing plenty of walking. Besides, I'm getting quite a lot of reading and writing done.'

'I'm delighted to hear it. I had feared that you might be becoming a little bored by so celibate a society. How long is it, Mungo, since you set eyes on a girl?'

'Quite some time,' Mungo said, and said no more. He was a little startled by this poking around. Mallachie Castle itself certainly did nothing to mitigate boredom of the sort Sedley was speaking of. There didn't seem to be a woman in the place. The entire staff consisted of a few morose elderly men.

'I don't think I'd venture to ask Ian such a question,' Sedley went on humorously. 'He is not a very simple person, and in a way I feel I am only just getting to know him again. As you have probably heard, he doesn't come to Mallachie very often. But I take a great interest in his fortunes. In spite of the disparity of our years, he and I have always liked each other. One doesn't know how these things—affinities, they may be called—come about. But it is very pleasant when they do. As, for Ian, they have again done in his joining forces with you.'

'Yes, of course.' Mungo didn't find this speech of Sedley's easy to reply to. Could so perceptive a man as the novelist possibly be so far at sea as he appeared to be in supposing himself liked by Ian? It seemed so. Sedley had spoken more unaffectedly than was common with him. Seeing this, Mungo felt he might be put in a false position, and have to lie his way out of it, if the conversation came to rest on Ian's supposed affection for Leonard Sedley. So he boldly gave the talk a shove forward. 'Did you and Lord Brightmony,' he asked, 'feel such an affinity from the first? Was it what made you decide to set up house together?'

'Ah, but it was so long ago!' Sedley smiled whimsically. 'And one is scarcely able to give an account of some of one's dead selves. But, yes. We recognized confirmed bachelors in each other—almost from the first, I suppose —and a joint establishment seemed not a bad idea.'

'Was he as devout then as he is now?'

'He was already a good Anglo-Catholic. But, no—it was then much more only a part of the man. I confess, Mungo, that had I known then how David would develop— But I need say no more.'

'Do you think it has been a good idea, all the same?' One of Mungo's reckless questioning bouts had come over him. 'Has your friendship confirmed itself with the years? Do you irritate each other a lot? Because it does seem to be an awfully solitary life you lead.'

'Yes, indeed. I was remarking on it a few minutes ago, was I not?' Sedley was perhaps making an effort to remain unperturbed in the face of Mungo's seizing the initiative in this way. 'We do get across one another from time to time. It would be unnatural not to. I shouldn't be surprised if you and Ian had managed a row or two already.'

'Oh, yes—we had a row about a girl.' Mungo believed that this odd conversation was now marked by confidence and frankness on both sides. 'I'll tell you about it one day.' He was about to add, 'I'm sure Ian wouldn't mind,' when he realized that this would be untrue. He and Ian were developing markedly different attitudes to Sedley. So he paused, disconcerted, and was aware of Sedley staring at him strangely. This somehow made him want to change the subject entirely. But he managed only another direct question. 'Had you come to live at Mallachie before you wrote *An Autumn in Umbria*?'

'It was some time after that.'

'Was your coming to Mallachie connected with your deciding pretty well to stop writing?'

'My dear Mungo, I am sure you have a future as a novelist. But, if not, you can certainly become a television inquisitor.'

'I'm terribly sorry.' Mungo was properly confused. 'Asking these questions is the most frightful cheek.'

'Not a bit, Mungo. And I propose to have my own turn later. If I may say so, there is a good deal about you that interests me very much. But tell me—why should you conclude that I have stopped writing?'

Mungo's confusion grew. This was not merely because he had made an ass of himself; it was also because he perceived that Sedley's ease of manner had become strained and spurious. Quite without meaning to, he had touched the author of *An Autumn in Umbria* at the quick.

'It's just,' he said weakly, 'that you haven't cared to

publish anything for some time. And it seems such a tremendous pity.'

'Ah! You see, Mungo, there are artists in whose career these intermissions—perhaps long intermissions—simply happen. So far as publication is concerned, I mean. But the work, the travail, may be going on—and own a complexity that forbids the giving of instalments, of bits and pieces, to the world. Not all *chefs-d'oeuvre* are like *Finnegans Wake*.'

'No—of course not. I can see that.'

'An artist loses his identity, abnegates his personality, if he ceases to work. You remember what Sainte-Beuve once said? *Je ne suis complètement moi que plume en main et dans le silence du cabinet.* You will come to feel it yourself—to prove it on your own pulse, my dear lad— one day.'

This was impressive, and Mungo didn't at all know why he suddenly found himself rather disliking it. He was even irked, he noticed, by Sedley's calling him 'my dear lad' —whereas when his tutor occasionally addressed him as 'my dear boy', or even 'most acute juvenile', he didn't mind a bit. But the main point, of course, must be that he had come on something uncomfortable in Leonard Sedley—and just how uncomfortable, he couldn't guess. Perhaps self-deception was an element in it. At any rate, Mungo—whose enquiring mind had so happily addressed itself to exhibiting to Ian his dangerous state of uncle- eclipse—just felt that he didn't, for the present, want to lift any further lid from Leonard Sedley. Perhaps he had invested rather heavily in Sedley as a great writer—a process which is held often to render disillusioning at least a first contact with the man behind the books.

'But of course,' Sedley was saying, 'there are other fac- tors which may make a writer fight shy of the printing press from time to time. A great deal of nonsense is talked

about the artist's independence of his public. One can
battle against active misconception—rising to it as to a
challenge. But mere disregard, the absence of any slightest sign of being wanted, may make one—well, may make
one resigned to bide one's time.'

'Yes, I can see that.' Mungo had been aware of Sedley
as pausing for a token of acquiescence.

'And one may have to fight against changes in taste,
or the almost universal vogue of what is precisely not
one's thing. When that happens, one can become very
lonely among one's peers. I don't know whether you ever
glanced at that novel of mine you mentioned: *An Autumn in Umbria*—'

'I've read it and reread it. It's a marvellous book.'

'My dear Mungo, I am most delighted and touched
that you should say so.' Sedley flushed as he said this,
and Mungo would have been very content to feel that it
was a flush of pleasure. Indeed, it was unreasonable to see
it as anything else. But was it conceivable that something
embittered, even a little crazy, in Sedley found only mor-
tification and annoyance in the praise of a callow grammar-school boy? Mungo had a sufficient sense of this
strange and disagreeable possibility to make him resolve
not to say anything too enthusiastic again.

'It's a novel,' Sedley went on, 'that now wears an old-
fashioned look. It has—I am foolish enough to feel—its
subtleties, its own accent, its modest depths. But it remains an almost Victorian affair. It tells a story! You
understand me? There is an action, a developing com-
plication of attitudes and relationships, which is resolved
and brought to a just close. Now, modern taste scarcely
admits of anything of the kind. A long time ago we used
to speak of *tranche de vie* realism, and we knew and
acknowledged alike its just claim and its limited scope.
And from it there stems today's dominant aesthetic of

the unresolved, the open-ended structure—if it *is* structure—in fiction. Have you noticed of late, on the television screen, a modish way of concluding—or rather of
fading out—debate? A few people, or perhaps a dozen
people, are presented to us as engaged in serious argument. But the minute comes when the "feature", as it is
called, must yield place to a news bulletin or—as they
say—a "sports-night", and we begin to hear music. The
music grows in volume, and the picture starts to darken.
Clearly the contestants are still arguing. But not for our
benefit. We are left, very literally, in air.' Sedley made
a whimsical gesture. 'Nowadays one is expected to end
novels like that.'

'And you won't play? But why should you? You've
got your own achievement to build on.'

'Thank you, my dear Mungo. But I am only telling you
why I—well, why I bide my time. Perhaps—who knows?
—I shall be like Landor, and dine late.'

'I'm sure you will.' Mungo, because he went in for loyalty, said this stoutly. But he had felt something a little
fusty in the argument. It all sounded plausible enough,
but it didn't, somehow, add up to a valid explanation of
the silence of Leonard Sedley.

'And perhaps it doesn't matter—if one's name proves
to be written in water.' Sedley said this on rather a noble
note. 'One has had a go, as you young people say. One
has had one's vision.'

'Yes, of course.' Mungo noted dispassionately that Sedley was given to tags out of other people's books. That
last one was from *To the Lighthouse*. But he did appear
to hold genuine views on the craft of fiction. So for a
moment longer Mungo pursued this. 'If it's *not* in water,
if you *are* to be remembered, what would you most like
to be remembered for?'

'The inquisitor again!' Sedley said with amusement. 'At

the tail-end of a programme, too. "Finally, Professor X, will you say, very briefly, what are your conclusions about the mystery of human existence." Just that note.'

'No, that's not fair.' Mungo, feeling more at ease with Sedley than during the past few minutes, had received this fancy with his grin. 'I'm not asking a question as comprehensive as that.'

'Very well. I'll try to give you an answer.' Sedley fell silent for a moment, as if paying Mungo's true question the compliment of serious thought. But his reply, when it came, seemed disappointingly whimsical. 'I'd like to be remembered as a supreme illusionist.'

'An illusionist?'

'It's the name that large-scale conjurors used to give themselves. The real swells, who used enormous mirrors.'

'The mirror of life? Dr Johnson said Shakespeare's plays are that.'

'No, it's not of that that I'm thinking. There's quite enough of real life around, if you ask me, without our industriously stacking up more of it in mirrors. Art as a mode of knowledge, you know, was brought to its logical terminus in the absurd by the Dadaists. You recall how Duchamp put a navvy's shovel in an exhibition and labelled it "shovel". One doesn't, when one is being serious, want to do that. No! We do, indeed, collect our materials from the actual world, since nothing else is available to us. What do I possess to frame a novel out of? Myself, you, Ian, David—whom you will. And then comes the conjuring.'

'Ian said something like that about a story I wrote in Oxford.'

'Did he, indeed? He may have been remembering my holding forth to him in just this vein.' Sedley was pleased.

'But he seemed to feel the conjuring to be rather immoral.'

'Amoral, perhaps; but immoral, no. Our allegiance is wholly to the illusion we create. And even if the illusion is itself impermanent, itself written in water, it has had its moment. The intenser it has been, the greater our triumph. Of course we all want to write what will outlive marble and the gilded monuments of princes. But that's not the real—or at least the only—test of our achievement. The intensity of the illusion while it holds; the clarity with which we have seen, and the conviction with which we have asserted what never has been and what never will be: that is the test of our success as artists.'

Having delivered himself of this, Sedley made one of his pauses for comment. But Mungo failed immediately to manage anything in that line. His silence was the product of a divided mind. He wasn't too impressed by the propositions Sedley had offered him; for one thing, they didn't seem adequate to *An Autumn in Umbria*. On the other hand, he had never heard an author talk about writing before, and perhaps one had to get the hang of a creative mind's way of going about it. Mungo's tutor wouldn't talk in Sedley's fashion; he would try to define his terms more rigorously, and would convey a more logical and disciplined effect. But Mungo didn't often remember what his tutor said, whereas he was pretty sure he wasn't going to forget at least Sedley's main assertions. He now seized on this last thought for the purpose of civility.

'I'm going to remember what you've said,' he offered, 'and think about it quite a lot.'

'Ah, but you have your own ideas on these matters.' Sedley had glanced at his watch, and stood up. 'You must tell me about them—and something about yourself as well. Are you and Ian coming up to the house for dinner tonight?'

'Oh, yes—I think so. I doubt whether we have more

than a few sausages in stock at present.'

'An excellent reason for joining David, the ghostly
Father, and myself.' Sedley appeared to have been put in
good humour by the ingenuousness of Mungo's revelation. 'Perhaps we can have a further talk then.' He picked
up his cap, and flicked a finger idly at one of the garish
flies stuck in its brim. Then, as if reminded of what was
going on in the river, he turned round to look. Ian was in
the act of making a long, powerful cast, his eyes fixed
upon the widening ripples of a rise. The sinuous movement ended in immobility. Sedley watched for a further
moment, and then nodded to Mungo and walked rapidly
away.

17

IAN HAD DECLARED (as part of a gloomy build-up of
Mallachie for Mungo before their arrival there) that his
uncle David's table was served only with pulse and tap-
water—except on saint's-days, when there were locusts
and wild honey as well.

Fortunately this turned out to be untrue. Lord Brightmony certainly drank only water, and had an air of quite
failing to notice the little that he ate. But Leonard Sedley
was fastidious and Father Balietti greedy, so that the
meals and the wine weren't at all bad. Moreover the
morose elderly servants, who knew very well that young
Mr Cardower would successively become Lord Brightmony and Lord Auldearn, showed their proper feudal
feeling by seeing to it that Ian and his friend got the
best of what was going. But all this hadn't rendered any
of these occasions exactly convivial, and tonight looked
as if it might be worse than most. Ian's second spell with
his rod had been disastrous. He had hooked an enormous
salmon, played it for no end of a time with a mature skill,
and then lost it through some miscalculation or unreadi-
ness at the very moment he had appeared sure of it in the
net. As a result of this, he was in a foul temper. And
Mungo (who was perhaps jealous of the salmon fishing
after all) was rebuking this bad behaviour as they walked
up to the Castle.

'Just take the trouble to be civil, will you?' he said.
'You're battening on your uncle for the sake of those ab-

surd fish, and the bargain is that you show him the light of your countenance in return. Repeat: the light of your countenance. Not that vintage Cardower glower.'

'Oh, shut up, Mungo!'

'You can scowl at that religious caterpillar Balietti if you like. Not that it's very civil to a dependent in your uncle's house.'

'Don't try to teach me my manners, Lockhart, you. Or I'll bash you.'

'I don't see you bashing someone your own size. You tried once, and it didn't work. I don't believe you could bash Pons—and he's a midget.'

'He's nothing of the kind. Get Pons furious, and he's pretty well the Mighty Atom itself. I could bash him, all the same.'

'No, you couldn't.'

'Yes, I could.'

The enjoyment derived by Mungo and Ian from conversations of this sort was obscure but indubitable. On the other hand, they both at times wondered whether there wasn't a precarious side to it; whether it didn't guy some genuine antagonism lurking somewhere in their minds. But as the security of their relationship was an unuttered article of faith with them, they never let this fragmentary perception constrain them to pull their punches.

'And there's another thing,' Mungo went on. 'Sedley. You're at least not in a state of Sedley-eclipse, so you might treat him at least with decency. He's fond of you, as a matter of fact.'

'Rubbish.' This was Ian's most withering word.

'And—what's more—he believes that you are fond of him.'

'For God's sake, Mungo, what have you two been yattering about?'

'The stalwart and handsome Ian Cardower.' Mungo paused wickedly. 'Who is exciting to watch, as he performs his little water-ballet up to his belly-button in the flood. It hadn't occurred to me, I'm afraid. But of course I hastened to agree.'

'Oh, Lord!' Ian halted in his tracks. 'Look, Mungo— let's pack up tomorrow and go back to Fintry. If your aunt will have me, that is. Life seems simpler there.'

'No salmon. And a gent from London has the shooting rights. Of course he'd jump at being introduced to you, and let you slaughter as many of God's creatures as you cared to. But at least we can't leave until Friday.' Mungo had turned serious. 'Your uncle's having people to lunch, just to meet you. Your visiting Mallachie is quite a thing to him. No kidding.'

'Oh, all right.'

'Besides, I aim at enjoying more of your uncle's conversation myself.' Mungo was mocking again. 'I want his version of the Cardower family history.'

'As I've said before, you're bloody inquisitive. I suppose you intend to use us all for copy. And I don't go poking about in Lockhart family history.'

'There isn't any to speak of.' Mungo was silent for a moment. If he was to be candid with Ian, as he much wanted to be, he would have to tell him here and now that, strictly speaking, Lockhart family history was something with which he, Mungo, had nothing to do. But this, he found, he couldn't do. He couldn't, on the strength of what was little more than intuition, however lively, claim as true what Ian had once propounded as a tasteless joke. 'Perhaps,' he said, 'there's just a very minor family skeleton rattling in the cupboard here and there. I say, are you hungry?'

'Of course I'm hungry, after flogging that water all day.'

'I had an exhausting afternoon myself—sustaining a literary conversation with a real live novelist.'

'Not alive exactly. I'd be prepared to bet you had the impertinence to ask him why he stopped scribbling.'

'Yes, I did. It gave him an opportunity for quite a lot of profound remarks.'

'I suggest you ask my uncle about it. Check up on whether his view of the silence of his dear old friend corresponds with Sedley's own.'

'That's quite an idea. I think I will.'

'And then you can write one of your short stories about them. Something sad and tender. Two elderly queens living out the fag-end of their days in the solitude of a mist-enshrouded Scottish castle. A real castle, I'd make it—not a merely titular one like Mallachie. A kind of Moray Castle of Otranto. With plenty of Gothic effects.'

'Good idea. As a matter of fact, I'm beginning to feel Sedley would go quite well into a sinister setting.'

'You would!'

'The raven himself is hoarse. That sort of thing.'

'Yes. And it was the owl that shrieked, the fatal bell-man, which gives the stern'st good-night.' Ian's ill-temper had departed, at least for the moment. 'But, no. Better go easy on *Macbeth*. The people over at Cawdor might have you up for libel. Serve you right. Scribble, scribble, scribble.'

This improving conversation brought Ian and Mungo to their dinner.

It was an awkward dinner—physically awkward. Lord Brightmony and Leonard Sedley sat at either end of a refectory table a good deal too large for common domestic occasions. Mungo sat on Lord Brightmony's right and Ian on Sedley's. Between Sedley and Mungo, but nearer to Mungo than to Sedley, sat Father Balietti. As Lord

Brightmony chose to spend most of the meal in meditative silence, Mungo and Balietti were more or less in a *tête-à-tête* situation, as were Ian and Sedley. Balietti, although his more genuine interest appeared to lie in eating as much as he could, owned an impressive acquired skill in making polite conversation at the same time. It was—Mungo thought—no doubt one of the chores he was hired for.

'I understand,' Balietti said smoothly, 'that at Oxford you and Ian became friends almost upon the first day on which you met. That is extremely pleasing.'

'It quite pleased us,' Mungo said. 'But why should it please you?'

'Ah.' Balietti was only momentarily brought to a stand by this bald question. 'I find it much to Ian's credit. It shows that he has a proper sense of his birth. As a Scot, I mean—simply as a Scot.' Mungo had perhaps produced a stare which elicited this elucidation. 'He is drawn at once to another Scottish boy. And just the same may be said of you. Don't you think it was your both being Scottish that was a little responsible?'

'Well, it may have been with Ian. I've never asked him, so I don't know. But as for me, I've never managed to think of Ian as very seriously Scottish. Or not until lately. Certainly at first he struck me as being as English as he could be. I think I still see him pretty well like that. And it's not just his having been at schools in England since he was nine or thereabouts. It's simply that his sort of Scot—his class of Scot—stopped much bothering about being Scottish a couple of hundred years ago.'

'That is a most interesting point of view.' Father Balietti's mouth seemed to be full of soup, but his voice remained like butter. 'Would you say that there is nothing characteristically Scottish about your host?'

'I don't know that I would.' Mungo glanced rather ner-

vously towards Lord Brightmony, whom Balietti's question seemed not designed to draw into the conversation.
But Lord Brightmony was quite obviously not even listening. 'Lord Brightmony is a bit granitic, wouldn't you
say? And that's said to be a Scottish quality.'

'At least the epithet is apt. But tell me something more
about Ian and yourself. It is said that in every close companionship there is a leader and a led. Is this true of you
two? And, if so, who is which?' Swallowing his next
spoonful, Balietti produced a smile designed to give this
last enquiry an apposite lightness of air.

Mungo was suddenly aware that it was quite a question.
He heard himself say what he'd said before: that it was
Ian who knew all the ropes. But his eye was on Ian as he
spoke, and he saw what was almost startlingly relevant.
Ian was doing as he'd been told—which was to treat Leonard Sedley with decency. In a way, perhaps, it didn't
take all that effort. Ian's upbringing had given him a
more than adequate technique for making himself pleasant—either because it genuinely pleased him to be so, or
just because he felt it to be part of the day's work.
Actually, Mungo thought, it was amusing to see how
much it was Robert Cardower who was more or less isolated at the end of the table with Sedley: the interrogative expression which every now and then flitted across
Ian's face was no doubt the accompaniment of his begging
Sedley to say just what he thought about this or that. Not
that Mungo was amused, since the thing was an abrupt
revelation of responsibility coming as a total surprise to
him. He'd really thought of himself as toted around by
Ian—this less as a matter of comparative strengths of
character (or of Ian's being by a whole nine months the
older of the two) than of an entire social context. Oxford
was much more naturally Ian's context than it was
Mungo's, and so was almost everywhere that they had

been together. It was as if Mungo had willingly taken on the role of an apprentice. Now he saw that this was far from being the total situation. Although it was in a tone of ingenuous irony that he'd talk about the ropes, he saw that in fact he'd greatly overestimated the purchase, the attached system of blocks and pulleys, that they represented. He saw all this, quite simply and completely, in those seconds in which he held under his observation an Ian Cardower who was obeying orders.

His discovery didn't gratify him at all. He remembered how, in the darkness of their tent outside Perugia, Ian had suddenly granted him a kind of *proxime accessit* status to Lord Auldearn himself as the possessor of a sound judgement. And now, as then, Mungo doubted himself very much. He had a good opinion of himself in quite a variety of ways, and didn't see why not; if he was really going to be a writer he'd need all the self-confidence he could muster. But he still didn't honestly see himself as a sage. As Ian's friend he'd give himself, so far, a fairly decent mark; but he doubted whether he could put in much of a claim as a guide and philosopher. Had it been for any responsible reason that he'd held forth on how Ian ought to behave to Sedley? Or had he grabbed at this simply as the next useful material in a verbal rough and tumble of the sort they occasionally found amusement in?

'Sedley,' he heard Father Balietti say, 'is quite opening up. I sometimes fear that the serious and contemplative life which we lead at Mallachie is not wholly to his taste— or not to the taste, let us say, of the whole man. And he can talk brilliantly when stimulated. Ian is stimulating him.'

Mungo, although he didn't fancy the tone in which Balietti employed this phrase, saw that it was true. Across Balietti's prattle he could catch only a little of what

Sedley was saying, but he was aware that it had a different pitch and pace—and probably a different quality—
from the conversation he had turned on for Mungo's
benefit during those afternoons by the river. As Mungo
caught this effect, he felt uneasy. And the feeling prompted
him to a rush of his rash questions.

'I suppose you've known Mr Sedley for a long time.
Would you say he's still the man who wrote *An Autumn
in Umbria*? I'm sure he can be brilliant still. But do you
think he still really knows about people? Or is his sensitiveness a bit in a decline? Is he likely to get his feel of a
situation wrong?'

Mungo had had the sense to deliver himself of this
inquisition in a lowered voice. But the result was, in fact,
awkward. Lord Brightmony, who was only a couple of
feet away, and who ought to have been paying him at least
some attention during the meal, chose to attend to him
now—and on the basis of having perfectly heard what
had been said.

'Mungo, your question is no doubt based upon a
sensitiveness of your own. You are aware that Leonard,
although he may have talked to you on literary matters
out of a distinguished and well-stocked mind, is indeed
judged not quite to have fulfilled the particular sort of
promise of the famous book you have mentioned. But why
should he? Why should his life have continued to run on
those then predictable lines? All is flux; nothing stays
still. Do you know who said that?'

'Somebody called Heraclitus, I think.'

'That is very good.' So highly did Lord Brightmony
approve Mungo's passing this odd little educational test,
that he actually looked at him squarely and gravely. And
Mungo was reminded of Lord Auldearn, who had directed upon him just this scrutiny. It was as if his features
were being studied like a passport photograph. He didn't

have any difficulty in telling himself why. 'Nothing stays still,' Lord Brightmony repeated, '—and least of all in the mutable mind of man. From your point of view, which I believe to be, broadly, that of the secular artist, Leonard may have changed for the worse. But does it, perhaps, come to no more than this: that his prime concerns are no longer yours? He will meet you as he can. He is so meeting Ian now—and to Ian's advantage, I do not doubt. You understand me?'

'Yes, I suppose I do.' Mungo felt prompted to add that the homily he was receiving went rather stiffly with grilled salmon and hock. But he was at least judicious enough to suppress this.

'Leonard and I have been each other's companion for a long time. Our first friendship formed itself, perhaps, amid some darkness of the spirit and the flesh. Our concerns are different now, as Father Balietti would explain to you were you to have some serious talk with him.'

'I think I understand, sir.' Mungo was quite sure he was never going to have any serious talk with Father Balietti. He was of a divided mind as to whether he wanted any more with Leonard Sedley. But Lord Auldearn's heir was a different matter. In one way or another Cardowers tended to be arresting. And Lord Brightmony was interesting primarily because his spiritual aims weren't in the least spurious. He mightn't be so securely regenerate as he believed—although he did, for the matter of that, look at you, or not look at you, in a way that suggested him as aware of retaining a hunk of his particular old Adam. But the main point about him was that some struggle went on. He might be torn, but he wasn't baffled; whereas with Sedley it was perhaps the other way round. As for Balietti, Mungo felt, it was just a pity that Lord Brightmony had made such a bad buy.

'We shall take these matters up again after dinner,' Lord

Brightmony said. 'I have one or two questions to put to you which would be out of place now. They arise out of something that Leonard told me when he came back from your cottage this afternoon. I hope, by the way, that the cottage is comfortable? Is there anything that I could tell my people to supply, or do?'

'Oh, no—nothing at all. Ian and I like it very much.' Mungo found it easier to say this, which was perfectly true, than to find an appropriate response to the earlier part of his host's speech. He thought he could make a fair guess as to what Sedley had come back to Mallachie with: it was the Vera affair as it had been sketchily communicated to him. At Mallachie such a topic would probably turn out rather more than mildly embarrassing.

18

AFTER DINNER THEY went into a room called the saloon. It wasn't in the least the sort of place that sometimes gets that name in a great house. It was long and low and about as bleak as could be, with nothing much more than high-backed chairs and bare tables dotted here and there. The only token of comfort was a bright fire in a big grate, and as the late summer night was keeping very reasonably warm off its own bat there really wasn't much point in that. Ian had nicknamed this apartment the public bar. It would, he said, be possible to keep up your spirits in it only if there were a chap behind a counter, ready to draw you unlimited pints of bitter or mild.

'Ian,' Lord Brightmony said, 'I don't know if you remember—but on your last visit, which was unhappily some time ago, Father Balietti challenged you to a game of chess, and you defeated him. I suggest that you give him the chance of having his revenge now.'

'Yes, of course.' Ian was being as nice to his uncle as to Sedley. 'I'll get the board and pieces at once.'

'And I shall look forward to presiding over the combat,' Sedley said. 'But I am a much better player than either of you, and shall have to resist the temptation to offer a nudge now and then.'

Mungo for some reason distrusted these amiable exchanges. Perhaps it was merely that he had been reckoning on a quick get-away. Perhaps he sensed something contrived about the proposed disposition of things. Or

perhaps his interest in what Ian's uncle was going to say
to him didn't quite match his alarm. Any way, it happened. Ian and Balietti sat down to their game at one
end of the saloon, rather like Ferdinand and Miranda in
the interior of Prospero's cave or whatever. Sedley drew
up a chair between them. And Lord Brightmony, who
would have made quite a good Prospero of the modern
beardless sort, motioned Mungo to a seat beside him near
the fire. Mungo felt like Caliban when about to be
given the works.

'I think you know,' Lord Brightmony began, 'that I
am my father's heir, that my brother Robert is mine,
and that Ian is his?'

'Yes. I've come to understand that quite well.'

'I mention the circumstance only as in part explaining
the solicitude for Ian which must excuse what I am about
to say. You may think me impertinent, Mungo. If you
do, say so—and that will be the end of the matter.'

'I think I can promise you not to feel it anything of the
sort.'

'You encourage me to venture the remark that I judge
you a straightforward young man.' There was a pause,
during which Mungo was conscious of having no urge
to make gratified noises. 'What I have heard from Leonard
is that you and Ian had a quarrel over a woman. Is that
correct?'

'Yes, it is. We had a bit of a row over a girl.' Mungo
felt that this was a more accurate way to describe the
matter. 'But I thought I was speaking to Mr Sedley more
or less in confidence. He oughtn't really to have passed
on to you something about Ian which he'd had only at
second-hand.'

'Leonard shares my anxieties. Was this incident
occasioned by one or the other of you committing an act
of fornication?'

'Of fornication?' This outrageous demand for information had bobbed up so suddenly that Mungo was at a
loss. He had to tell himself, for one thing, just what was
meant by a word which he vaguely regarded as biblical or
technical. You were a fornicator if you were unmarried,
and went to bed with somebody else who was unmarried.
That was it.

'Oh, yes,' he said. 'Both of us, actually.' He wondered
whether this ready admission had a displeasingly jaunty
sound. 'We're not at all inclined to boast about it, and I
don't know why I told Mr Sedley at all.' Mungo wondered
whether this was quite true. 'Ian and I ended up not a
bit pleased with ourselves, as a matter of fact.'

'I would be glad to think that you had repented such a
sin. For a grievous sin it is, however the worldly may
judge.' Lord Brightmony's gaze was on the floor. 'Yet
perhaps there is a certain reassurance in it. I can see that
you and Ian have become close friends, and have remained so in spite of this reprehensible episode into the
nature of which I will not further enquire. So tell me,
please. Is yours and his a virtuous attachment?'

'Yes, it is.'

Mungo's answer, flat and pat, came without effort. He
found he hadn't the slightest impulse either to stand on
his dignity or be vulgarly amused. He wondered how Ian
would have reacted, if the queer question had been pitched
at him. As it ought to have been, for that matter, if it was
to be pitched at anybody at all. The morbid imaginings
of the Cardowers ought to be kept on the closed circuit of
the family. But perhaps that was wrong. Perhaps Ian's
uncle-eclipse, at least on one of its sides, had been genera-
ted by his uncle David's having fired off such obsessional
questions at him in his vulnerable years. Whereas Mungo
was going to experience nothing traumatic in anything,
however bizarre, that the poor gentleman found to say.

This thought made Mungo glance at Ian down the length of the saloon. The chess seemed well launched, and both players were concentrating on their play. Sedley had risen, and was wandering restlessly to and fro at the far end of the room. Mungo tried to remember how long a stubborn game of chess could take. Until this one was over, there was no chance of a getaway from the Castle. Meanwhile, Lord Brightmony was conducting an ordered retreat from what might have been called an exposed position.

'Leonard and I live much out of this world,' he was saying. 'We are all the more subject to what a young man like yourself may consider irrational—or even pathological—anxieties. And I fear our manner of life bears more hardly on him than on me. Glance at him now. Is there not something thwarted about him? But perhaps you will say that a sick imagination is again running away with me.'

'I wouldn't say anything so impertinent.' Mungo paused. 'And I think I see what you mean. Oughtn't he to be having a shot at the world, sir, even if he does live out of it? Publishing something, I mean. Or have you persuaded him that anything of the sort is frivolous and wrong?'

'It is a question I have to ask myself, Mungo.' Lord Brightmony had accepted without displeasure Mungo's going over to the attack in this way. 'Would you agree with me that all art ought to be dedicated to the glory of God, since it is only a pale shadow of the divine abundance?'

'I'm afraid that's not quite my language.' Mungo was ceasing to find himself embarrassed. 'But I can see myself wishing that it was.'

'I can only say that Leonard's art has fallen back, baffled, from anything of the sort. You and I have agreed that *An Autumn in Umbria* is a remarkable book. Yet, at

the same time, there is a spirit of negation in it. There is
no love.'

Mungo had no reply to this, except for a cautious and
wondering glance. It wasn't necessary to believe Lord
Brightmony quite mad just because he spent hours wandering around his house muttering prayers, or a sex-
maniac because he was troubled by images of sexual trans-
gression. Lord Auldearn's mad doctors had been right
in refusing to lock him up—and equally right in saying
he was worth listening to. For here he was, an unbalanced
and eccentric person whom Mungo couldn't conceive
himself as living with, nevertheless saying something very
serious which Mungo felt to be true.

'The created universe, Mungo, is a labour of love. All
its minute particularities—such as the infinity of wildly
strange creatures at the bottom of the deepest seas—are
just that. And a man can only create, can only truly
create, those imagined beings whom he loves for their
uniqueness. Everything else is only cleverness and steril-
ity.'

'Are you saying that Mr Sedley realizes the truth of
that—a truth which perhaps you have taught him—and
accounts himself an outsider in terms of it?'

'It would be a great evil in me to make Leonard feel
an outcast. His talents, could he continue to exert them,
would doubtless afford harmless pleasure to many. But
something has laid a spell upon them, has frozen them at
their source. Have I been the cause of this? You are an
artist too. Perhaps you can tell me.'

Mungo shook his head and kept his mouth shut. The
challenge was an extravagant one which it was not for
him to take up. And again he glanced across the room.
The game had progressed, but in whose favour he couldn't
tell. Sedley had come to a halt behind Ian's chair, and was
studying the board. It was a peaceful tableau, with no

stress or strain to it at all. Mungo turned back to Lord Brightmony, resolved to continue this conversation, but on a different tack.

'I've gathered,' he said, 'that Mr Sedley is a kinsman of yours and Ian's, although rather a distant one. But it sometimes seems to me that nearer relations influence Ian a good deal. I mean just the fact of their existing, or having existed. He thinks about his family a lot, and sometimes it makes things difficult for him. Do you think that's possible?'

'I believe you may have in mind my late brother, Ian's uncle Douglas.' For the second time that evening Lord Brightmony allowed himself more than a moment's study of Mungo's face. It was what Mungo was coming to think of as the long-lost-kinsman glance. 'Is it so?'

'Well, yes.' Mungo was now regretting his temerity. 'I have heard of him. But I'm not trying to be inquisitive.'

'Why should you be?' On reflection, Lord Brightmony seemed to think poorly of this demand, for he hurried on. 'You are Ian's closest friend, and candour in these matters is due to you. There must be candour—confidence, indeed, in the fullest sense.'

There was silence, Mungo not feeling himself called upon to speak. Now—he told himself—it's coming. He rather felt that, if it was to be done at all, the job ought to be done by Lord Auldearn. Still, he liked Lord Brightmony. He'd quite made up his mind about that. So Lord Brightmony could go ahead. This, however, didn't happen. Lord Brightmony stuck to his theme.

'You have heard of Douglas, perhaps, from your family? But your parents, I think, are dead.'

'Yes. I live with an aunt.'

'Ah, yes—Miss Guthrie of Fintry.' Lord Brightmony said this much as if he were saying 'Miss Macdonald of the Isles'. Mungo, although a little discomposed by this

indecisive hovering, as he felt it to be, before the small
family secret he shared with his host, found time to be
amused by a courteous attribution of territorial grandeur
to a hillside farm. He thought he knew what prompted
it. Lord Brightmony knew himself to be embarked, with
whatever delay, upon a topic which demanded all the
delicacy he could command.

'It is unhappily true,' Lord Brightmony went on, 'that
one of your aunt's generation would have heard much of
Douglas. He was two years younger than I, and three
years older than our brother Robert, Ian's father. When
we were young men Douglas and I lived together in this
house for a good part of the year. But it proved not a
happy arrangement, and he found other quarters. He
was, in fact, a rootless person—but that, alas, is not all
that must be said of him. His morals were impaired. But
all this—about one who remained very dear to us—you
have probably heard.' Lord Brightmony paused, and
gazed sombrely into the fire. He was a handsome man,
and had given what Mungo thought of as a Victorian
tone to this speech. With Mungo sitting attentively beside him, and his unconscious nephew playing chess with
a priest in the background, he might have been worked
up very nicely as the pivot of a Royal Academy picture
called, perhaps, 'The Family History', or 'The Spectre
from the Past'. This fancy had occasioned a certain inattention in Mungo. He had to emerge from it hastily,
and agree that he had heard certain broad facts about
Lord Douglas.

'My brother died—in miserable circumstances which I
need not detail—when Ian can have been no more than a
very small boy indeed. But if it is your suggestion, Mungo,
that the shadow of this unfortunate uncle has a little
hung over him nevertheless, I will not say that I myself
find it altogether improbable. For one thing, poor Douglas

has been a divisive influence among us. My father, whom I gather you know, has never visited Scotland since what may be called the final and humiliating scandal of Douglas's last days. Yet Douglas had been, I think, his favourite son. So you may judge how deeply he felt about it. My brother Robert—a very charming man, surely, but of a light and volatile spirit—sends Ian here from time to time, but never comes himself. His wife and daughters scarcely know the place. And yet it is not the palatial Bamberton Court, Mungo, but this modest house which you are in now, that is to be regarded as the principal seat, as the reference books say, of our family.'

'Shall you continue to live here when you become Marquis of Auldearn?'

'Most assuredly. But will Ian? I fear not. He sees shadows here.'

There was a pause. Mungo, having marked that plural noun, held his peace. Lord Brightmony, for the moment at least, had nothing more to say. But the silence, before it could become awkward, was broken, indeed shattered, in a startling fashion. From the farther end of the room there came an exclamation, something like a cry, and the sound of a quick succession of objects tumbling on the floor.

A chair, a table, the chess-board, and the chess-men: all these had been knocked over and scattered. Across the evidences of this unaccountable misadventure Leonard Sedley and Ian faced each other. Both were strangely immobile and very pale. Righting the table and chair, picking up the chess-board, resourcefully gathering the scattered pieces in the skirt of his soutane, Father Balietti was labouring to obscure the nature of the crisis.

'But how very clumsy of me,' Balietti was exclaiming. 'A single inadvertent movement, and all this disaster!

My dear Ian, our game is ruined, I fear.' He tumbled
the chess-men on their board, and at the same time glanced
swiftly at Sedley. 'For shall we be able to return to the
status quo ante bellum? I judge it improbable.'

'Call it impossible,' Ian said, and walked across the
room to his uncle. Lord Brightmony, frowning and with
compressed lips, watched him approach—whether in mere
perplexity, or with anger or dismay, it was impossible to
tell.

'I was losing badly, so it must be called Father Balietti's
game.' The commonplace words came from Ian in a voice
Mungo seemed never to have heard before. 'And I don't
think anything has been broken.'

'Then no more need be said.' Lord Brightmony looked
gravely at his nephew. 'And on another occasion you
must make a fresh start.'

'Yes, of course. But it's later than I thought. Mungo
and I must go.'

'Ian, what on earth was it all in aid of?'
Mallachie Castle was behind the young men. In the soft
Highland darkness they were striding through the park at
a pace that challenged a tumble. It was a very still night.

'For the Lord's sake, man!' Silence had greeted Mungo's
first question. 'Stop creating, and speak up.'

'He pawed me. Sedley pawed me. You saw how he
was standing behind me, seeming to watch the game? But
his mind wasn't on that sort of game at all.'

'Stop creating, I said. Be sensible. How could he paw
you? At your end of the room you were in as bright a
light as we were. It would be a ridiculous thing to do.'

'He put his hand on my head.'

'Well, why shouldn't he?' Having received what seemed
not very shocking news, Mungo made up his mind what
line to take. 'As I understand the matter, he's known you

off and on since you were a kid. The poor chap's fond of you, and believes you to be fond of him. I've told you that. So all he intended was a token of the fact—a token of simple affection. There's nothing indecent about having a hand put on your head. Bishops are doing it all the time. Probably the sight of Balietti sitting opposite you put it into *his* head. A kind of whimsical echo of being confirmed.'

'He ran his fingers through my hair.'

'Oh.' This silenced Mungo for a while. 'But, Ian, what happened then? What did you *do*?'

'I jumped up. I just couldn't stand it, or take it. I jumped up, and everything went tumbling.'

'Did you say anything?'

'Yes, I did.'

'Well, what?'

'I called him something. Something I'm not going to repeat.'

'I don't take it as a compliment that you think my ear as chaste as all that. Now cool off.'

They walked on in silence to the river. It seemed a long way. When they were inside the cottage it was Ian who first spoke.

'Shall we pack up now, or in the morning?'

'Neither, I hope. We've got to cut this thing down to size first.'

'Mungo, I resent your talking about me as creating. It's as if I were a hysterical girl.'

'All right. It's only a phrase, and I'm sorry. Do you mind my saying you over-reacted?'

'Not if you admit there was something to react to.'

'Well, then—there was. Sedley has done something extremely silly, and knows it.'

'Perhaps you think I ought to be satisfied with an apology?'

'Not quite that. Not that way on, as a matter of fact.'

'Mungo, what the hell do you mean?'

'The apologizing, or whatever it's to be called, had better be done by you. First thing in the morning will be best.'

'You've taken leave of your senses.'

'No, I haven't. Just listen. You can't help being attractive to Sedley. You can't give yourself a squint and a hump and a clubfoot. But the thing's been no more, you know, than a sentimental indiscretion on the part of an ageing man, and it's up to you to mitigate it as a disaster for him. Your uncle and he are important to each other, and the *status quo* there you *can* help to maintain. I think your uncle is a very remarkable man. But he'd be inclined to be harsh, I believe, to any overt expression of ways of feeling that he hopes he has mastered and repressed in himself. So it's only fair to get the whole thing played down. Tell your uncle you haven't been sleeping well, or something like that. Tell Sedley your nerves have been a bit on edge lately. Say any damn thing—briefly and quietly. They're both rather formal people, and will respond to a ritual gesture, or spot of decorum.'

'I'm to paper over the cracks?'

'Exactly that.'

'You seem to be a bloody sight more concerned about those old men than about me.'

'Ian, say that over again slowly, and you'll see it's rot.' Mungo managed a grin. 'In fact, you'll be ashamed of it.'

'That's true, at least. Sorry.'

'Then just go on listening for a moment longer. The well-intentioned advice of Mungo Lockhart is advanced directly in the interest of Ian Cardower.'

'Don't be so verbose. It's about time we were going to bed.'

'All right. But meanwhile just hold on to your seat.

When you jumped up in that absurd way, and let out a
great yell, and knocked over a perfectly harmless table
and chess-board, and called a distinguished elderly novelist—'

'Oh, stow it, Mungo. Stuff it.'

'Well that's from the same region of discourse.' This
time, Mungo's grin was wholly unforced. 'When you were
doing all those things, you were putting on a classic turn
as the boy with disastrous uncles. Uncle One, Douglas
Cardower—so I'm booked for a life as a squalid woman-
izer. Uncle Two, David Cardower—so—'

'You do most tediously spell things out, Mungo. Your
novels are going to be quite awful.'

'So they are.' Mungo drew a deep breath, kicked off
his shoes, yawned, and began scrambling out of his clothes
while still crossing the floor to his bedroom. He paused
at its door, with his hand on the latch. It might have been
Howard 4, 4. But nothing further came into his head, and
he simply said good-night. Ian—once more—was going
to do as he'd been told.

19

HE DID IT with commendably little delay. He went up
to the Castle after breakfast, and was away much longer
than Mungo had expected. When he got back to the
cottage he grumbled about missing a morning's fishing,
demanded his lunch, and said briefly that he supposed
Mungo had been right. About the previous night's embarrassment, he added, he'd uttered no more than a dozen
words, but the effect seemed to have been an easing of
tension all round. Leonard Sedley had walked part of the
way back with him.

'What did he talk about?' Mungo asked.

'Never mind what he talked about. There are a lot of
things about which you're a damn sight too curious.'

Mungo realized with a shock that Ian was in one of his
very darkest moods. Something must have happened to
occasion this, and it was something that Ian didn't want
to talk about. It was Mungo's impulse to challenge such
an infringement of an unspoken compact between them.
Then he reflected that he himself had felt unable to tell
Ian of his own convinced belief—for by now it was entirely that—that he was Ian's uncle's son. The reason for
this inability, he didn't quite know: perhaps it was simply
that romantic illegitimacy was a notion, or a fact, just
too silly to talk about. But still, whether silly or not, it
was a pretty large thing to keep from his best friend.

There came to him a sudden perception that it must be
precisely this, and nothing else, that Ian was now keeping
from *him*. He, Mungo, had been taken to Bamberton to

be inspected—on the initiative, as it must have been, of
Ian's father. Then he had been brought to Mallachie for
the same purpose; and he was sure that Lord Brightmony's
persuasion—and Sedley's too, for that matter—had been
the same as Lord Auldearn's. And now the thing had
been broken—if that was the word—to Ian. Ian now
actually knew that they were cousins of a sort. And Ian
was finding it very difficult to talk about. So Mungo
waited. He felt he had to wait. The initiative was very
much Ian's to welcome him, so to speak, into the family.
And surely this was exactly what Ian would immediately
want to do? He had thought about Mungo as a possible
brother-in-law (what might be called the Mary Cardower
episodes witnessed to that); so surely he wasn't going to
jib at this other and much less substantial relationship—
which, anyway, he'd once advanced as an idle joke?

Thinking in this fashion, Mungo kept mum. They sat
down opposite each other to munch bread and cheese and
gulp brutally swamped malt whisky. Ian had produced a
single flare of straight hostility, and Mungo rather hoped
he'd do it again. It might at least start explanations. But
for a long time Ian kept mum too. He *wasn't* hostile,
Mungo decided. He was simply, in some mysterious way,
totally out of his depth. The river might have got into
those ridiculous waterproof breeches and be carrying him
he didn't know where.

'Damn and blast!' Sitting up abruptly, Ian had chucked
a last crust savagely through the open door of the cottage.
'I suppose I can clear out in good order as soon as this
lunch-party of my uncle's is over. I'm about through with
this place. There are things I want to do.'

'I've had an idea, as a matter of fact.' Mungo hadn't
failed to mark the singular pronoun. 'Those friends of
yours near Fochabers, the ones that absolutely stink of
fish—'

'The D'Arcy-Drelincourts.' Ian was looking at Mungo strangely, and only half attending.

'Yes. Obviously another ancient Scottish family—'

'Don't jabber. What the hell ought we to be caring about ancient Scottish families? All that just buggers things up. But go on.'

'The D'Arcy-Drelincourts—lords of the salmon-falls, the mackerel-crowded sea.' Mungo had been so confounded by Ian's enigmatical outburst that he had momentary recourse to nonsense. 'Don't you feel their particular fishy fume calling to you?'

'As a matter of fact, I've been thinking about it.' Ian brightened a little as he said this. But it didn't escape Mungo that the statement wasn't true. Ian was simply grabbing at something which hadn't been in his head.

'Well, then,' Mungo demanded, 'why don't you go?'

'It might be an idea. And I could—at least I suppose I could—ring them up and ask if I might bring a friend for a week. It's a big house, and I expect they could find us a couple of garrets.'

'My child, you could angle for an invitation—but I continue not to angle for fish.' Mungo's dismay—for that was what he was conscious of feeling now—took shelter behind a doggedly facetious idiom. 'You go, and I'll stay put.'

'Stay here at Mallachie?' Ian asked sharply.

'Yes—why not? It will give us a rest from each other. Have some more whisky.' Mungo watched Ian reach for a bottle with what horrifyingly revealed itself as a trembling hand. 'I rather think your lugubrious uncle approves of me,' he went on desperately. 'He knows of my one carnal sin, but otherwise rates me as pure and—'

'Dry up, for Christ's sake!' Ian brought this out in such a burst of real desperation that Mungo saw he must make a drastic reappraisal of the situation. 'Of course uncle

David has lent us this cottage for the season, and won't
in the least mind how we come and go.' Ian took a gulp
of whisky in a fashion so random that it dribbled down
his chin. 'And just what do you plan to do with yourself,'
he demanded roughly, 'if I go off?'

'Lie on my lonely pallet, sobbing bitterly, I suppose.'
Mungo waved in the direction of his typewriter. 'Don't
you know I have a novel to get on with?' Pausing, and
getting no response, he decided to try provocation. 'Besides, I propose to haunt the Castle, and get to know a lot
more recent Cardower history.'

'To put into your rubbishing romance, I suppose. I tell
you again, I've never known anybody so full of impertinent curiosities.'

Mungo felt what he supposed was his blood going to
his head. But, strangely, something else swam up there
as well. It was the knowledge that what had come from
Ian was not an insult but an appeal. The contemptuous
words, decoded in terms of their normal relationship,
represented not exactly a plea for quarter, but certainly a
plea for time. Whatever had happened had got Ian
thoroughly disoriented.

'Then that's fine,' Mungo said. 'Your turn to skivvy
round.' And he went out to sun himself on the river-
bank.

The arrangement fulfilled itself a couple of days later—
days so constrained and miserable that it was a relief
when Ian departed. Mungo told himself that now he'd
settle down and work. He'd go up to Mallachie to dine, if
only because it seemed to be expected of him, but for the
rest of the time he'd work like mad. At least it wasn't
true that he had the slightest wish to put any of the Cardowers into his book. If he could sufficiently lose himself
in his story he might even stop uselessly beating his brains

over Ian's strange behaviour. You can't write a novel, he
supposed, and remain uncomfortably curious about anybody outside it.

Evenings apart, it was unlikely he'd see much of Leonard Sedley. For Sedley had been making those afternoon
trips to the river-bank not in the least to enjoy the improving conversation of Mungo Lockhart, his *cher* but
undeniably juvenile *confrère*. About this Mungo had been
under a flattering delusion. Sedley's talk had been nothing
more than a circumspect cover for his desire—not really
all that indecorous a desire—to watch another young
man gracefully catching, or failing to catch, salmon. And
for *that* young man his companion wasn't in the least a
substitute: a circumstance which somehow for Mungo
preserved Sedley his dignity. The eminent novelist (or ex-
novelist) wasn't promiscuous. Mungo could stand waist-
deep in those chilly Highland waters until the cows came
home, without rousing in Sedley anything more than a
polite willingness to converse instructively on the aesthet-
ics of fiction.

So he was surprised when, a couple of days after Ian's
departure for Fochabers, Sedley turned up as usual at
the cottage. Seeing him coming down a path to the river,
he hastily shoved aside his typewriter—this out of a feeling that it would be awfully embarrassing to have a pro
looking over his shoulder as he clattered away at his artless tale. Mungo was at the stage of feeling that the novel
absolutely wouldn't do; that its immaturity and inepti-
tude piped and burbled from every line of it; and that he
was bloody well going to finish it, all the same.

Of course Sedley wasn't deceived; he couldn't be, seeing
he knew exactly what Mungo was engaged on. But his
apology for interrupting work seemed sincere without
being in the least fussy. He then took it for granted they
were going to talk, leading the way to the river-bank and

the tree trunk that had been dedicated to their former conversations. The river, minus Ian, had rather a vacant look, but Sedley eyed it for a minute with complete satisfaction. When he spoke it was gently, but with a directness that startled Mungo for a moment.

'It was so very sad that I upset Ian the other evening as I did. Do you remember, Mungo, how Othello speaks of "heat, the young affects in me defunct"? Scholars say the text is corrupt, but the sense is clear. Not, mark you, that the Moor is being very honest with himself, for he plainly has the power of a lusty lover in him still. But I am a doddering old gentleman, moved by certain quiet affections from time to time, and according them the recognition of a tone, a gesture, maybe.' Sedley produced something between a soft laugh and a sigh. 'However, it is entirely one's own fault if one is misunderstood.'

'I'd hope,' Mungo said firmly, 'Ian would never think of so small a thing again.'

'Ah, but he will! There are areas of feeling in which Ian doesn't enjoy your sense of security.' Sedley waited, but Mungo said nothing. His psycho-analysing of Ian, he felt, hadn't been particularly useful. Perhaps it had been intrusive, even allowing for the fact that he and Ian were sworn brothers, or whatever was the best way of describing it. He certainly wasn't going to air the theory of uncle-eclipse in Ian's absence and for the benefit of Leonard Sedley. Not that he was in the least eager to feel towards Sedley other than admiringly and respectfully. Sedley was not only the first author he had met in the flesh; in *An Autumn in Umbria* he had written a book which Mungo knew he himself couldn't equal if he lived to be a hundred. And Sedley's subsequent silence or nearsilence as a writer was more than a mere mystery. It attracted sympathy—almost something like compassion —as well as curiosity.

'But we'll drop Ian for the moment,' Sedley said. 'After all, you've sent him about his business for a time—his business being to fish as many waters as possible while the season lasts. It must be wonderful to have ambitions as simple as that.'

'Ian has a good many other things in his head besides fishing.' Mungo wasn't too pleased even with mild and whimsical denigration of his friend. 'And as for sending him about his business—'

'Come, Mungo, be honest. Those people at Fochabers were your idea. And a good idea, as things stood. I'm grateful to you. However, I haven't come over to talk about Ian. I've come over—or been sent over—to talk about you.'

'Sent over? I don't understand you.'

'By David. But also, in a way, by the whole family. I suspect them of having been writing round to each other. Of scratching one another's heads, one might say. They feel the whole thing is delicate, and I don't say they're wrong.' Sedley paused, and eyed Mungo intently. 'I'd find this easier if you could give a hint that you *do* a little understand.'

'You seem to be talking about something rather serious. So you mustn't ask me for guesses.' Mungo said this stiffly. Leonard Sedley was an intimate friend of the family. He was even some sort of remote relation. But it wasn't proper that he should have been sent to say—to reveal, as they must judge it—what Lord Brightmony had failed to get round to a few evenings before. It wasn't proper. It was even—Mungo fleetingly thought—rather odd. And Sedley himself appeared to be aware of what was going through his mind.

'Of course, Mungo, you're quite right. And I don't see why it should be me who has to break the ice. Except that I'm a very old family friend—which is precisely what I hope you will remember as we talk. And it is, no doubt, a family friend to whom it is natural to turn in so odd a state of affairs. Then, again, you intend to be a writer, and it's a writer that I've been. That could be seen as a bond of sorts between us, I suppose.'

'Yes, of course.'

'You can't be unaware, my dear Mungo, of how these people feel towards you.'

'The Cardowers in general? Well, I suppose not. They've all been extremely nice to me, as Ian's friend. But there's this big social gap—in outlook, and assumptions, and moment-to-moment manners, and everything else. I have to ask myself sometimes if I'm at sea in it. If all their niceness is as simple and spontaneous as I'd like to think it.'

'There's a sense—but an innocent and honourable sense —in which it is not. Let me come to the point. Has it ever occurred to you, Mungo, that you may be Douglas Cardower's son?'

'Yes, it has. In fact, I've become sure of it.'

As Mungo got out this affirmation he felt the force of the cliché that speaks of getting a load off one's chest. The sensation brought him to his feet and to facing Sedley squarely. Sedley, too, seemed relieved; he put his two hands on the tree trunk, and eased himself into a more relaxed posture.

'You see,' Mungo said, 'Ian once made a joke about it.'

'A joke?' Sedley's eyebrows went up. 'I'm afraid I can't see how he could possibly—'

'It was in Italy. I'd invented a kind of psycho-analysing game with Ian. Or not a game exactly.' Mungo felt the danger of incoherence. 'I really did think I could get him clearer to himself about—about one thing and another which rather bothered him. And this joke of Ian's about

Douglas Cardower—which *was* just a joke—was a kind of paying me back. You see, I'd learnt about Douglas Cardower having been a tremendous libertine, and having had any number of illegitimate children—'

'Quite so. It was a very odd joke to make to you, all the same.' Sedley spoke coldly. 'It's almost a new light on Ian.'

'No, no—you don't understand. We say anything to each other, Ian and I. So you see—'

'I'm sure you do. You have, or seem to have, one another's confidence completely.' Sedley's mouth hovered into the motions of a smile. 'Still, it was exactly the sort of thing that your generation describes as simply not on. To put it bluntly, it was a joke about the chastity of your mother.'

'Yes, I know. As a matter of fact, Ian was uncomfortable about it almost as soon as he'd come out with it. But there's another thing. He rather challenged me to deny that I hadn't already dreamed up the idea myself. And I had, you know. It's this business of what he called the Myth of the Birth of the Hero. I believe there's a book called that.'

'There well may be.' Sedley's gaze was still intently upon Mungo's face.

'As children; we've all indulged fantasies of—'

'Yes, yes, Mungo. That's obvious stuff. But this particular fantasy had been coming to you now that you were grown up?'

'It sounds idiotic. And I hadn't nursed it or elaborated it. It's partly, I suppose, that I have the kind of mind that is always starting to tell itself stories.'

'Quite an arbitrary story on this particular occasion?'

'Oh, no. I'm not really as daft as that. For a start, you see, I never knew the people I'm told were my parents. And there's money comes to me mysteriously through a lawyer in Edinburgh, a Mr Mackellar. And I'd found out that at least I hadn't been—been conceived in wedlock, or whatever the jargon is. I suppose you may say that set my rash imagination to work.'

'Let us not asperse our imaginations, Mungo.' Sedley spoke with a sudden grimness. 'They're what we hope, or have hoped, to earn our keep by. And I assure you that building up stories about oneself needs no apology to *me*.' Sedley took an impulsive step towards Mungo, almost as if intending to lay a hand on his shoulder. Then he checked himself. 'And the imagination, you know,' he said gently, 'is surely the organ by which we sometimes learn a truth about ourselves. But get this clear. You haven't been indulging a purely private fantasy. Lord Auldearn, who used to be spoken of as the best brain in the Lords, believes that you are his grandson. David and Robert both believe that you are their nephew.'

'That's what I've become more and more aware of, really: *their* belief. And, you see, there was something in their heads—in Ian's father's and grandfather's heads— awfully early on. In fact, *they* were imagining things well before I was.'

'How could you tell that, Mungo?'

'It was a bit indefinable. I'd call it something in the quality of their interest in me. And now what's believed by the family is perfectly plain—so you're not in the least springing a surprise on me. What I haven't yet got hold of is their evidence.' Mungo paused. 'Lord Auldearn showed me a photograph of his son Douglas, and I could see that I'm not a bit like him. So it isn't *that*.'

'No, Mungo—it certainly isn't your good looks. They're there, but they're quite different from Douglas's.' Sedley said this with a sudden faded coquetry which was startling. 'They have grounds—as Hamlet says—more relative than that. You come from Fintry, near Forres, and you are Mungo Guthrie Lockhart. What more they've been fishing up, I just don't know. Of course, there are your manners.'

'What have my manners got to do with it?'

'I think I'd rather say your bearing. Perhaps they wouldn't have fallen so in love with you, if you'd been— well, a more rustic character.'

'What do you mean by saying they've fallen in love with me?'

'*C'est une façon de parler*. They think they see in you, no doubt, what was attractive in Douglas when his years were as yours are now.'

'I see.' Mungo didn't care for much in this—including that final literary cadence. 'Do they know about Mr Mackellar and the money from Edinburgh?'

'I don't think so. That must have been something arranged long ago, and by—by somebody else. Of course I'm sure they'd now want to push it up.'

'To push it up! Please, what do you mean?' Mungo had flushed in a way that showed he didn't really need to ask this question.

'The money. To get you launched, my dear lad. The Robert Cardowers aren't particularly wealthy, but Lord Auldearn is a very—'

'You think I'd do that? Take money, because of the accidental coming to light of some casual'—Mungo searched for a word—'liaison that happened twenty years ago? You think I would?'

'Don't let's get side-tracked by that.' Sedley looked like a man conscious of having made a mistake. 'At least the family isn't lacking in delicate feeling about the thing. They've asked themselves whether *their* discovery ought to become *your* discovery as well—or Ian's, even. They've been far from thinking it's anything particularly grand or grateful they have to communicate. They'd have answered themselves No, I think, but for knowing that you your-self were wondering about your birth.'

'But they couldn't know that!'

'Why, Mungo, you told Ian, didn't you?' Sedley's almost covert smile hovered again. 'And the Cardower family grapevine is always in singularly good trim.'

'I see.' Mungo was conscious of a strange dismay—not in his head but somewhere in his chest. 'And Ian knows all this—all that these other people have come to believe?'

'He hasn't spoken to you about it?' Sedley asked gently.

'No. But *I* believe he knows—has just come to know. And I don't feel it has made *him* fall in love with me.'

'Ah!' Sedley, too, was on his feet now, and regarding Mungo gravely. 'I'm not—as I think you can guess—as much in Ian's confidence as I'd like to be. But I have a great respect for his intelligence. He's a far abler man than his talkative father—or, for that matter, my very old friend, his uncle David. He's going to be of the same weight as his grandfather, to my mind. He's your equal in wits, wouldn't you say?'

'Of course I would. But that isn't—'

'If you were pitted against each other, it would be a stiff struggle. However, my dear Mungo, we must stick to the point. I can't think Ian would have made that joke to you on the basis of nothing at all. It might even have been an abortive shot at bringing the thing into the open and discussing it. Do you remember the occasion as hav-ing that feel, at all?'

'It might have. But I don't think so.' Mungo had to fight off a sense of mere confusion. 'If any member of his family had told him about—about what was being be-lieved, I wouldn't have expected him to keep mum to me.'

'He might have been told in confidence.'

'I wouldn't expect him to accept a confidence about me.

We're wholly in *each other's* confidence—as you said yourself.'

'Yes—of course.' Sedley hesitated. He seemed almost to be wondering how not to take this conversation further. Then he spoke impulsively. 'Listen, Mungo! There's something I haven't said. And it's certainly something I haven't been commissioned to say—for the simple reason that nobody else has thought of it. Except, perhaps, Ian himself—quite recently.'

'I don't know what you mean. Tell me, please.'

'Just one moment. Did you find it quite easy to persuade Ian to clear out for a week in order to ease our small embarrassment of the other evening?'

'Yes, I did. I was rather surprised, as a matter of fact. And I thought that, when he came back from the Castle on the morning after that awkwardness, he was a little strange, actually.' Mungo paused, and saw no virtue in this understatement. 'In fact, he seemed rather queerly shattered.'

'Indeed?' For a moment Sedley occupied himself with examining his well-manicured nails. 'Then let me be frank with you. What occurs to me is that, just possibly, he has gone off to think the thing out.'

'To think it out? This other-side-of-the-blanket oddity? I don't see—'

'Or even positively to set some investigation afoot. Ian's highly intelligent, as I said. He mayn't merely know what the others know, and be resting there; in fact, it looks as if he has really had your own sort of intuition about that for some time. But when suddenly he was *told* by David —say on the morning of his coming to the Castle to make his touching apology to me—he may in that instant have seen a possibility that hasn't entered their heads. A pretty stiff possibility!'

'A possibility?'

'A challenging possibility, which I happen to know some relevant facts about myself. Did I tell you, by the way? I was quite as close a friend of Douglas as of David twenty years ago. It could be rather an onerous position at times. There were things about which it was best to decide that one had better hold one's tongue.' Sedley paused for a moment, stood up, and looked down at Mungo smilingly. 'I've never had a clue, you know, about *your* having come into the world. Please remember that.'

There was a silence. Mungo had opened his mouth to say he made nothing of this. But it wouldn't have been true—or not quite. He had never, perhaps, formulated what would be the ultimately strange thing, but it had lurked, somewhere in his mind, all the same.

'But here you are,' Sedley said. 'The big surprise! So if Douglas and your mother were legally married—which is what I had reason to suspect but judged it pointless to go digging after—just where do you all stand now they've dug *you* up? Perhaps Ian is wondering.'

'It wouldn't make any difference.' Mungo's head was swimming. 'It wouldn't make any real difference. Not after all these years.'

'Of course it would make a difference. As long as the Cardowers take your illegitimacy for granted, nothing more is called for from them than an easy benevolence. But if Ian has seen the possibility of your legitimacy, he has seen the possibility that neither his father nor he will ever be Marquis of Auldearn.'

'But that's all rubbish!' Mungo cried out this passionately. 'A thing like that couldn't come between—' He broke off, arrested by something implacable in Sedley's face.

'Have some sense, Mungo. Are you telling me that Ian regards the family title as rubbish?'

'I didn't mean that. He thinks the world of it, although

he's careful to conceal the fact. I meant he couldn't for a moment believe I'd—I'd go after the thing. Not any more than that I'd steal the coins in his pocket.'

'I don't know that you'd necessarily have much choice in the matter.'

'We're talking, for a start, about something that's still wildly improbable.' Mungo had a sense, perhaps irrational, that he was fighting with his back to the wall. 'It may be difficult to stop off being a lord. I don't know about that. But I'm almost sure you can refuse to become one. You renounce your claim, and then it simply passes to the next chap. That would be Lord Robert, and after him of course it would be Ian.'

'Ian may not be so sure of what you'd do as you are—or think you are. My dear Mungo, don't imagine I like this. I've been absolutely nerving myself to be open with you, to speak out the truth as I see it. Ian has suddenly taken alarm—I can only guess why—and has resolved to arm himself.'

'*To arm himself?*'

'With the facts in the first instance, whatever they may be.'

'He'd have come to me.' Mungo's voice was no longer steady. 'I'm sure he would.'

'Where do you think he is now?'

'With those people near Fochabers, of course. The D'Arcy-Drelincourts.'

'Is he?' Sedley, silent for a moment, had raised his hands gently—so that they were poised, Mungo thought, like a composer's above his keyboard. 'Ring up and find out.'

20

F OR TWENTY-FOUR hours Mungo fought a losing battle with himself over Leonard Sedley's challenge. To use the telephone to check up on Ian as one might do on a faith-less marriage-partner seemed wholly horrid; seemed the sort of treachery one would never redeem. For hours he sat in front of his typewriter and the beastly half-baked concoction he was calling a novel, without the ability to tap so much as a single key. It was a paralysis not remotely of the common inspiration-seeking, pen-chewing order. It was something outside his experience. So much was it this that it frightened him.

He went doggedly up to Mallachie to dine. What Sedley had been sent to him to say—as distinct from what Sed-ley had gone on to say off his own bat—would, he sup-posed, have to be referred to by Lord Brightmony. Uncle and illegitimate nephew (if that was the way such a re-lationship was expressed) would surely be obliged—even if reticently and without fuss—to join in some acknow-ledgement of what was now the admitted kinship.

But Lord Brightmony said nothing to the point. He was even more reserved than usual, and of this Mungo could think of only one explanation. Sedley's second shot (for it had come to feel very much like that) had now been fired at Lord Brightmony too. Sedley had owned up to having kept a secret of Douglas Cardower's that he ought not to have kept; that it was immoral to keep now that this young man calling himself Mungo Lockhart had been established as being who he was. Lord Brightmony, in fact, had before him the same facer that Ian had.

It was a situation that contrived to be at once hateful and absurd. Mungo's impulse was to speak out about it himself, and perhaps all that prevented him was the constant presence of Father Balietti. Mungo imagined—but he was getting into a state in which imagining things was easy—that Balietti's manner towards himself had modulated through deference into obsequiousness. Perhaps the big news had been broken to him too, and he was casting a provident eye ahead. As for Sedley, he was no help at all. Sedley was in a queer sort of abstraction which reminded Mungo, most bizarrely, of Mungo Lockhart when 'stuck' before his typewriter—confronting a story which just wasn't going to come out. Perhaps this regularly happened to Sedley. He had, after all, intimated to Mungo that he was engaged in labours of literary composition still.

So Mungo sat at table with these three elderly men and felt very alien to them indeed. With Ian gone, the world to which they all in one way or another belonged was no longer the world he had entered quite naturally and acclimatized himself in. It was a remote world, a long, long way from Forres and Easter Fintry.

But what if it was all true? What if improbability piled upon improbability was true? It would mean that absurdity piled upon absurdity was equally true: that he was the Hon. Mungo Cardower; that he would become Mungo Cardower, Viscount Brightmony; that he would become the Marquis of Auldearn, and end his days prowling around Bamberton Court in carpet-slippers. These concepts had no reality. They were as absurd as dreams. It would take more than parliament, it would take more than the Lord Lyon King of Arms and the Scottish Court of Chivalry to chivvy him out of his own honest identity.

This last jingle cheered up Mungo's word-mongering soul for perhaps as much as thirty seconds. Then he became so gloomy that there was nothing for it but to excuse himself immediately after dinner, and get back to the cottage. Making his way there through the deepening dusk, it occurred to him that it was a gloom very like Ian's sudden glooms. First cousins, he supposed, might well share some temperamental affinities. But he now very much didn't want to be Ian's cousin—whether first, second, third, or several times removed. Not on either one side of a blanket or the other.

He could ring up Ian, he told himself next day, not to find out whether Ian was where he had said he was going to be, but simply to contact him and let him know there was something they must talk about. This was sophistry. It eventually took Mungo to the telephone all the same.

He spoke to a manservant, who judged that Mr Cardower was not among the guests. But perhaps he was expected. Mr D'Arcy-Drelincourt would know. Mr D'Arcy-Drelincourt (who, to Mungo's present mood, sounded irksomely upper-class) said No, Ian Cardower wasn't with them at present. No, he hadn't been expected, nor—alas—was he expected in any immediate future. It would, of course, be extremely jolly if he turned up. Mr D'Arcy-Drelincourt, who by this time perhaps scented a little more in the enquiry than appeared, offered one or two further tactful remarks, and rang off.

Mungo, putting down the receiver on his own part, sought relief in uttering obscene words aloud. They weren't of the slightest help. He had spied on Ian. He had spied on Ian and had, in a sense, found him out. It was an action belonging to a wholly hideous world. It was like opening a man's letters and getting some disreputable hold on him.

But these were extravagant thoughts, and Mungo detected them as such. He wasn't doing too well, his mind wasn't doing too well, let alone his sense of what was honourable between friends. He needed help. Only a few hours before, he'd have said that in almost any conceivable exigency the help he'd want would be Ian's. Perhaps —he felt dimly—that was the true answer now. But it wasn't a practicable answer, and he'd better think again. At this point sanity abruptly returned to Mungo. He passed from a state of extreme bewilderment and confusion to one dominated by a single clear conviction. He ought to go and see Lord Auldearn.

Lord Auldearn was the head of the family. It was a family, indeed, that Mungo had not the slightest intention of allowing himself to be publicly declared to belong to. But that, somehow, made no difference. It was to Lord Auldearn he ought to go.

He had done his telephoning from the Castle; he went in search of the Castle's owner now. It was an hour at which Lord Brightmony was liable to have withdrawn for the purpose of private devotion in the chapel, but in fact he was pacing up and down a verandah in the late afternoon sun, with some work of edification open in his hands. Leonard Sedley was sitting near by, indulging himself in the worldly distraction of a game of patience. Mungo didn't waste words.

'Sir, I've been thinking over something very strange which Mr Sedley has talked to me about—I believe with your approval.'

'Ah, yes.' Lord Brightmony closed his book, and he and Sedley exchanged a swift glance which seemed to Mungo, in his keyed-up state, like that of two crooks in a crime-film. 'I have been corresponding both with my father and my brother Robert—and consulting Leonard, who is my very old friend. It was Robert who first had a groping perception of the truth. It is a truth which we have all come to feel should be acknowledged, although of course no breath of it would pass beyond the family except with your own express consent. I don't think I can say more, Mungo, except that we have all formed an affectionate regard for you.'

'Thank you very much.' Having said this, Mungo wasted no words. 'I've decided to go and see Lord Auldearn. Can you tell me, please, if he is at Bamberton?'

'My father is almost certainly at Bamberton. He never moves from the place.' If Mungo's announcement had taken Lord Brightmony a little aback, he was now indicating by his manner that he acknowledged its propriety.

'Then I shall go this evening—if I can be in Inverness in time for the night train. Is that possible, do you think?'

'If no time is wasted, I imagine it is,' Sedley said. He had given Mungo a curiously speculative glance, but seemed neither surprised nor perturbed. 'I tell you what, Mungo. I'll drive you there myself. And we'll stop at the cottage for anything you may want for a night or two. That way, we'll have plenty of time.'

Mungo found himself not too keen on this, but he couldn't refuse. He very much wanted to get clear of Mallachie with speed. It was even possible that the attraction of Bamberton was in part a matter of its being six hundred miles away.

'Then so it had better be.' Lord Brightmony nodded composedly. 'But you must have a sleeper, Mungo. Have you enough money? I can find you plenty in a few moments.'

'Thank you, I'll manage.' Mungo spoke stiffly, remembering that he still had time to collect cash from a post office. Then he realized that Lord Brightmony had spoken precisely with the unconsidered helpfulness of an uncle to a nephew. 'But thank you very much, indeed,' he added. 'It's awfully kind of you, and I hope I'm not being uncivil, rushing away like this.'

To this Lord Brightmony returned no more than a gentle shake of the head. It was almost as if what Mungo had said—or the tone in which he had said it—had afforded this sombre person pleasure. Sedley, it confusedly came to Mungo, could surely not after all have communicated to him the startling suggestion that the harmless illegitimate boy might not be illegitimate at all. The elder Cardowers might have been so attached to the reprehensible Douglas that they were prepared to be benevolently disposed to what the eighteenth century would have called one of his by-blows. But it was inconceivable that even Lord Brightmony, although he was bound, in any event, to become Lord Auldearn if he survived his father, could view with kindness a youth who might occasion a scandalous and sensational overthrow of the settled expectations of the family.

'You will come back to us,' Lord Brightmony said with sudden authority. 'You and Ian will come back to us, I hope, until Oxford requires your presence.' And Lord Brightmony shook hands.

'Well, well,' Sedley said to Mungo as he opened the door of his car. 'So you didn't run Ian to earth?'

'At those D'Arcy-Drelincourts? No, he hasn't been there, and they don't expect him.' Mungo spoke shortly. He was hoping for not too much conversation with Sedley between Mallachie and Inverness. But he clearly couldn't be too abrupt with somebody who was taking a good deal of trouble on his behalf. 'I don't understand about Lord Brightmony. I mean, about what he knows, or thinks he knows.'

'It won't take us five minutes to reach the cottage and collect your things.' Sedley put the car in gear. 'You mean about the possibility of there having been a legally valid marriage? I believe it hasn't entered David's head. David wasn't present when Ian and I talked about it.'

'Ian talked about it—to *you*?' Mungo's incredulity was scarcely civil.

'Oh, yes. I hope I haven't been disingenuous, my dear Mungo. It was the other day, when we had straightened out our small misunderstanding, and I was strolling back with him towards the cottage. He wanted to know about Scottish marriage laws. I said simply that I knew they have their peculiarities, and that he'd have to consult a solicitor, and perhaps take counsel's opinion, if he was to be sure of his ground.'

'To be sure—?' Mungo checked himself in the act of repeating this phrase. He hadn't liked it at all. 'Are you saying that's what Ian's doing now: enquiring about the law?'

'I suppose it well may be—and about the whole business of checking records, and so forth. By the way, have you thought of taking legal advice yourself?'

'Of course not!' Mungo felt really angry. 'You talk as if I might be thinking of planning and plotting against the Cardowers—'

'The other Cardowers, it's conceivable you ought to say.'

'—as if I were a kind of Tichborne Claimant.' Mungo had ignored the interruption. 'I haven't the slightest intention of seeing lawyers.'

'Not even Mr Mackellar, as I think he is—the solicitor through whom money comes to you?'

'No. Or not until I've seen Ian's grandfather.'

'Was it Mr Mackellar who let you know about the date of your mother's wedding—her wedding, I mean, to somebody called Lockhart—not many months, as I think you implied, before you were born?'

'No, it wasn't.' Mungo found that he furiously resented

Sedley's 'somebody called Lockhart'. 'It was a friend called
Roderick McLeod. I don't count him as a lawyer, because
he's still just a solicitor's clerk in Elgin. As a matter of
fact, he's the only person I've let know about this. I wrote
to him at the beginning of the week—the day we had
our talk by the river.'

'And Mr McLeod hasn't yet replied to your confidence?'

'No, but he will. Roddy will take his time. He's sensible.'

'And what do you suppose his sensible advice will be?'

'I don't know.' Mungo was glad that Sedley's car had
now drawn up at the cottage, for he resented the catechism
he was being subjected to. 'He'll probably tell me to mind
out.'

'To mind out? Yes—I think you must certainly do
that.'

Mungo made no reply to this, but jumped from the
car, and hurried into the cottage. He had to decide
whether to gather all his possessions together as if he were
leaving for good, or just to take what he needed for a day
or two. *Were I from Mallachie away and clear*—he mut-
tered to himself—*profit again should hardly draw me
here.* But it wasn't quite true. In fact, before this ghastly
mess blew up, he had been becoming rather fond of the
place. In any event, it would be cavalier to do anything
that would suggest he was shaking its dust from his shoes.
So he simply shoved a few things in a rucksack and went
out again. Sedley had turned the car and was looking at
his watch. They drove off, this time in silence. Sedley had
perhaps sensed Mungo's restiveness.

But just what had his talk been in aid of? Mungo felt
that Sedley had been trying to get something across to
him—but for some reason obliquely rather than forth-
rightly. Did he know something that he feared Mungo
simply wouldn't take if it was pitched at him straight?
Had he been making a wary progress towards some

further stiff disillusionment about Ian's attitude? Mungo remained a good deal under the spell of Sedley—or at least of the author of *An Autumn in Umbria*. So for some minutes, as they ran through Mallachie Park, he brooded uneasily over what seemed enigmatical in Sedley's attitude. What Sedley was saying, he decided, was that he, Mungo, was involved in a situation which he simply didn't grasp the brute worldly dimensions of, and which he had no chance of keeping control of in terms of his own impulses or standards. And he was perhaps saying that circumstances had made Ian an enemy, and that Mungo must acknowledge that cold fact, and plan in terms of it.

Mungo was bracing himself to have this out with Sedley, when he was suddenly called upon to brace himself in a wholly different sense. Sedley, who seemed not a very practised driver, had turned the car a little too fast and sharply through the lodge gates giving on the main road. And towards these gates another car—a large car—was turning from the opposite direction. There was a collision and a nasty jolt. Mungo found himself looking across a crumpled wing at the other—and not very obviously damaged—vehicle. It was a Rolls-Royce. In the front, impressively immobile in face of this futile assault, was a disdainful chauffeur. And in the back were Ian and his grandfather.

'So where do we go from here?' Sedley murmured. He lifted his hands from the steering-wheel in a gesture Mungo had noticed before; they might have been poised above a piano or a typewriter. '*Wohin der Weg?*'

21

In its literal sense, Sedley's question seemed not worth answering. It was clear that the little company so abruptly brought together would have to repair to Mallachie and there sort itself out. But Mungo hardly heard the question. He was wondering whether Sedley used a typewriter, and remembering him to have claimed, whether whimsically or not, to be a superior hand at chess. The fabricator of *An Autumn in Umbria* might almost have been asking himself what feasible moves lay ahead.

Obviously there had to be an initial parley on the spot. Lord Auldearn's chauffeur had unfrozen for the purpose of assisting his employer out of his car. Ian had jumped out on the other side. Sedley, having succeeded in backing his car into the side of the drive, scrambled out of it, and so did Mungo. Sedley and Lord Auldearn advanced upon each other, limply shook hands, and entered upon the leisured and casual expressions of courtesy, in the main unconnected with their present small misadventure, which the decorum of their age and station required. This left Mungo and Ian confronted with one another.

'I thought I'd better fetch our grandfather,' Ian said.

'I hope,' Mungo said, 'that Lord Auldearn hasn't found the journey too tiring. I was going off to visit him at Bamberton, as a matter of fact. But here we all are.'

There was a silence, as if each young man found a good deal to digest in the other's words and tone. It was broken by Ian—but with no more than Mungo's name, urgently spoken, before he was interrupted by an unexpected de-

velopment in the larger scene. A raucous and impatient
honking had made itself heard from the direction of the
high road. But as the high road itself was unimpeded by
the late collision, it was necessary to suppose that a third
vehicle, and one of altogether inferior social pretension,
was demanding a clear path to Mallachie. This proved
to be the case. A taxi-cab, carrying on its roof a board
saying *New Elgin Auto-Hire*, had drawn up behind the
Rolls. Its clamour, however, was abruptly silenced, as if
upon some peremptory command from within. Then its
door opened, and there emerged Roddy McLeod and Mr
Mackellar S.S.C.

Lord Auldearn—whose temper could scarcely have
been improved by two solid days of automobilism—
turned and glared at these intrusive persons. He might
have been feeling that what he had on his hands was at
least no more than a family party, although a perplexed
one, but that now here was the vulgar world as well. And
because he was very old, and for long unpractised in the
conduct of minor *contretemps*, he went, for a moment,
rather badly wrong now.

'Are you'—Lord Auldearn demanded of the new
arrivals—'a couple of damned journalists?'

'Sir!' Mungo had taken a quick pace forward. He wasn't
going to have his mysterious former patron (who had
given him a very decent lunch) abused in this arrogant
and mannerless fashion. 'May I introduce Mr Mackellar,
my solicitor, from Edinburgh? And Mr McLeod, who is
at present with a firm in Elgin?'

'How do you do?' Having no means of knowing that
these descriptions represented a more than commonly in-
opportune embroidering of fact in the interest of fancy,
Lord Auldearn surveyed the two legal gentlemen grimly
as he growled out this civility. Then he turned to Mungo.
'At least you lose no time in telling us where we are.'

Mungo was without a reply. He couldn't very well begin explaining that Mackellar had described him as his
client on the occasion of lunching him at his club, and
that he, Mungo, had been freakishly reviving the joke.
For that matter, perhaps there was some truth in it. Mackellar could only have turned up like this because Roddy
had taken a drastic initiative in summoning him—and
summoning him for the purpose of looking after Mungo's
interests, whether real or supposed.

However that might be, Mungo's manner of introducing
the two newcomers was having a complicated effect. He
was conscious of a harsh hostility in Lord Auldearn's tone.
He was equally conscious of—and a good deal more un-
nerved by—a spark as of covert approval which had
momentarily glinted in Lord Auldearn's eye. For the
aged nobleman—this was the truth of the matter—was
suspecting him, Mungo, of engineering a vigorous (and
probably unscrupulous) *coup de main*. And this the aged
nobleman in his secret and unregenerate heart admired.
And he admired it because it reminded him of Douglas
Cardower—the black sheep of the family and his favourite
son.

Mungo's intuition, having carried him so far, now
carried him a little farther. In Lord Auldearn no son of
Robert Cardower could stir quite the same feeling as a
son of Douglas Cardower. Such a son, whether legitimate
or not, had only to bob up with some appearance of pre-
sentability to put the nose of Ian Cardower quite out of
joint with the head of his family. In fact there was a sub-
text to this uncomfortable comedy, and in it Mungo had
been made suddenly aware that his role was that of the
Prodigal Grandson.

Mungo was badly shaken by this glimpse of folly in an
old man's heart. And—for full measure—he suspected
that Lord Brightmony was of the same way of feeling as

his father. He wondered whether Ian had arrived at any sense of the injustice being done him. He didn't believe it could have any sequel in the material sphere of property and succession. If Mackellar S.S.C. were to step forward at this moment waving documentary evidences of a marriage between Douglas Cardower and Mungo's mother, then at once these two old men (for Mungo thought of Lord Brightmony as being much of an age with his father Lord Auldearn) would stifle their secret feelings and fight like mad. All the senior Cardowers would do that— and perhaps Ian too. To a man and woman, they would close their ranks against the Perkin Warbeck, the Lambert Simnel, who had appeared among them. But—Mungo reassured himself—all this was nonsense. Mackellar was *not* going to step forward with documents. Such things happen only in old plays, or in novels. Yes—Mungo thought—*novels*.

'Bestir yourself,' Sedley was saying briskly. 'We're driving up to the house.' He opened the door on the passenger's side of his damaged car, and gestured to Mungo to get in. 'I shall be interested in what Ian has to say for himself.'

'*I'll* be interested in what *you* have to say for yourself.'

'I beg your pardon?'

'Just that.' Mungo had hardly heard his own staggering words because of the clatter with which the scales had, so to speak, been falling from his eyes. Now he raised his voice. 'Ian and I,' he said, 'are going to walk.'

'I'm sorry I lied to you.' Ian said this stiffly, and with his gaze directed straight ahead up the drive. 'I apologize.'

'Did you lie to me?'

'By implication. By pretending to fall in with the idea of going to the D'Arcy-Drelincourts. I knew I must consult my grandfather, and you perfectly well know why.

I may say at once that he doesn't agree with me. He doesn't believe you've been on the make.'

'But I have?'

'On the other hand'—Ian had ignored Mungo's question —'he says you must be stopped. He distinguishes between the grandson (on whom he dotes, if that's any satisfaction to you) and what he calls the claimant. So I'm at odds with him there too. It's going to be for me to say, you know. And you may make your mind easy. Whatever you have the shadow of a title to, my dear cousin, you shall have.'

' "My dear cousin"—that, and in that tone, is a good start to just what Leonard Sedley had been hoping to hear a lot of.'

'What the hell do you mean by that?'

'I mean, chiefly, that I want you to belt up, Ian Cardower. No, that's wrong. Listen! You've said half a dozen words you're going to regret. Well there's not much in half a dozen words. But now—please, Ian, please—*keep quiet*! Just for the length of this walk to the Castle. Do you promise?'

'I promise. And I blame you for nothing. For instance, you've done quite right to bring in your lawyer.'

'That gets something wrong for a start. I wrote to Roddy, who is my oldest friend, just because I was in a bit of a puzzle when you'd walked out on me. And Roddy has routed out Mackellar on his own initiative. And Mackellar hasn't got in his pocket what you and your grandfather fear he has. He may have something—but not the melodramatic twaddle you've been led to think. Listen, Ian! For how long has this business of you and me as cousins of a sort been going?'

'Almost from the start, it seems. I've had that from my ... from our grandfather. As a suspicion, it began on the night we dined with my parents at the Randolph. It was when you explained to my father that your mother was a Miss Guthrie of Fintry.'

'All right, Ian. And then, just as a notion, it drifted into your head, and mine too. Later, we tried it out as a kind of joke, and no harm done. We saw that it could be true that I was your uncle's illegitimate son, and still no harm done. All your people came to see it. Rather notably, they seemed to like me all the better for it. But there was no point in making it explicit. You have delicate feelings, you Cardowers.'

'We Cardowers.'

'O.K. And right, so far?'

'Right.'

'Next point. How lately did the story get this further turn of the screw: the assertion of there having been a legally valid marriage between your uncle Douglas and my mother?'

'No time ago, at all. But that's not the point. You see, it's absolutely—' Ian broke off. 'Look here,' he said, 'there are things it's frightfully difficult to say. Because, you know, he *was* your father.'

'All right. He was my father. But just go on.'

'It's absolutely in uncle Douglas's wretched picture. It seems there was one unfortunate girl he married in a perfectly legal way and then persuaded that the ceremony had been a hoax. He'd have been in a regular fix if she hadn't fortunately died of it all. And he several times used popular misconceptions about the Scottish marriage laws—'

'Yes, of course. We all know he was the bad Lord Douglas. But what I'm asking is this: who unloaded all this on *us*—more or less on our cottage doorstep—and when? It was your uncle David's precious companion, Leonard Sedley—and no longer ago than the day after you had bitterly humiliated him. That's my guess. Is it right?'

'I didn't humiliate him.'

'Don't be so thick. Of course you did. Yelping because a licentious hand was teasing your virgin locks.' Mungo's spirits were rising. 'He just couldn't take it, Ian, however nicely you apologized. And he decided to gain his revenge by running up this professional job.'

'Mungo, you're cracked.'

'It's Sedley who's cracked. A bad case of the Iago complex.'

'For Christ's sake, let up!' Ian had come to a halt and was facing Mungo squarely. 'First uncle eclipse, and then the Iago complex. Can't you be *serious*?'

Mungo found this so funny that he laughed aloud. For he couldn't, of course, remember ever in his young life having been confronted with a more serious half-hour. Still, the battle was won. Ian would never now say to him, nor would he ever say to Ian, the unforgivable things that had been planned for them.

'It's quite simple,' Mungo said, and began to move forward again. '*Solvitur ambulando*, in fact.'

'I don't see you need be so gay.'

'But I am gay. Even as a bird out of the fowler's snare escapes away, so is my soul set free. But you don't deign to sing the metrical psalms in your whistle-kirks.'

'What on earth is a whistle-kirk?' That Ian's chin was coming clear of the water was attested by this irrelevant curiosity.

'It's a kirk with an organ in it—and therefore only fit for Episcopalians.' Mungo now stretched his arms above his head as he walked, and looked contentedly about him. 'That post-and-rail fence along the drive,' he said, '—could you hurdle it?'

'I could vault it.'

'But I can hurdle it.'

Mungo hurdled it, ran on, turned, and hurdled it again.

On this repeat performance he unfortunately misjudged the dip of a shallow ditch, and came down with a breath-expelling wallop. He stood up, very dusty, to the accompaniment of Ian's comradely laughter.

'And now I'll go on,' he said soberly.

22

'YOU HAVE MADE a somewhat leisured matter of joining us,' Lord Auldearn was saying some twenty minutes
later. Lord Auldearn had seated himself at the head of
the long refectory table in the dining-room of Mallachie,
and was plainly proposing to preside over quasi-judicial
proceedings. He looked hard at Mungo. 'Young man,' he
demanded, 'have you been fighting?'

'Not fighting—hurdling,' Mungo said blithely, and
glanced round the room. Lord Brightmony was present,
but not Father Balietti. Mackellar and Roddy were sitting
at a far end of the table. With Ian and himself, that was
the lot. There was no sign of Leonard Sedley. 'It was a
fence, you see,' Mungo amplified. 'Ian thought he could
only vault it, but I said I could treat it as a hurdle. And
so I did. But I mucked it, the other way on. Are you waiting for Mr Sedley?'

'It is certainly desirable that he should be present.'
Lord Auldearn looked a little puzzled. 'I understood that
he was following us. He will no doubt be here in a
moment.'

'I don't think so. It's my guess that from this time
forth he never will speak word.'

'Mungo, this is no occasion for talking nonsense. We
have a very serious matter to consider. To consider and,
if possible, to compose.'

'I'm sorry, sir. But it isn't quite nonsense, as I'll explain.
May Ian and I sit down?'

'My dear boy, don't play at formalities. This is a family

matter, as you very well know. Sit down, both of you.'
Lord Auldearn made a gesture which seemed more weary
than his voice. 'And, Mungo, if you think it useful that
you should begin our discussion, please do.'

'Then that's fine.' Mungo sat down, and offered everybody present a cheerful smile. He had resolved that it
was his line to keep the temperature low. 'I'm sorry Mr
Sedley isn't here, because it would be better if I said
what I have to say in his presence. But it can't be helped.
I think you'll find that he really has asked for his cards.'

'Has *what*?' Lord Brightmony demanded.

'I'm sorry. Has handed in his checks. Decided to go
away. You see, he knows that I know. It came to me in a
moment—and I saw that its having come to *me* came to
him the moment after. These are frightfully spontaneous
things.'

'This talk is idle,' Lord Brightmony said severely. 'And
it appears to asperse Leonard, who is indeed not here to
defend himself. It will be more proper that Mungo be
silent for a time, and that we go about the matter another
way.'

'I think not.' Lord Auldearn said this gently and with
decision. 'Mungo, you were quoting the last words spoken
by Iago, and apparently with some serious intention.
Please explain yourself.'

'Well, it's just that I've been explaining it all to Ian
in terms of what I called an Iago complex. And that
was only because we have a game—Ian and I—of sometimes talking a sort of outmoded psychological jargon.
So I won't use it to you, sir, because I'm afraid you really
would think it frivolous.'

'I wonder.' Lord Auldearn was now looking at Mungo,
thus all disarmedness, very searchingly indeed. 'I think
that, on the whole, I should like to be favoured with it
too.'

'Very well. Iago is the type of the failed artist. I think
he wrote no end of plays and things—with perhaps a bit
of a success now and then—before he gave it up and
joined the army. The root cause of his failure as an artist
was that he had no impulse himself to enter into the lives
of other enjoying and suffering human beings. He just
wanted to get a sensation of power out of manoeuvring
his characters—puppets, really—into various rather horrid destinies. He took that instinct—Iago did—into actual
life after he'd failed as a writer, and started in with his
funny business on flesh and blood people. That's the
whole truth about him—except, of course, that he was
jealous of, or hated, relationships he couldn't understand.
I suppose this is a quite old-fashioned and boring view of
Iago, but it seems to me the true one.'

'It is at least an odd preface to our affair.' Lord Auldearn looked with a sudden glint of malice down the
table and at Mr Mackellar. 'I even feel that your legal
adviser judges it irrelevant and injudicious. But please
go on. Are you dignifying our absent friend with the
stature of an Iago?'

'Oh, no! It's just that he has exhibited rather the same
pattern of behaviour. In a way, he interests me rather more
than Iago does.'

'Does he, indeed? He would be flattered.'

'It's because he has an aesthetic—quite a specific aesthetic—which has lent a pattern to his fatuous attempts
to muck us all up. I'm afraid this sounds fearfully pretentious.'

'You are afraid of nothing of the sort. Don't waste our
time.'

'No, sir. Well, it's an aesthetic of illusion. The artist
creates precisely what is not, and the measure of his
achievement lies in the completeness or intensity which
his illusion achieves. It may be only for a moment that

the illusion holds. But if for that moment it is absolute, then he has succeeded in his aim.'

'It seems not a very elevated view of the artist.'

'Oh, no—of course it isn't. I'm just trying to explain why Mr Sedley has acted so freakishly. He's been a baffled sort of person for a long time, chiefly because he's lost the ability to create people and understand them—love them, even.'

'That may be true,' Lord Brightmony said. 'But is it relevant?'

'Just let me go on, please. Mr Sedley hasn't liked me at all, particularly as Ian's friend. And—only quite recently —he's come very much not to like Ian either. So what he's been doing is trying to bring off a malicious joke. He was going to exploit a bit of—well, of family history to bring us to a shameful and embarrassing public quarrel. Ian and I were going to say things to each other about each other's motives and feelings that would make it impossible for us ever to be friends again. That was to be the joke.'

There was a silence, during which Lord Auldearn glanced at his son as if inviting comment on these extra-ordinary statements. Lord Brightmony, however, appeared to have withdrawn upon silent prayer. So Lord Auldearn turned to Ian instead.

'Ian, would you describe yourself as suddenly converted to Mungo's view of the matter?'

'Yes, I would. It's bewildering, but there it is. I was to suspect Mungo of making his way among us in order to poke around in the family history to his own advantage, and Mungo was to see me as believing I had to take every means to outwit him. Mungo says the whole business of uncle David's supposed secret marriage to his mother will turn out to be a sudden invention of Sedley's. Sedley felt I had humiliated him, and his imagination got to work.'

'Humiliated him, Ian?'

'Yes—because one evening I made a silly scene. We'd been—'

'That, certainly, we need not pursue.' Lord Brightmony had emerged abruptly from his devotions.

'All right, then, I won't.' Ian turned again to his grandfather. 'But for a time, you see, the secret marriage was to be colourable—I think that's the word—because uncle Douglas is known to have played some odd tricks with the marriage laws. I ought to say Mungo and I think Sedley must be a bit cracked, as well as astoundingly malicious. He imagined he had far more grip on his plot, so to speak, than was actually the case. It's true that Mungo and I were beginning to be uneasy with each other—'

'Even to suspect each other,' Mungo interpolated calmly.

'Yes—even that. But his big scene, with the two of us chucking low accusations at one another before the entire assembled cast: that, I just don't believe he could conceivably have brought off.'

'That is a belief,' Lord Auldearn said drily, 'that it will be salutary to maintain.'

'You do see that we're right, don't you?' Mungo demanded.

'I think I may say I do. As for Leonard's being—like all the rest of us—a little mad: I see no difficulty in that at all. Do you think, by the way, that he supposed he was going to remain undetected in this ramshackle piece of wickedness?'

'Oh, *I* think that!' Mungo broke in with this. 'You see, there's the convention of the Calumniator Believed, and there's the convention of the Invisibility of the Villain—'

'Be quiet, Mungo.' Lord Auldearn was not amused. 'Let us not have your dramaturgical lore outstay its welcome, David, is that note perhaps from our friend?'

One of the melancholy manservants had tiptoed into the dining-room, handed Lord Brightmony an envelope, and withdrawn. And Lord Brightmony was reading the message with unchanged features now.

'Leonard writes that he is called away. And he judges that he will not be continuing his domestication at Mallachie.'

'There is really nothing more to be said.' Lord Auldearn, if exhausted, was also in high good humour; he might have been a company chairman winding up a successful shareholders' meeting. 'The only potentially awkward or delicate aspect of our affair proves to be a fabrication. Ian can return to his salmon, and Mungo to his typewriter. Mungo remains very much of the family, but with no explicit relationship given out to the world.'

'I regret that I must disagree with your lordship.'

It was Mr Mackellar who said this, and the words represented his first contribution to the entire proceedings. Lord Auldearn glared at him.

'Be so good as to explain yourself, sir.'

'It appears to be taken for granted that my client, Mr Lockhart, emerges from all this as still the natural son of the late Lord Douglas Cardower. I have to submit that the assumption is highly injurious and prejudicial. Lord Douglas was a notorious libertine. Falsely to ascribe any man's paternity to such a person is in my view slanderous and actionable.'

'Then your view is stuff and nonsense, sir.' Lord Auldearn was suddenly thunderous. 'And your description of my late son so impertinent that I must ask you to quit this house at once.'

'You will be so kind as to listen to me.' Mackellar hadn't budged from his seat. 'I am not here as your guest—any more than as a damned journalist. I am here as the representative of a legal interest of which it is your duty, and Lord Brightmony's duty, to stand apprised.'

'Very well.' Lord Auldearn was breathing heavily. 'Have your say. And then withdraw—taking that futile youth with you.'

'Roddy isn't a futile youth!' Mungo was staring at Mackellar S.S.C. round-eyed. 'I don't know what this is about. But it's obviously important—and it's Roddy who has had the gumption to get it here.' Mungo was quite as angry as his putative grandfather. 'What's more, I think it was when he saw Roddy and Mr Mackellar that Leonard Sedley knew his nonsense was going to be no good. In fact, Roddy's been the means of saving us from frightful howlers. Please apologize to him, sir.'

'Very well. I apologize to Roddy.' Lord Auldearn was looking at Mungo as if he couldn't believe that this wasn't a most authentic Cardower. 'And Mr Macculloch—'

'Mackellar,' Mackellar S.S.C. said grimly.

'And Mr Mackellar shall be heard.'

'Thank you.' With much deliberation, Mackellar drew a file of papers from a briefcase at his feet. 'It will not, I judge, be necessary to exhibit these at this stage. But they are available if required.' Mackellar paused weightily, and Mungo transferred his wondering gaze to the mysterious documents. It was like *The Way of the World*, he was thinking. A little black box is brought on in the final act, and with its aid everything is cleared up. In fact, and although Sedley had withdrawn in confusion, there was to be a bit of a sensation-drama after all.

'My lord,' Mackellar said, 'it appears to be your persuasion, and indeed that of your entire family, that Lord Douglas pursued his chosen courses so vigorously that he must be supposed to have fathered every fatherless lad in Moray and Nairn.'

'That does seem the idea,' Mungo broke in. He had only a dim intuition of what was coming, but he felt extra-ordinarily light-hearted. 'Wide as his command, scattered his Maker's image o'er the land.'

'Mungo!' Lord Auldearn said, 'this is mere buffoonery. Persist in it, and you shall leave the room.'

'I'm very sorry, sir. Mr Mackellar, please go on.'

'It is true,' Mackellar continued, 'that certain coinci-dences of topography and nomenclature have aided your misconception. But as it is a question of your own lands and your own tenants, there appears to be involved a degree of inattention that is to be deprecated.'

'It is not your business, sir, to deprecate anything,' Lord Auldearn snapped. 'It is your business to get on with your attorney's trade. Pray do so.'

'One moment.' Lord Brightmony had raised an arrest-ing hand. He was (Mungo thought) quite as chilly an aris-tocrat at bottom as was his alarming father. But his religious slant did appear to make him chary of the sin of pride. 'It is understood in the family,' Lord Brightmony went on, 'that I look after the Scottish estates. And for a long term of years I have been less attentive to such matters than is right. If there was some negligence, it is only too likely that I am responsible.'

'That is as may be.' Mackellar was a little thrown out of his stride by this confessional episode. 'The fact remains that there is an Easter Fintry and a Wester Fintry in this part of the world. Just as there is an Easter Golford and a Wester Golford, an Easter Milton and a Wester Milton, an Easter—'

'We take your point,' Lord Auldearn said. 'Proceed.'

'And there are Guthries on every gooseberry bush.' Mackellar S.S.C. paused, as if startled by his own use of this reckless figure of speech. 'At least there are, or were, Guthries of Easter Fintry and Guthries of Wester Fintry

—the two families being unrelated. With the Guthries of Wester Fintry I have no concern. But no doubt Lord Douglas had, in pursuance of his customary diversions.'

'It is a certain Eliza Guthrie whom we have thought to see at the root of this perplexed business.' Lord Auldearn spoke in quite a new voice. 'Did she come from this confounded Wester Fintry? No doubt she did. She was simple-minded, and there was an obscure scandal to the effect that Douglas put her through a mock marriage ceremony which he pretended was valid. Rubbish straight out of a Victorian novel. I had to pay those damned Guthries money to keep quiet, and eventually to go away. An irregular marriage can be a very tricky thing here in Scotland.'

'You're clean out of date, sir.' Roddy McLeod spoke loudly and unexpectedly. The charge of futility had very properly rankled in him. 'The law hasn't admitted such a thing these thirty years. You don't know your own law any more than you know your own tenants. And now we'd better let Mr Mackellar continue.'

'I can be very brief,' Mackellar said, with the ominous weightiness of one who sees some considerable oratorical flight ahead of him. 'Turning to the Guthries of Easter Fintry—'

'One more moment.' Lord Brightmony had again raised his arresting hand. 'It is a point about poor Leonard, perhaps unknown to some of you. In the period we seem to be considering, he was much more Douglas's intimate than mine. And I fear the truth is indeed appearing. Poor Leonard has been proposing to make much irresponsible mischief out of his knowledge of the deplorable seduction of Eliza Guthrie.'

'My client's mother was *Isobel* Guthrie of *Easter* Fintry.' Mackellar had got into his stride again. 'She was the sister of the present Miss Elspeth Guthrie, my client's aunt, and now, as then, of this same Easter Fintry. It is very likely that neither you, my lord, nor Lord Brightmony has ever troubled to set eyes on the place. I will remark, therefore, that Easter Fintry is a gentleman's residence of modest character, and no longer encumbered with land.'

'Good God, man—are you an estate agent too?' Lord Auldearn's patience and residual civility were wearing thin. 'Get on with it.'

'I am sorry to say that in early womanhood Miss Isobel Guthrie had the misfortune to form an attachment to a married man, a member of a highly respectable profession, then resident in Elgin. My client, Mr Mungo Lockhart, was in fact the issue of this brief irregular connection. A few months after his conception, a certain Andrew Lockhart, being possessed of a full knowledge of the facts, married Miss Isobel Guthrie and thus provided the child in the womb with a legal father. Unhappily both he and the child's mother were drowned not very long after my client was born. And since then, as you know, Mungo has lived with his aunt.'

'Why has not all this been made known before?' Lord Auldearn asked sternly. 'Why should these facts not have been communicated to my grandson's friend, Mr Mungo Lockhart—who, despite an intermittent indulgence in unseasonable levity, is quite obviously a responsible young man, and of the soundest practical judgement?'

'Quite so, quite so.' This encomium (although it was perhaps really a requiem over a departed Mungo Cardower) impressed Mr Mackellar considerably. 'I must explain that I have been bound by the terms of a trust. My client's natural father felt that his social and professional responsibilities made it inexpedient for him to acknowledge his child. But he established—as was very proper—a fund for the child's education, the administration of which he placed in my hands. The true circumstances were to be communicated to my client upon his twenty-first birthday, or earlier at my discretion, provided that both the donor and his wife were dead. That situation has now come about. Mr Macgonigal died many years ago, and Mrs Macgonigal within the last fortnight.'

'You did say Macgonigal?' Mungo heard himself ask. He was slightly dazed.

'Certainly, Mungo. Macgonigal.'

'And what, please, was his highly respectable profession?'

'He was a dentist in very good practice. And I am happy to communicate to you the fact that, at the likely close of your university career, there will be a residual credit of some £300 available for payment into your bank.'

'Thank you very much.' Macgonigal the dentist's son stood up and walked over to Lord Auldearn. 'Sir,' he said, 'here I am. And on my own feet.'

'May they take you over plenty of hurdles yet.' Gravely, Lord Auldearn rose and shook his lost grandson's hand.

Later in the evening, Mungo and Ian walked down to the cottage. The river, almost invisible, was flowing past them with a deep strong murmur.

'Do you think,' Ian asked, 'we'll ever see Sedley again?'

'Bugger Sedley! Of course not. And not ever speak of him, either. An Iago's bad enough. A downright incompetent Iago is the end.'

'He was busying being an artist, and all that. It was hard cheese on him coming up against another top-class specimen—a staggeringly intuitive type.'

'Don't be a bloody idiot,' Mungo said. Being a little drunk with happiness, he privately thought that Ian had quite hit the nail on the head. He was silent for some moments. 'Ian,' he said, 'this has been a marvellous day.'

'Unflawed?'

'Utterly.'

'I don't believe you—that you're all that damned pleased to have got clear of us.' Ian's mockery was familiar and comfortable in the dusk. 'Your imagination was touched. It must have been—at the thought of being descended from chieftains and kings.'

'Not my imagination, and not even my pride. My vanity, perhaps. Talking of imagination, isn't it odd that it was the Cardowers—wary aristocrats, and all that—who went wildly to town on it, and not your scribbling friend? I caught the infection, I admit, but not until your people had done a lot of meaningful goggling at me.'

'It was an understandable error. It's ridiculous that there should have been two families called Guthrie.' Ian was silent for a moment. 'None of it would have happened if some unknown don hadn't decided to shove us both into Howard 4, 4.'

'Solemn thought.'

'That £300 would go some way towards setting you up in a pub. The Macgonigal Arms.' Ian, being a Scot of sorts, was sentimental at heart. He enjoyed the luxury of having somebody to whom he could offer outrage like this. He began further and obscurely to indulge this feeling by skimming flat stones across the river in a manner that would have scandalized his uncle's water-bailiff. '*Now*,' he said inconsequently, 'will you consent to pay your addresses to my sister?'

'To Mary? If only I could!' Mungo chucked himself down supine on the river-bank, raised his legs in air, and in that position executed certain ankle-tapping steps of a Scottish reel. 'I'm in love with Anne, and I'm going to dance at her wedding.'

KNIGHT MEMORIAL LIBRARY

DATE DUE			

STACK

ONE WEEK

STEWART
MUNGOS DREAM